Sad Desk Salad

Sad Desk Salad

JESSICA GROSE

wm

WILLIAM MORROW
An Imprint of HarperCollinsPublishers

This book is a work of fiction. References to real people, events, establishments, organizations, or locales are intended only to provide a sense of authenticity, and are used fictitiously. All other characters, and all incidents and dialogue, are drawn from the author's imagination and are not to be construed as real.

FIRST EDITION

Designed by Diahann Sturge

Library of Congress Cataloging-in-Publication Data

Grose, Jessica.
Sad desk salad / Jessica Grose.—1st ed.
p. cm.
ISBN 978-0-06-218834-2 (pbk.)—ISBN 978-0-06-218835-9 (ebook) 1. Young women—Fiction. 2. Blogs—Fiction. I. Title.
PS3607.R6537S24 2012
813'.6—dc23
2012027369

12 13 14 15 16 OV/RRD 10 9 8 7 6 5 4 3 2 1

To Hanna Rosin and Anna Holmes, the best bosses a girl could ever ask for

Sad Desk Salad

MONDAY

Chapter One

The alarm on my iPhone goes off at 6:20. I crawl out of my rumpled bed and shuffle to the kitchen, where my morning coffee is waiting. I've set the timer on the Krups so that I can start sipping a cup by 6:22. By 6:23 I'm sitting upright on our mottled brown corduroy couch. My MacBook is open and pinwheeling awake at 6:24.

I turn on the TV and flip to the *Today* show, which I keep on low in the background. Every day I watch the *Today* show and never *Good Morning America* or *The Early Show* or whatever clowns they have on Fox. George Stephanopoulos is intrinsically smug, so I can't hold with *GMA*. *Today* has Natalie Morales, whom I implicitly trust. This morning Savannah Guthrie is interviewing the parents of a four-year-old who can't stop coughing. While I'm watching the wretched toddler in her mother's arms, I hear my computer chirp an alert.

MoiraPoira (6:25:22): Good morning, sunshine.

Alex182 (6:25:24): Merrrr

That's my boss, Moira, who IMs me immediately after I log on. I'm Alex, one of four writers at a website for women called Chick Habit.

The website is Moira's baby. She started out fresh out of the University of Dublin working at a tabloid newspaper in Ireland called the *Evening Mews*. When she was twenty-four, she famously discovered the hotel in the Canary Islands where the bad-boy goalie of Irish football, Eamon Best, was getting married to a very orange British reality television star.

Moira rented a room overlooking the beach where the ceremony was being held and got the exclusive scoop on the bride's Swarovski-crystal-encrusted gown-kini. Alledgedly, she even managed to plant a recording device in the floppy ear of a stuffed bunny rabbit tucked away in the couple's Gran Palmas suite. That's how she got the dirt about the groom arranging an illicit rendezvous with one of the equally orange bridesmaids mere hours after the nuptials. For this, Moira was promoted to features editor before her twenty-fifth birthday.

At twenty-nine she was poached by one of the fancy women's glossies and moved to New York. She was bored with the magazine instantly—all the women who worked there had young babies and well-appointed apartments north of Sixtieth Street. Moira had dead houseplants and sex with guys in the bathrooms of posh members-only clubs. She was like a Bengal tiger in one of her fancy colleagues' chintz-covered living rooms. When an opportunity arose for her to start Chick Habit, with its 'round-the-clock posting and frenzied pace, she jumped at the chance.

But it wasn't just the fusty ladies at the established magazine that made her want to set out on her own. She wanted to be part of something that was much sharper and a little meaner. She also wanted it to be "empowered." I've been working for her for six months and it still isn't 100 percent clear to me what that word means to her, except that I am encouraged to express my deep hatred for Gwyneth Paltrow and write about period sex. What is clear is that the site is hitting a nerve. Even the posts that have less than a thousand page views get upwards of fifty comments from variously engaged silly, militant, and under-employed young women.

Moira has me do the first post of the day, every day, in part because I'm the only Chickie she can count on to wake up before seven. "You're so Japanese," Moira always says, which, since I'm not actually Asian, is her vaguely racist but pretty amusing way of telling me that I'm dutiful. I wasn't so focused before I had this job, so I appreciate her attempt at a compliment. I have about ninety minutes to find something, read it, consider it, and then spew out something publishable by eight A.M. That's the most time I will get for a post all day.

MoiraPoira (6:25:30): Glad you're so chipper this AM, kiddo. Here are some links to choose from. The first is about a campaign to stop female genital mutilation in Somalia. The second is about some former beauty queen in Mississippi who is now a meth-head and held up a supermarket. The third is about a study that shows how women can close the gender gap among physicists. The fourth is about a new law in Nebraska that outlaws late-term abortion.

These topics are among the most serious that Chick Habit covers. The eight o'clock post is the hard-news post, which comes right before the first gossip roundup. Moira gave me this assignment because these are the kinds of things I used to write lengthy features about in college. Topics for this post fall roughly into three categories: sad foreign ladies, dead babies, sexist statistics.

The female-genital-mutilation link is from the *Guardian* and I feel like I wrote a post on the horrors of FGM just a couple of weeks ago. Sad foreign ladies are good for audience interaction (typical comment: "The patriarchal domination of our world's most vulnerable women makes me stabby!") but bad for traffic. My last post on a woman in Iran whose brothers beat her for going to school only got eight hundred page views. Same goes for sexist statistics. Maybe it's worthwhile to write about how only 4 percent of philosophers are women, but most of our readers couldn't care less. Or, more accurately, they just don't care as much as they do about Lindsay Lohan's latest trip to rehab.

When I started this job in January, I didn't really think about the traffic to my posts. I still remember the first post I was really proud of. It came through our tips line—a woman in Memphis wrote to tell us that prosecutors declined to try her rape case because she wasn't the perfect victim; she had consumed a few exotic-berry wine coolers before she was violated, and she had a prior record for stealing a strappy tank top from Walmart.

I wrote about her story, and it felt really good to give voice to someone whose rights were being stifled.

And 147 people read about it.

At the time the lack of reader interest stung a little—why didn't they care more about something so meaningful?—and I was worried about impressing my new boss. But Moira never used to pressure us about whether a post had a hundred views or a hundred thousand. Then last month she received a message from the lackeys of Tyson Collins, the Southern billionaire who owns the faceless cable conglomerate that owns Chick Habit: Our page views were growing impressively, but not fast enough. Each of us Chickies was given a monthly quota of views—one million a month. If we surpass the quota we get a bonus. It's made us all much more territorial, not only because of the money, but because of the implied flip side: losing our jobs if we only get 999,999 page views. I've been trying not to let this vague but serious threat affect my work.

> **Alex182 (6:25:55):** I guess I'll go with the meth lady. She looks festive.

I do a search on the woman's name—Desiree Jiminez—and find stories about the hold-up in the local Jackson paper, on CNN's website, and from abcnews.com. I scan all three stories and discover that Desiree was Miss Congeniality and first runner-up in the 1997 Miss Mississippi pageant. I find her Facebook page—she hasn't put up any privacy protections, so I can see all her photos. There's one of her with crown and all, atop a podium at a day-care center in Choctaw County. Her hair was magnificent back then: a halo of bleached blond fluff teased into a perfect sphere floating above her head. According to cnn.com, in the intervening decade she fell on hard times and several ex-cons. In the mug shot they show, she has a tattoo on her upper right arm that says STEVE in gothic lettering. Her hair is no longer magnificent. It hangs in lank brown bunches next to her face.

While I'm reading up on Desiree's exploits, my boyfriend, Peter, gets up and ambles over to the coffeepot. I'm still clad in his old boxers and a frayed T-shirt that says JE T'AIME, MONTREAL!—what I slept in the night before.

"Hey, Al, what's on the Interwebs this morning?"

"Methy former beauty queen . . . Big hair," I mutter.

"Oh yeah? Sounds thrilling."

Peter is one of those incorrigible morning people, and almost every day he tries to talk to me while I'm doing the first post. He walks briskly through our low-slung garden apartment, his nearly black hair catching the light, and when I look up to admire him in his boxer briefs, he takes the opportunity to engage me in conversation. I've told him over and over again that I can't really talk while I'm working but this does not seem to deter him.

In a few minutes he'll shower and put on his suit—he works in finance, at a place called the Polydrafter Group. He's an analyst specializing in media, and I only have a faint idea about what he does all day—though I do know there are a lot of Excel spreadsheets involved. Before I met him at a friend's birthday party I was only attracted to artists: skinny guys in tight pants who were always talking about their latest installation at some unfortunate gallery in Bushwick. The breakup with my last boyfriend, Caleb, a mercurial mixed-media artist, was brutal. About a month before we parted ways, he said I was too neurotic and dramatic for him. I took this to mean that he wanted to be the spaz in the relationship. Peter doesn't mind so much that I'm intense. "It keeps things exciting," he tells me.

I've also cleaned up my act considerably since I met Peter, curbing my emotional and alcoholic excesses for our life together. I've always heard that animal trainers put goats in the stable with particularly high-strung racehorses because the goats are calm yet stubborn and the Thoroughbreds chill out. Peter's innate goatishness—he likes me for who I am, but he still doesn't take any guff—has made our relationship the best thing in my life. I never thought that I would find joy in planning and cooking meals for someone (so Suzy Homemaker!), but I love Peter so much that I relish the idea of nourishing him. I'd like to think that he inspires me to be a better person.

As Peter is putting on his blue tie with the gray stripes, the one I bought him for his last birthday, I am putting the finishing touches on my post about Desiree. It's 342 words and I title it "Desiree Jiminez, Former Miss Congeniality, Holds Up the Piggly Wiggly." I make sure to put her name at the beginning of the headline, so my post will show up when people Google her. After ten minutes, it's got 4,332 page views, and I feel like I can relax a bit. I get up on my tiptoes to kiss Peter before he walks out the door. He's six foot one to my five foot seven, and in his fancy work shoes the height disparity seems even greater. As we're embracing I catch him sniffing my hair.

"Alex, are you going to shower this morning?"

"Maybe?"

"I think you'll be happier if you do."

"Okay, okay, I'll try."

When I watch him leave through our tiny front door, ducking his head so he doesn't thwack it on the concrete, I fully intend to head to the bathroom. But I can picture Moira's angry IM in my head—"WHERE ARE YOU?" in all caps—and it pulls me back to the couch instead. Eight turns into nine and I'm sucking down room-temperature coffee, trying to find my next post. I've pinned my slightly filthy dark blond bangs back with a bobby pin I found on the floor so that they stay out of my eyes and don't make my forehead break out.

Moira hasn't sent me anything good. I keep refreshing my RSS feed, watching hundreds of new stories tumble down the screen. The same image flashes in my head when I am particularly stressed. It's of that classic *I Love Lucy* episode in which Lucy and Ethel are working at a candy factory. The bonbons keep coming down the conveyor belt in an endless stream of confection. The ladies are so overwhelmed with chocolate that they end up shoving it in their mouths and in their hats in an effort to keep up. This is what I feel like most of the time, constantly behind the wave of nonessential information.

I am responsible for ten posts every day. Theoretically they can be about almost anything, as long as Moira approves, but lately they're mostly about celebrity drama and civilian controversy. Some can be hundred-and-fifty-word shorties, but at least four have to be meatier, at least three hundred words long, preferably closer to five hundred. Sometimes I find the posts myself, and sometimes Moira assigns something to me. In some ways it's a dream job—I get to make a living writing all day. In other ways, it's not.

For example, around 9:15 nature calls, and I feel I must take my laptop with me into the bathroom. The last time I left my computer for more than ten minutes, a seventies TV star died, and Moira was livid that I wasn't there to throw up a hot pants–filled slideshow.

At 9:37 I'm still sitting on the toilet. I've become so absorbed in trying to find something to post on that I haven't moved. Finally, the jackpot, courtesy of the *Christian Science Monitor*: A trend piece about the small but growing number of women who are having water births.

Alex182 (9:37:42): I'm going to grab this *CSM* piece about the ladies who give birth in bathtubs.

MoiraPoira (9:38:03): Brilliant. I'll let the other girls know you've got it.

The other girls are Ariel, Tina, and Molly. They all work from their respective apartments in Brooklyn and Queens. I've become tentative friends with Ariel, even though we see each other in person once a week, tops.

Ariel, who goes by Rel, is the most like me. We even went to the same YMCA summer camp (filled, absurdly, with Jews like us) in the Adirondacks, though our stays there didn't overlap. We have the same heavy-lidded amber-colored eyes I've only ever seen on other Jewesses and the baseline familiarity of nice Jewish girls turned hipster. We might wear thrift-store sweaters, but we wear them with the Tiffany bean necklaces we got for our bat mitzvahs.

But the similarity is mostly superficial. Ariel has had a much more exciting and expensive life than I ever did. She went to a ritzy private school in Riverdale and wound up in rehab before her twenty-second birthday for that tiny heroin habit she developed at the New School. She spent most of her college years at bars on the Lower East Side and backstage at various secret rock concerts. That she looked like a Jewish Olsen twin (petite and waifish, brunette rather than fair) certainly helped her get behind the velvet rope. When I describe Ariel to other people, I make sure to include this bit of pivotal information: She once fucked a Stroke.

Now that she's thirty, she lays off the junk (but not the booze). However she still has that cloak of coolness about her shoulders. She came to Chick Habit from *Spandex Magazine,* a notorious downtown rag that was founded in the midseventies by drag queens, where she was the culture editor. Her IM handle is a reference to Todd Solondz's indie film classic about an unfortunate tween called *Welcome to the Dollhouse*. I spend most of our conversations wondering why she bothers to talk to me.

Wienerdog (10:03:14): Moira is really up my ass today

Alex182 (10:03:29): What's her damage?

Wienerdog (10:04:11): I told her I would have the clip of last night's ANTM up at 11, but it turned out to be a double episode and now I can't get it done until 12.

Then she called me a "lazy article," whatever the fuck that means.

Alex182 (10:04:38): That is so annoying.

In fact, I think Moira's demands are generally reasonable and that Ariel sleeps much later than she claims to. But chatting with Rel always turns me sycophantic.

Wienerdog (10:20:12): Molly is sort of being an eager beaver.

Alex182 (10:20:39): I know. Every afternoon she asks me for work because she's already finished whatever Moira gave her for the day. Whenever I tell her I don't have anything for her, she's all, "Sorry I'm so persistent!"

Wienerdog (10:21:02): "My real weakness is I just work *too* hard!"

None of us really knows Molly very well, and what we know we find irritating. Moira just hired her as our editorial assistant to pick up stray posts here and there and do research for the rest of us. She's nearly fresh out of Yale, save for a brief interlude at *People*. I want to be empathetic—she's just a go-getter!—but she makes it difficult, especially since the posts she wants to pick up always seem to be mine.

I let my conversation with Rel go idle for a while so I can

finish up on water births. There is a photo accompanying the story, which depicts a woman in brownstone Brooklyn grimacing in an inflatable tub in the middle of her living room. Her family looks on in the background. A woman who is identified as her younger sister has the most horrified expression on her face: Her mouth is slightly agape, and her eyes are wide. I crop the sister's face out and zoom in on it, and write 578 words about this completely grossed-out sibling, including a borderline-jerky joke about hippie placenta eaters.

These days it feels like I get paid to be a bitch. It makes me feel pretty terrible when I think about it, but the meaner I am, the better my posts do—and I can't afford to miss my quota. In fact, my occasionally nasty sense of humor is what got me the job at Chick Habit. I had been working for the website of a moderately successful music magazine called *Rev* (not to be confused with *Rev: The Magazine for Reverends*). I was getting paid about the same rate as I did babysitting in high school, so to make rent, I took some DJ gigs on the side. At least the *Rev* name was good for something, even if it wasn't good for a living wage.

I had a blog that a whopping three hundred people read regularly, and at least three of them read it from prison. I have the snail-mail letters they sent me from a minimum-security lockup in Georgia to prove it.

Moira noticed a very critical review of a Duncan Sheik album I had written. If memory serves, I suggested that he was "a eunuch" who should "stop cooing about yoga." In return for my vitriol, a commenter called me a "mean cunt."

That particular comment really affected me—for a few

weeks afterward I'd go back and look at it every day. I'd have the same two dueling reactions whenever "cunt" flashed before my eyes: Part of me would feel hot-faced shame. Why did I have to be so bitchy? Why couldn't I be more measured in my criticism? What if Duncan Sheik actually read it? The other, smaller part of me would think, Fuck that commenter guy. I'm allowed to have strong opinions and express them in whatever way I please. And besides, that review was funny.

At least Moira thought so. She called me in for an interview on the basis of that eunuch insult. I met her at a wine bar in the East Village, and she offered me the position as Chick Habit's third full-time blogger before our second glasses of Pinot arrived. It would be much more money than I was making at *Rev*—a respectable $45,000 a year—but no health insurance (not like I had any at *Rev* in the first place). She was also offering me a much bigger audience: Chick Habit had been around for about six months at that point, and it was pulling in about three hundred thousand page views a day.

Both Peter and my mom were excited when I got the job offer at Chick Habit. "I read about that site in the *New York Times* last week!" my mom exclaimed over the phone. "You should definitely take it."

Even though it didn't have quite the gravitas that I had desired when I graduated from Wesleyan four years ago, I was pretty excited myself. A few years in New York had made me a realist, rather than an idealist. No one was going to pay me to write indulgent multi-thousand-word articles about the world's woes. Chick Habit was, though, going to pay me to write occasional blog posts about those woes, along with the gossipy and cultural stuff that gets more pickup anyway. I knew even then that I would get noticed more if I wrote eight hundred words on the significance of the food poisoning scene in *Bridesmaids* than if I blogged about a climate-change bill.

Saying yes seemed like the easiest decision I ever made.

I file the bathtub birthers to Moira at 11:12; she gives it a once-over and schedules it to go live at one P.M., which is the blog equivalent of prime time. We get the most readers around lunchtime, when girls in offices all over the East Coast eat their sad desk salads and force down bites of desiccated chicken breasts while scrolling through our latest posts. We get another traffic bump around four, when our West Coast counterparts eat their greens with low-fat dressing.

Even though I no longer work at an office, I run out to get my own version of sad desk salad. There's nothing in the fridge except a half-empty container of milk and some congealed Thai food from three nights before. I throw on the same black eyelet muumuu that I have worn every day this summer so far—I don't bother to put on a bra—and scurry across the street. It's a clear July morning. The sun is so bright I need to hold up a hand to shade my eyes.

At the bodega across the street I'm ordering the same mixed greens with my own limp chicken cutlet when I realize I don't have my iPhone on me. "Shit! BRB," I tell Manuel, who is making my salad. It's come to this: I spend so little time talking aloud during the day, I've started speaking in Internet abbreviations to people in real life. He gives me a quizzical look right before I dart back outside and into my apartment for the smart phone. I'm back to the bodega in under two minutes; there are no angry e-mails or texts from Moira. Thankfully Cher has not died while I was in transit.

While Manuel is folding balsamic vinaigrette into my salad with half-clean tongs, the phone rings. I seize up a little, because I assume it's Moira, but when I look down at the screen, my mom's sweet, broad face is smiling up at me. I step toward a cooler filled with coconut water in a back corner to answer.

"Hi, Mom."

"Hi, puffin. Just calling to say hello on my break between second and third period."

My mom is the only person besides Moira whose phone calls I will take during my workday. She is a high school teacher at Manning prep, which is in the small Connecticut town where I was raised. Since my dad died, my mom has started proctoring summer school in order to pad her nest egg and afford expenses on the house. Mom teaches freshman English and has read every word I've ever written; before Dad passed, he taught advanced chemistry, and hadn't.

Almost exactly two years ago, my father was playing an evening game of squash against Mr. Hibbert, the head of the math department, when he keeled over. He died right there on the court, before he got to the hospital. When my mom called to tell me what had happened, her generally loud and chipper voice was so muffled and faraway it sounded like it was coming from another dimension. My best friend and then-roommate, Jane, was the one who picked me up off the floor of our apartment; I had crumpled down to the tiles in our kitchen and couldn't move my legs.

Rev let me work remotely for a while, and right after the funeral I went to Connecticut to help my mom regain some sense of everydayness. I was still numb. My dad was always this stoic, immovable figure in my mind, the voice of scientific reason in my head. Sure, he could be a hard-ass, but that was part of his charm. That he could be as ephemeral as anything else disrupted my sense of the world.

For my benefit, Mom tried to put on a happy face, but I would hear her crying at different times throughout the day. Voices carried in our old Victorian, and even though she tried to muffle the sound of her tears in her dressing room pillows, I could still make out nearly every sob and gasp.

About three weeks after Dad died I woke up to the sound of her crying long after midnight. The next morning I confronted her—tenderly—in the kitchen.

"You can cry in front of me, you know. I want to be here for you," I told her.

She looked shocked, and like she might cry again. Then a deep sigh seemed to travel through her slender body—which was starting to look downright bony. Before the tears started flowing she sniffed and straightened her robe, a crisp blue pinstripe that she'd been wearing every morning since I was a child. "You're the kid here," she said. "I want to support you, not the other way around."

After that, I stayed with my mom for just one more week. I sensed that my being there didn't actually make it easier for her—she wanted to get back to her routine. My mom's attitude toward profound disappointment and woe has always been to fill her days with productivity. The other teachers at Manning, close neighbors, and various friends that she had made through our temple were there to help, so I knew that I wasn't leaving her to the wolves.

Before I left, I gave the house the best scrubbing I could (not really my forte) and sent my dad's clothes to the Salvation Army at my mother's request. "Are you sure you don't want to save anything of his?" I asked her. "Not even his beaker cuff links?" Dad wore them on the first day of school every year, his own private sartorial chemistry teacher joke.

"If you want them you can keep them," my mother said faux-cheerfully. "But I can't keep his stuff here." This is the way she's always dealt with things, by putting a positive gloss on them and moving on. "There are no problems, only challenges," says the poster on her classroom wall. I pocketed the cuff links but sent everything else away.

I don't really have time to talk to her right now, but I felt too guilty to send her straight to voice mail, so we have a quick chat. When my salad is ready I tell her I need to rush on back home.

"I'm so proud of you for your exciting job!" Mom says, which is what she always says when the topic of Chick Habit arises. When we hang up, I turn to Manuel and apologize for talking on the phone in the bodega.

He smiles at me and says, "Your voice brightens up the place." I give him a ten for a seven-dollar salad and tell him to keep the change.

When I get back home I catch sight of myself in the mirror and grimace, hearing my mother's sweet yet firm voice in my mind. If she could see me now, unwashed and underdressed, she would have trouble hiding a look of abject horror. I decide to sit at the desk that's in the corner of the bedroom rather than slouching back on the decrepit couch. I eat my limp greens as I search my RSS feed once again. I check my Chick Habit e-mail account. Occasionally story tips will come through that way. Today all I see is spam from chirpy PR women trying to sell me on stories about eco-friendly makeup and an e-mail from someone who claims to know me from college.

"I'd always admired your work at school," the note says, "and I'd love it if you'd link to a piece from my literary quarterly about the Langi women of Uganda. My writer spent six months living among them."

I get e-mails like this all the time from acquaintances asking for link love. I am sure the piece is smart and worthy, but at this point I know that Moira will laugh me offline if I ask if I can post on some ten-thousand-word bit of earnestness from a journal no one's ever heard of.

I listen to the air conditioner clanking in the window that faces the sidewalk, feel the clammy air pushing inside. I'm just about to cross the threshold into goose-pimpled anxiety when I find a new blog that's getting a ton of attention today—a series of videos of people crying while eating.

I write a hundred words and post a quick link back to that site. "Who hasn't cried into her ice cream after being dumped?" I ask the commenters. Moira schedules the post for twelve forty-five. Our readers respond by posting tales of weeping while eating pizza after their best friend ditched them and sobbing into their salad after fighting with their boyfriends.

This is when the commenters are at their most charming.

Writing mini posts like this makes you feel like you're hosting the sweetest virtual sleepover party ever thrown.

The love fest ends abruptly when the water birth post goes up fifteen minutes later. About a quarter of the commenters are on my side. Someone called rebekahb writes, "Ugh, I hate hippies. I would die if my upstairs neighbor was giving birth in her apartment. Isn't that a violation of the lease?" And 75 percent of them want me fired: "I thought this site was supposed to be supportive of women and their choices. Giving birth the way nature intended is a choice that every woman should be able to make without getting made fun of. I'm appalled by this and writing a letter to the editor." That one is at least civil. This one, from a frequent commenter with the handle Weathergrrrl, is not: "Alex Lyons is a fucking traitor." You'd think I'd be more immune to mean comments by now, but it still feels like I'm trapped in a bathroom stall while a gaggle of girls stands at the sink, gossiping about what a terrible jerk I am.

Moira, of course, is delighted:

MoiraPoira (2:05:33): Your birthing post already has 25,000 page views and 256 comments!

Alex182 (2:05:41): I know, but have you read any of those comments? They want me crucified for crimes against womanity.

MoiraPoira (2:05:58): You have nothing to feel bad about. You had a decidedly un-fuzzy response to that water birth article, and it was your honest response.

They shouldn't care what some 25-year-old ninny thinks about the fact that some woman in Brooklyn shot a baby out into a bathtub.

Alex182 (2:06:10): I know, I just feel bad.

MoiraPoira (2:06:17): Love, grow a pair.

Moira and I have some version of this conversation every time I write a controversial post. From what I've observed, she's never had even a pang of guilt about anything she's written, even when she broke the news about Lily Allen's miscarriage back at the *Mews*. And Moira's right. I can't have it both ways—I need to stand by what I've written.

The comments affect me less than they used to. I try my hardest not to read them whether they're positive or negative, though most days I break down and take a peek at a few. Okay, several. But I never read every single one of them late into the night until Peter forcibly removes the laptop from my hands. I'd never do that!

The positive ones are ego inflating, and the negative ones can be soul raping, but if you let them get to you too much, you start pandering to the audience. You write toothless, feel-good posts about everything so you'll be above criticism. This involves lots of exclamation marks: "It's so great that Britney has finally found a solid guy and is no longer flashing her business everywhere!!!!" Even when you're writing about celebrities, this feels icky.

One of the reasons I look up to Rel is that she never seems to be affected by responses to her posts. Whenever commenters start attacking her, she starts attacking right back. "I can't believe you care that I'm insulting one of the Real Housewives," she'll write. "Get a fucking life." But reality stars are one thing—they put themselves out there as public figures. What about the girl in the background of that photo, the one caught in an odd grimace watching her sister give birth? Did she ask for her face to be plastered all over the Internet? I try not to think about these questions. It bogs down my posting schedule.

During the next hour I do two more short posts. One is about a woman who has found her long-lost cat seven years after it went missing. The other is about what size Marilyn Monroe *really* was (12, but a 1950s 12 is like a current 6). I'm just searching for a good image of Marilyn that we have rights to when Molly IMs me.

> **Prettyinpink86 (3:52:11):** I heard you're working on a Marilyn Monroe post. Can I do some historical research for you? I have access to the Life archives. Or if you're really slammed today I would be happy to write the post! I have seen every one of her movies and I dressed up as Marilyn last Halloween! LOL!

Somehow I feel like her offer to write about Marilyn is not motivated by the goodness of her heart. Moira's always talking about how adorable Molly is and how she doesn't "know how we got along" without her. I think we got along just fine.

> **Alex182 (3:53:42):** I'm almost done with the post so don't worry about it.

Prettyinpink86 (3:54:23): Okey dokey!

I'm looking for one more longish post before I can start relaxing. I scroll through my RSS feed again; I see a story from one of the medical websites I subscribe to that looks promising, about a new study that shows how women are more likely to buy sexy clothes when they're ovulating. That seems like a perfectly ridiculous premise to pick apart. I spend 378 words writing from the point of view of my eggs, describing how they ran up a $400 bill at Frederick's of Hollywood the last time they busted out of my ovaries, how they can't resist the stripper heels. I call the post "Your Ovaries Want You to Dress Like a Whore." When Moira posts the piece, at four fifteen, I'm back in the commenters' good graces: "OMG this is hilarious!"

Even silent Tina IMs me her approval:

TheSevAbides (4:20:11): Nice one on that ovaries post. I LOL'd.

Alex182 (4:20:13): Hey thanks! I was really into the one you did today about Michelle Obama's state dinner fashion.

TheSevAbides (4:21:15): Word.

I think I like Tina, though I'm still vaguely intimidated by her. She is this impeccably dressed black woman who used to work as a freelance stylist before she started at Chick Habit. She had a Tumblr called What Chloë Wore, in which she dissected the always-batshit outfits of the actress Chloë Sevigny. The blog was a side business until she designed a graphic that ricocheted around the Internet for months, of Chloë wearing high-waisted hot pants, suspenders, a Zen expression, and nothing else. Under that image was the simple tagline "The Sev Abides."

The Sev Abides meme got Tina 674,530 readers in one day. Sure, they fell off after that, but it put her blog on the map. The *New York Times* Thursday Styles profile was next ("Fashion Don't Becomes a Blogger Do"). Shortly after that, Tina stopped posting photos of the Sev every day. She started posting photos of what she was wearing instead. Moira says that it was the photo of Tina in spiky, lobster-clawish Alexander McQueen heels that got Tina the job at Chick Habit. Tina's always polite to me, but she's a bit of a cipher. I can't tell whether she's just being cordial or if she actually hates me.

At this point in the day I don't need to have any more ideas; I merely need to read and condense. That's because my last post of the day is always the same—a gossip roundup that culls links from the web. Since I've been doing this for half a year now I can tell you every single person that has dated any Kardashian for more than three days. I go to the website of every major tabloid and get URLs for the most recent stories. I write a sentence or two about each one. My favorite today is the quote from Bret Michaels's wig stylist, who claims that his real hair is just as lustrous as the fake hair she manages for him. By the time I file to Moira it's five fifteen—and I'm done.

I take stock of myself. I've migrated back to the dun-colored couch with my laptop. No matter where I start on the couch, I always end up slumping in the crack between the cushions. I'm sitting among the spare change and the crumbs from the toast I always eat here. It's a near-perfect day outside. *Sally forth!* my inner camp counselor says. *Go for a run, or even just a walk. Go to the supermarket and get provisions for dinner! Breathe fresh, non-basement air!*

Then Rel IMs me.

Wienerdog (5:20:49): Dude.

Alex182 (5:20:51): What?

Wienerdog (5:21:13): Some asshole started a blog about us: http://www.breakingthechickhabit.com

I can't resist clicking on the link. The first thing I see when I go to the site is the headline: "Top 5 Things Alex Lyons Should Do Instead of Writing in Public." I *can* resist finding out what they are. I click off the site and notice that my mouth is hanging open.

Alex182 (5:21:58): Oh my fucking god.

Wienerdog (5:22:12): We need to get drinks asap and figure this shit out. I'm calling the other chicks.

Alex182 (5:22:34): Copy that.

I text Peter. He texts back immediately. "A hate blog about u? R u ok? Do u want to talk?"

I tell him I'm okay. "Going out 4 drinks with the chicks—call me when ur getting out of there."

"K. Don't be too late. Got to talk to u about something."

I tell Peter I won't be too late and finally get in the shower. I am in such a rush to see the girls that I don't have time to consider an outfit. That's right: I put the unwashed eyelet muumuu back on. But this time I also put on a bra (I *am* a lady), and deodorant, and, just to cover that musty old couch stink, a generous spritz of green tea perfume. I make sure I have my phone in case Moira e-mails with some late-breaking emergency news (e.g., Demi Moore had an affair with the least attractive Jonas brother; a beloved diva croaked). I throw it into an old *Paris Review* canvas bag along with my keys and my wallet and I run out the door.

Chapter Two

I spend the entirety of the ten-minute F train ride to the Lower East Side tugging at the too-short hem of my dress while my sweaty legs stick to the plastic seats. I periodically unstick my gooseflesh and hope that no one in my subway car notices the sucking sound.

As we whiz past East Broadway, I try to make sense of the hate blog. Chick Habit has become a phenomenon since I joined. Our traffic grows every week, and we have a reputation as the too-cool-for-school girls of the Internet—opinionated and just a tad bratty. Whenever a newspaper or magazine wants to know what women think about, say, some politician's mortifying shirtless Twitter photos, they call us for a token comment. I think Rel may have been the first person to ever use the phrase "dong shot" on National Public Radio. Considering our current status, my mother's explanation for the hate blogger would most certainly be: "Oh, they're just jealous!"

I can almost accept someone's hating me because I get to be part of the Chick Habit coven. It's much harder to accept the idea that someone just hates me.

This is the precise thought that I am rolling around in my head as I walk into Oahu, the newish tiki bar where Rel suggested we meet. I'm surprised she picked this place—it seems a little generic for her. I can't tell if we're there ironically or because we're genuinely supposed to be excited about fruity drinks as big as our heads.

I'm doubly surprised to see Rel and Tina already perched at a round, faux-bamboo table. Rel is notoriously late. I've seen her in getting-ready mode, and it involves no fewer than three outfit changes, two screaming phone calls with her boyfriend, and at least four trips down the Internet rabbit hole to check Facebook, watch a video of a sleeping corgi on a treadmill, and tweet angrily at someone who's wronged her. I guess this time around Rel was upset enough to step away from the laptop.

Rel and Tina are so deep in conversation that they barely notice when I sidle up to the table.

"Hey, where's Moira?" I ask.

"We decided not to invite her," Tina says.

"Why?"

"I don't want her getting involved with whatever we decide to do, and there's no need to freak her out yet," Rel explains. "I didn't invite Molly, either. I don't trust that kiss-ass."

Before either Rel or Tina says anything else, an extremely thin and familiar-looking blond waitress wearing a lei and an orchid-print romper approaches our table. "Can I get you anything?" she asks, smiling.

"Yeah, we're going to have a flaming scorpion bowl. Three straws," Rel says, smirking.

"No problem," she says, and as she walks away Tina whispers, "Holy shit, was that Amber from cycle three of *America's Next Top Model?*"

"Oh my god. Yes! That's why I recognized her," I say.

"We're getting distracted," Rel says impatiently. "We're here to talk about that fucking hate blog."

I snap to attention. "How did you even find that thing?" I ask.

"I have a Google alert on my name," Rel replies.

Tina doesn't say anything, so after a little pause I ask, "Well, did you guys read it?"

"Hell fucking yes I read it," Rel says. "And that's why we're sitting here right now. Whoever started that site needs to be destroyed."

"I didn't read it," I admit. "What do they say about you all?"

Rel makes a face. "Mostly they talk about what a smack whore I used to be, and how I used to go home with guys and pass out in their bathrooms. It actually doesn't bother me that much because it's true, and I'm totally honest about that on Chick Habit. What *does* bother me is when they say that my writing is really shitty and that I hate black people because of something that I wrote about Flavor Flav. Which is total bullshit."

"I don't think you hate black people. You just hate ugly people," Tina says, not unkindly.

We both look at Tina, who doesn't usually say things that are so snappy. She fidgets with the mini turban she's wearing and looks down at her shoes, which of course are the fabulous four-inch Cherokee wedges circa 1977 she scored on eBay last week.

"They say that my style is derivative, and that I only got successful by using some celebrity," Tina finally says. "Also, they found some photo of me from when I was sixteen. I know my jerky high school boyfriend probably sent it. He's still unemployed and lives in his parents' rec room in Dallas. My skin's terrible and I'm wearing a frumpy Starter jacket."

"Hey, I didn't know you were from Dallas," I say. This is the most open that I've ever heard Tina be. Whenever I try to ask her seemingly benign things about her life, like, "What do your parents do?" she clams right up. I don't even know how old she is. She's got really high cheekbones, which make her look more mature, but her skin is baby smooth. She could be anywhere between twenty-five and forty. Hearing about the Starter jacket in the photo makes me think she's somewhere in her early thirties—that's what the high school kids wore back when I was in middle school. "And hey, everyone wore Starter jackets back then. That's not so bad!" I reach out to touch her shoulder.

"You can only say that because you don't know what they said about you yet," Tina replies, shrugging me off.

I don't have time to respond because Amber has arrived with our scorpion bowl: about a gallon of viscous orange-pink liquid in a wide-mouthed ceramic jug covered with hula girls whose clay bikinis stick out from the side. With little ceremony Amber places it on the table in front of us and whips out a six-inch-long match. She sets the bowl on fire and looks satisfied as the flame reflects in Tina's vintage glasses.

After the flame has died down all three of us stick in our straws and start slurping. After a few huge gulps I take a deep breath and ask, "Okay, so what did they say about me?"

"They said that you're more hypocritical than Sarah Palin," Rel says.

"They said that you're more judgmental than Phyllis Schlafly," Tina tells me.

"And they have this video . . . ," Rel says, her voice trailing off.

"*What* video?" I ask. I immediately recall the video my college boyfriend Adam took of us having sex when I was nineteen. We were in love, after all. I was a little smart about it: I refused to let him film my face, so I'm fairly sure there's no way anyone could prove it's a video of me. And besides, he's not enough of a dick to expose me in that way. Is he?

"This video from your college a cappella group. I believe it was called Causing Treble?" Tina says, unable to suppress her laughter.

"Oh. My. *God.*" I feel instantly nauseous, like the scorpion bowl is clawing its way back out of me. I'm not sure if this is worse than the sex tape.

"Your solo performance during 'Bohemian Rhapsody' really is priceless. I replayed the part where you sing the word 'Scaramouche' about forty times," Rel says.

"The Schlafly crack was one thing," I say. "But dredging up the a cappella? This means *war.*"

I am trying to be funny, but I am actually hurt by all of this. I joined Causing Treble my first day of freshman year. I was in choir in high school, and it hadn't yet occurred to me that I didn't need to bring everything about my high school persona to college. That video must have been taken during my final show, and the mental image I have of myself from that day makes my entire body shudder. Even my sphincter is cringing with embarrassment, thinking about the fringed poncho I thought was so fashion-forward then, and the really awful bright red dye job I had that was more Ronald McDonald than Angela Chase.

I thought those embarrassing memories of my dorkus past had been buried forever. I wasn't always the savvy, non-poncho-wearing individual I am today. Until eighth grade I went to the local public school, an unsophisticated, cozy place filled with the offspring of Manning teachers and an assortment of locals. Sometime around the fifth grade I started writing. My early works included a poem about how much I hated mimes called "I Hate Mimes" and a play about the beheaded wives of Henry VIII called *Ouch!* My mom saved every one of these pieces of juvenilia—I stumbled on them neatly organized in file folders the last time I went home for a visit.

My graduating class from junior high had about sixty people in it, and we felt like extended family, so even though I would probably have been considered a bookish loser in most middle schools, I was spared from the pain of that kind of cliquish categorization. There weren't enough of us to shun each other like the mean girls always seem to on TV.

Because I could attend Manning for free, there was no question that I would go there for high school, even though it wasn't in the same stratosphere as Andover or Deerfield. It was filled with kids who got kicked out of those kinds of prep schools for selling LSD out of their dorm rooms. Still, my parents wanted to give me the best education possible, and while Stanton High would have been cozy, it didn't offer a single AP course and was best known for its high concentration of students with gonorrhea.

But even if it weren't embarrassing enough to have my mom as my freshman English teacher, I was shy and a little immature when I started at Manning, and certainly not prepared to interact with the gilded children of the elite who made up most of the population. You'd think that my fellow faculty kids would band together. Not so. Olivia Jordan, who had been one of my closest friends at Stanton Middle, rode her shiny "Rachel" haircut and lacrosse prowess to popular glory—and left me behind in the dust. I found comfort and friendship in the typical dork haven: the Drama Club.

I also edited the campus literary magazine, the *Manning Monitor,* and counted the days until I could ankle the Abercrombie hell for someplace way cooler. When it came time to apply to college, Wesleyan was my very first choice. It wasn't too far from home (I may have been ready to get out of Manning but I still wanted to have access to a home-cooked meal and free laundry), and it had a reputation for being bohemian but also rigorous. But most important, its creative writing department was supposed to be fantastic.

My mom was ready to hop in our 1994 Volvo and drive me to Middletown immediately when I found out that I got in, but my dad balked. He and my mom had scrimped on luxuries for themselves for years so that I could go to that YMCA camp followed by nerdy enrichment camps when I was in high school. He didn't want to spend on a private education for something so unstable. "Why don't you just go to U Conn if you're hell-bent on becoming a writer?" he pleaded. "I might as well take all our savings out and set fire to them."

I don't know what my mother told him about my so-called

writerly potential, but it must have worked—they agreed to enroll me in Wesleyan. I once tried to ask her how she convinced him to let me go but she just smiled and said, "I have my ways."

If the point of liberal arts college is to find yourself, then Wesleyan was worth every nickel. I made friends who truly understood me. I found a style that suited me—I ditched the poncho and stuck to short hand-cut jean skirts (to show off my legs, my best feature) and little boys' T-shirts I bought in bulk at the nearest thrift store. I lost fifteen pounds and got a pixie haircut. I had one semi-serious boyfriend, the aforementioned Adam, who in addition to being a casual filmmaker was also a stoner, and some scattered hookups after we parted that provided fodder for hungover Sunday brunches with the girls.

I also took as many theory and writing classes as I possibly could. Five years ago I could have told you a whole lot about Julia Kristeva and correctly used the word "simulacrum" in a sentence, but of course I remember none of it now.

I've grown up enough to know that I shouldn't care what the Internet public thinks about my eighteen-year-old self. Who among us didn't embarrass herself in some spectacular fashion in her mid- to late teens? But I guess a part of me hasn't reconciled the unformed, scared little person I was then with the person I am now. And I just want everyone to know my hair is *much* better than it used to be.

It's at this point that I see my face in the mirror behind Tina's head and realize that it's bright pink. Not just from the embarrassment; I'm two sheets to the wind and about to toss sheet number three. Ariel calls, "Hey, Amber, can we get us another one a these scorpion bowls? A frozen one this time, I don't want any of that flaming shit." Amber doesn't even seem to register that we know her name, despite the fact that she hasn't told it to us and is not wearing a name tag. I guess she must be used to randoms knowing about her by now.

Rel changes the subject abruptly, twirling a lock of long dark hair as if it were a cartoon villain's mustache. "You know who sucks?"

"Who?" Tina and I say simultaneously.

"Molly," Rel replies as Amber sets down another enormous bowl, this one covered in palm trees.

"Oh come on, she's harmless," Tina says. "She came over to my place last week to help me make a gif of Nicole Kidman's disappearing forehead wrinkles. She couldn't have been nicer. And besides, have either of you even met her in person yet?"

Rel and I have to concede that we have not. But we have seen her perky little dimpled face in all her Facebook photos, and Rel knows she wants to punch it. Also, she is *so* annoying over IM.

"Whatever, fine," Rel says. "She acts nice. I'll give you that. But there's something conniving about her. I can sense it."

"I sort of know what you mean. It's so obvious she wants our jobs it's pathetic. It's very *All About Eve*," I say.

"Yes! Exactly that. She's always trying to one-up me. I was taking a while to post last week and Moira was on my ass, and of course fucking Molly chirps at her, 'I could have a post for you in five minutes!'"

"Totally annoying," I say.

Tina's visibly uncomfortable with our dislike of Molly. "We're losing the thread here," she says. "We need to try to figure out who's behind this hate site."

Rel pouts for a second—she clearly wanted the smack-talking session to continue—but before she says anything obnoxious I help bring the conversation back to Breaking the Chick Habit.

"They seem to know a *lot* about us," I say.

"Maybe it's some disgruntled commenter?" Tina says.

"That would make sense," I say.

The three of us ponder this in awkward silence for a moment. The sea of commenters is vast, and their anonymity means it could really be anyone.

"You know, I just decided: It's a waste of time for us to sit here and speculate about who this bitch is," Rel says. "We just need to start tracking her down."

We decide that our next move is to find out who registered the Breaking the Chick Habit URL and what her—we assume our hate blogger is a girl, because who else would care so much about the content of a women's website?—IP address is. Unless our hate blogger is completely green, she will have hidden this information. But Tina says she knows a way to figure out who registered the URL, even if she's trying to mask it. That's another Tina revelation: that she's a secret Internet ninja.

Once we've decided on our plan of action, Rel tells us she has a surprise for us in her purse. "We need to go outside for me to show you," she says. We tromp out of the tiki bar together, leaving $40 on the table to pay for our bowls and for Amber. Even though she was a preening narcissist on *Top Model*, seeing her in person made me feel warmly toward her. I hope she'll use some of her tip money to pay for some new headshots so she can stop serving booze bowls to NYU students.

I haven't been this drunk on a weeknight since I moved in with Peter about nine months ago. When we first combined our mismatched tablewear in that small basement apartment, we entered a deep nesting phase, one that made me feel surprisingly relieved and relaxed. I had become self-destructive in the immediate aftermath of my father's death: carousing to an unhealthy degree, drinking mirthless whiskeys while covering mediocre bands for *Rev* at various seedy concert venues around New York City.

Cohabitating made that life seem even less desirable. Peter took pride in watering our meager backyard garden; I read Mark Bittman cookbooks and started making healthy meals that usually involved quinoa. But more than that: At the beginning of this year, Peter went from being an associate at a small firm to an analyst at a big one, and I started working at Chick Habit. Both of our jobs are nearly impossible to do with a hangover—forcing myself to have a smart take on Michelle Obama and the latest mommy blogs is unbearable unless my brain is at full capacity.

Yet here I am, about to get even more smashed: The "surprise" turns out to be a small plastic bag of weed, which Rel proceeds to furtively pack into a one-hitter that looks like a cigarette. "We're already wasted," Tina says, swaying on those four-inch heels. "Is this going to turn out well?"

Rel hands her the pipe and I guess Tina convinces herself that it's a fine idea, because she takes a long deep pull and her face relaxes instantly. She hands the pipe over to me. I take a deep pull just like hers and end up sputtering and coughing, and while I'm trying to breathe I fall backward into a potted tropical plant.

"Ahahaahaha the pot made you fall into a pot!" Rel can't stop laughing, and she says it over and over again like an autistic child: "Pot pot pot pot pot."

Tina and I are laughing, too, though the edges of my vision are starting to get a little fuzzy, and then Rel says, "It's such a fucking gorgeous night. Let's go to the beach!" It's true: The day's heat is no longer rising from the sidewalks, and there's a slight breeze against my bare legs. It's not yet August, when the entire city becomes soggy and fetid and unbearable. These July nights are perfect and fleeting.

I use Rel's back as a beacon to guide me down the stairs at Second Avenue, the straps of her sundress crisscrossing daintily over her shoulder blades. I don't really understand where we're going, just that I'm with Rel and Tina and everything seems hilarious. My apartment is just a few stops away and so I can gracefully hop off and go home to Peter in ten minutes or so. I look over at Tina and she's grinning broadly. Her face in repose is generally so reserved—lips pursed, eyes unsmiling—that seeing her look happy is infectious. For reasons obscure to me Tina starts singing Lisa Loeb's "Stay" really loudly right after we travel under the East River into Brooklyn. A bearded dude gets off at York Street, chuckling to himself, and then we're all alone in the car, so Rel and I join in, reaching a shouty crescendo with the song's last line: "AND YOU SAY / I ONLY HEAR WHAT I WANT TO . . ."

Suddenly I realize the train is outside, and I look out the thinly cracked window at the broad boulevards below. I start smelling the Atlantic's particular brine. I can tell that we're getting farther and farther from the tiki bar. I also realize that we've blown past my subway stop and I don't even know how far. I take out my phone and see that I have two missed calls and three texts from Peter. The texts are increasingly anxious.

> Peter Rice (8:48 PM): Hey! Hope you're having fun with the girls! Call me when you have a second.

> Peter Rice (10:55 PM): Haven't heard from you. Have a big day tomorrow so I'm getting into bed.

> Peter Rice (12:59 AM): Can't sleep. Where are you??? Hello??

My iPhone says it's 1:22 now. "Shit, I have to call Peter!" I exclaim. My face flushes three times, first with guilt because he's probably sitting at home worrying about me; immediately after because I'm annoyed that his feelings have interrupted my buzz; finally, a third time because I feel guilty for being annoyed.

"*Busted!*" Rel shouts.

I fumble at my phone, finally getting to Peter's number. He picks up after one ring.

"Alex, where are you?"

"Hey, baby! I'm on the F!" I say it brightly, hoping that he'll hear that I'm kind of drunk but still safe, and he won't want to start a fight over the phone.

"How are you getting reception?" he asks, the confusion outweighing the palpable concern in his tone.

"We're outside!"

"What do you mean you're outside?" Peter's voice is rising, incredulous.

"We're going to the beach?" It comes out as a question because I still am not 100 percent sure where we're headed.

"Are you going to Coney Island at one in the goddamn morning?"

Rel is sitting next to me and can hear what Peter is saying. "We sure are!" she says, loud enough for him to hear.

"Alex." He says it evenly but I detect a tinge of condescension. The tone sets me on edge and instinctively makes me want to contradict him.

"Mmmm?"

"This is a really bad idea."

"It's going to be okay, I promise!"

"I'm too tired to argue with you. Have fun on needle beach with a bunch of crackheads," he says, and hangs up.

I can't tell if he's pissed that I didn't call him earlier or if he's more worried that I'm going to get hurt among the syringes and dirty condoms that litter the Coney Island boardwalk. Or maybe it's that he's a tiny bit jealous that I'm out with Rel and Tina while he's in bed by eleven so he can be shiny and fresh for work in the morning. His call takes me out of the moment, and I look down at the mottled floor. It's unclear how for long I've spaced out for when Tina shouts, "Oh my God we're *here*!"

The last stop on the train is Stillwell Avenue. We walk out of the subway onto Surf Avenue and the smell of the ocean smacks us in the face. The last time I was at Coney Island was for a big music festival and the clean sea waft was marred by the overwhelming scent d'Portapotty. Not tonight. The rickety wooden Cyclone looms over us as we stroll. It's light enough for our path to be clear, but dark enough so that we can't see the hot dog wrappers and the discarded bottles of suntan lotion that surely surround us. Tina seems to know where she's going, so Rel and I hang back and watch her walk languidly toward the boardwalk. Rel reaches for my hand and holds it the way a small child would.

When she spots the beach, Tina takes off her shoes and breaks into a run. Rel drops my hand and follows on her heels. I start running, too. The only people in sight are a couple of Russian teenagers huddled together on a bench off to our left. They don't even look up as we come whooping past, throwing our light summer frocks and our canvas bags onto the sand.

Tina's the first one in the bracing Atlantic salt water. "IIIEEEEEEEEEEEEEEEE," she shrieks as she hits the waves. I'm already running so fast into the surf I don't have time to register the temperature until I'm struggling to catch my breath in the chest-deep water.

Rel is smart enough to see us shudder and stays in the shallows. We join her back in the surf and loll around in the sand, letting the waves wash over us. For such a fashionista, Tina is wearing some seriously dumpy undergarments: Her baggy white Hanes droop around her hips. Rel's yanking up the waistband of her boy-cut briefs, and I'm trying to clear the sand out of my unassuming black bra.

Simultaneously, and for no apparent reason, we stop fidgeting. For what seems like forever we sit in silence and listen to the sound of the ocean. The salty air on my exposed skin makes me feel almost achingly alive, diametrically opposite to my days spent in our basement dwelling, shackled to my laptop.

Finally, Rel says, "This is the best possible end to a shitty day." Tina and I nod our heads in solemn agreement.

An early morning chill has descended onto the beach and I start shivering. I get up and paw around for my muumuu, which now has fine grains of sand attached to all the eyelets and sticks unattractively to my damp body when I pull it on. I reach down and gather my bag, instinctively grabbing for my iPhone. It's been about forty minutes since we arrived at Coney Island, and it feels like that's the longest period of time I've been away from an electronic device since I started working this job.

I wipe the sand away from the phone's screen and find another text from Peter.

> Peter Rice (2:34 AM): Please just come home.

TUESDAY

Chapter Three

The *bring bring* of my iPhone jolts me out of a sweaty half slumber at 6:20. I would estimate I've been asleep for about two and a half hours. I stretch my legs and feel sand crunching in between my toes. My first coherent thought is, Why is there so much sand in this bed? And then the previous evening's activities come roaring back to me.

I look over at Peter's side of the bed and realize that it's a mass of blankets and a depression where his body should be. I heave myself out of bed and go out into the living room, where Peter's sitting in the crack between the couch cushions, drinking coffee with a blank expression. The burgeoning crow's-feet around his pale eyes look deeper than usual, probably because he barely slept last night. And I know it's my fault.

"Hi," I say, padding over to him. With every shuffle-step my head throbs. I pick the salty muumuu up from the floor and slip it on. Tiny grains of sand skitter across our wood floors. "I'm really sorry about last night. I was freaking out about that hate site and I wanted to unwind with the girls."

"It's fine," Peter says tersely.

"I don't really think it's fine," I say, sitting down next to him.

"I'm not trying to control you," Peter says. "But you can't disappear like that for hours and hours and not tell me where you are."

"I said I was sorry!" I reply, a nasal whine appearing in my voice, which I hate. I collect myself and say, "I promise I won't let it happen again."

"It's more than that. I don't want to sound like your dad." Peter winces and pauses; he sometimes forgets about my father, and always feels guilty when he does. "But I feel like those girls are a bad influence on you. You've never done something like this before. Coney Island?"

I don't want to tell him that right after my dad died I used to do stuff like this all the time. So instead I become defensive. "Seriously?! It's not like we went to Baghdad. We went to the beach. And it's not like I was alone. Don't be so provincial."

"Fine." This time when he says it he just sounds resigned, and he stands up as if he's about to leave.

"Peter, come on."

"I don't want to fight you on this."

"Can't you appreciate the extenuating circumstances?"

"Sort of," he grudgingly says. Then his tone abruptly shifts. "I did read the hate blog last night."

"What? How did you even find it? I didn't give you the URL!" I am genuinely surprised, and then concerned.

"Promise not to get mad?"

"Maybe."

"I Googled 'Alex Lyons sucks' and it was the first thing that came up."

"Fuck." But I have to laugh.

"Have you looked at it yet?"

"Not yet."

"I don't know if you should. There's some pretty awful stuff on there."

"I'm a big girl, I can take it," I tell him, with zero certainty that it's true.

"They're just anonymous losers. Who cares what they think?"

I sit with that thought for a second. I don't want to tell Peter that it's not what they think—though that can be hurtful—it's what they could potentially reveal that's so worrisome. There are probably things I don't even remember doing that could be dug up and framed in a way that would make me look like a monster. But instead of following that horrifying train of thought, I decide to change the subject.

"What about you? Are you going to be okay at work today even though you didn't get much sleep?"

Peter sighs. "Yeah, I think it will be fine. I got a few hours and you know they have that fancy new Nespresso machine at the office. I'll just mainline caffeine all day." He starts palming the ceiling with his hand as we talk. The downside of living in the garden apartment is that our ceilings are so low I can touch them with the tips of my fingers. When he's anxious, Peter puts his whole hand up there. His ire seems to have dissipated, but I'm pretty sure he isn't going to fully forgive me for a few days. Still, I feel like at least one fire has been put out.

Peter walks over to the kitchen to put his coffee cup in the sink.

"I love you," I tell him.

"I love you, too," Peter says, and bends down to kiss me on the forehead.

I hate having even the smallest tiff with Peter, since I'm so grateful for his presence in my life. In the months before Peter and I met, I felt lost in such a profound way I couldn't even voice it. I dated a bunch of clones of my terrible ex-boyfriend Caleb—artists in every different medium. I went out every night and was drinking even more than when Caleb and I were together.

What brought me out of my downward spiral was the night I went home with this nebbishy, sleazy guy from *Rev* named Adrian who always wore an out-of-date leather jacket and tried to pass as twenty-nine though he was probably in his midthirties. Adrian was a writer for the magazine who came into the office only occasionally, but whenever he did he would loiter by my desk and ask me to go to concerts with him. I always turned him down, but when Adrian asked me to a secret Magnetic Fields show just after my dad died, I said, "Sure, why not."

I don't remember much of the show because I started chugging whiskey as soon as I got there. When Adrian asked me to go home with him, I slurred, "Whatever," and the next thing I knew a cab was ferrying us to his Lower East Side bachelor pad. As I watched this man I wasn't even attracted to roll on a condom, I knew I was about to cry. I pleaded with my drunk self: Don't cry in front of this troll. But as soon as we started having sex, I couldn't stop the tears from rolling down my face.

What was I doing in bed with this loser? What was I doing drinking and snorting my life away?

To his credit, Adrian noticed I was crying and stopped, but he looked annoyed. "Are you okay?" he asked. I shook my head and started crying harder. I started crying so hard that I had to run to the bathroom and throw up. I stayed in that sticky bachelor bathroom for half an hour, splashing cold water on my face and trying to pull myself together. When I emerged, Adrian was fully clothed in beat-up corduroys and a Samples T-shirt, and I could barely look him in the eye.

"Do you need me to get you a cab?" he asked, by then genuinely concerned.

"No, I'm okay," I told him, and rushed out of there.

The next day I had already turned this mishap into a comedy routine—"Having sex with Adrian makes me puke and cry"—but I knew that I had reached some kind of turning point. I only went out after work to DJ, and I stopped drinking more than one cocktail a night. I spent those morning hours before I had to be at *Rev* buffing up my résumé and sending out links to my best posts, hoping that some other publication would take notice so that I could start truly fulfilling those creative ambitions my parents had sacrificed so much for. My mom couldn't pay for my health insurance anymore—there was now only one income to save for her retirement when the expectation had been for two—so I needed to find something more lucrative, and fast.

I was so down on the idea of writing professionally, I even started applying to advertising agencies and branding firms. Copywriting was a kind of writing, I convinced myself, and one that could even give me a 401(k). When I told my mother about these applications on the phone, she sighed deeply. "I guess you should do what you feel like you have to do," she said. "But if you want my advice, you shouldn't waste your talent on diaper ads."

A few weeks into my new shit-together regime, I was DJing at a small bar in Park Slope, near where Jane and I lived together. It wasn't a particularly fashionable place—its only nod to décor was a string of chili pepper lights ringing the backyard—but they were paying me $200 for the evening and advertising me as if I were some semifamous DJ diva just because I worked at *Rev.*

I had just finished a set and was getting a club soda at the bar when a sweet-looking preppy guy with nearly black hair and very blue eyes appeared next to me. He was wearing a button-down shirt, acceptably stylish jeans, and Tretorn sneakers. He basically looked like all the guys who ignored me at Manning. I glanced at him and then turned away.

"Can I buy her drink?" he asked the bartender, undeterred.

"It's free for me because I'm DJing," I told him, hoping he would just go away.

"Well, can I buy you a drink somewhere else?"

"I don't think so."

"Why not?"

"Because you're a strange guy and I don't even know your name." I was still in a vulnerable place then, and I wasn't in the mood to fend off creepsters in shady bars. I saw his crisp exterior, dark hair, and square jaw, and (this really says something about my headspace back then) my first thought was, He looks like the "Preppy Killer," Robert Chambers.

"I'm Peter," he said, extending his hand to me.

"Alex," I said in a way I hoped telegraphed that I wanted him to leave me alone.

"I really liked your set and your DJ name. DJ Divine Hammer? A Breeders reference, right?"

"Yeah," I said, semi-impressed that he'd gotten it, considering how well pressed his shirt was.

"And you write for *Rev*?"

"Yeah—how did you know?" I was both delighted and slightly freaked out by this. I'd never been recognized by my writing before, so that part felt amazing, but the piece of me that read the *New York Post* too much was still thinking, Is this guy going to take me to Prospect Park and stab me a bunch of times?

"I read your stuff every day," he said.

"You and about fifteen other people." As I looked at his genuine smile and his non-murderer-y eyes, the squickiness I was feeling started to dissipate.

"I think it's really funny," he said, cocking his head toward me.

I was truly flattered by this, and we started talking about the bands that we liked. It turned out that this prep could out-indie me: He knew about obscure yet highly influential bands that had played a single show in someone's basement in Milwaukee in 1977. "I have that 9 Fingers bootleg everyone always talks about," he said, bragging.

"So what do you do?" I asked, bowled over by his level of rock nerdery.

"I'm a calligraphy grad student at Pratt."

I didn't know how to respond to that at first. I was trying to avoid artists, but also, that sounded like the most useless and idiotic graduate degree I had ever heard of.

"That sounds . . . interesting," I finally managed to say.

He laughed. "I'm just joking. I work in finance. I thought some artsy shit would play better with a girl like you."

I had to laugh at how accurately he'd pegged me. "I have to start DJing again," I told him.

"Can I have your number?" he asked, and to my surprise, I gave it to him.

He called me the next day.

Unlike my previous boyfriends, Peter always called when he said he would. During our first few dates, I put on my dizzy-girl-about-town act. I told him the having-sex-with-Adrian-makes-me-puke-and-cry story; I bragged about my DJing and my job at *Rev* and made myself sound like much more of a whirlwind than I actually was. Looking back, I think I was acting as loony as possible to test him: Caleb had always criticized me for being so dramatic, and I wanted Peter to get the full force of my drama to see how he would respond.

Peter was not turned off. Underneath that preppy exterior, we had a lot in common. He is also an only child, a late-in-life miracle baby. His parents had both been married before, and neither had children from those first, disastrous unions. Peter's mom in particular was desperate to have a kid, and so when he emerged on her forty-second birthday, she was immediately obsessed with him.

Unlike me, though, Peter's always been a golden boy: partial scholarship to Georgetown, secured a job as a junior analyst at a well-regarded financial firm by the fall of his senior year. I secretly think he's always followed the straight and narrow path in part because he never wanted to let his mother down. His parents retired at sixty-two and live on Long Island. They watch Fox News for approximately 40 percent of their waking hours. They are nice to me in a distant sort of way, although I suspect that in my absence they refer to me as a socialist.

When Peter and I first started dating we would go to shows together, and we always stood near the front and held hands. But soon we found ourselves at home more often than not. Being with him was so soothing and felt so natural that I could really be myself, not some histrionic fool. I didn't mind being a homebody when Peter was around. Sure, part of me was always going to be overwrought, but Peter accepted that as part of who I am, not as some terrible inconvenience to his lifestyle.

After Peter heads to work I get up to brush my teeth and see that it's almost seven. "Shit," I say aloud, and decide to ankle the teeth brushing. Instead I pour myself some coffee and dart back to the couch, flipping open my laptop. "Come on come on come on," I chant under my breath when I get the spinning rainbow wheel. Moira is going to be furious.

Finally my MacBook comes to life. I immediately go on IM.

MoiraPoira (7:01:33): WHERE THE FUCK HAVE YOU BEEN??

Alex182 (7:01:35): I'm really sorry! I overslept.

MoiraPoira (7:01:44): Molly was the only one of you

lot online on time this morning. So I gave her the first post of the day.

MoiraPoira (7:02:15): Sometimes I think she's the only one of you girls who really cares about this job.

Alex182 (7:02:28): It won't happen again.

MoiraPoira (7:03:12): It best not. I've sent you a bunch of links. Choose one and have something for me by 8:30. If you're a minute late filing, Molly gets your next post slot.

Alex182 (7:03:34): Roger that.

Damn brown-nosing Molly. Of course she was there to pick up my slack. I know I really shouldn't be mad at her—she's just doing her job, and I'm the one who screwed up—but I'm furious. Since the traffic pressure started, Moira's been emphasizing our constricted budget; she's made it very clear that no one is going to get promoted unless someone else quits—or gets canned. It really feels like Molly is deliberately trying to make me look bad so she can squirm her way up the ladder.

My laptop feels extra hot against my bare legs and all I want to do is rinse the Coney Island grit off my body, but I need to churn out at least one post before I can move from the couch. I click through Moira's links.

There's a story about a high school in Tallahassee, Florida, where ten girls in the tenth-grade class are pregnant. We wrote about those knocked-up teenagers when the story first broke two weeks ago. A reporter named Marti Grimes at the *Tallahassee Democrat* had written an article on the "Tallahassee Ten," and Tina had linked to the story and provided some clucking commentary about the pathetic state of sex education in some of our school districts.

The story was big news for a day or so but then receded. It generally takes the major news networks a week or two to pick up on these Internet firestorms, and so last night Diane Sawyer put on her best concerned expression and talked to some of those preggo fifteen-year-olds on *ABC World News*. I predict the Lifetime made-for-TV movie about the Tallahassee Ten will hit your cable listings in approximately six months.

I watch the clip online. "I'm pregnant, so what?" one of the girls asks the camera defiantly, her bulbous belly pushing out over the top of her too-tight jeans. "So was my mom when she was my age. And I turned out fine."

Diane Sawyer cocks her head to the right, purses her lips, and says nothing.

I throw the clip up with a headline, "The Tallahassee Ten: 'I'm Pregnant, So What?'" and manage to write two hundred desultory words describing Diane Sawyer's immobile face and the pregnant girl's churlish yet sort of inspiring attitude. Part of me admires her unwillingness to be shamed, even in the face of all that straining Botox.

Ten minutes later, the comments on the post are mixed. Most of them are about the sorry state of sex education in the Bible belt. A regular commenter with the handle Shananana says, "If only these girls had Depo shots this stuff would never happen." The normally churlish Weathergrrrl is even supportive. "You should publish things like this more often."

The room starts to seesaw right after I've read the first handful of comments, and I run to the bathroom, thinking that I might hurl.

I don't puke, but I do spend several minutes lying with my face against the cool tile floor, trying to decide if I should go to Breaking the Chick Habit when I can force myself into an upright position again. I weigh the pros and cons. Pro: I won't be able to stop thinking about what's on the site until I actually see it for myself. Con: I will actually see it for myself. Pro: It might not be as bad as I fear. Con: It will be worse than I could ever imagine in my darkest self-loathing nadirs, confirming all the anxieties I have about myself as a person and a writer. Pro: Maybe they think I'm pretty!

I use what little arm strength I have left to lift myself off the floor and propel myself back to the couch. An IM from Rel is waiting for me there.

Wienerdog (9:07:15): Ugh I feel like shit

Alex182 (9:07:44): I know, dude. I want to die.

Wienerdog (9:07:49): This is the worst.

Alex182 (9:08:01) I KNOW! And that little sycophant Molly did the 8:30 post instead of me. She is so far up Moira's ass I don't even know how she can type.

Wienerdog (9:08:04): Word.

Alex182 (9:08:07): I still haven't looked at Breaking the Chick Habit yet.

Wienerdog (9:08:11): Dude, that is ridiculous. Just look at the fucking thing already.

Alex182 (9:08:16): Are you sure?

Wienerdog (9:08:22): Yes. Sack up. It's not actually a life or death situation.

This is the second time in two days that one of my coworkers has told me that I need to grow some cojones and deal. I tell myself four times: You are not a wuss you are not a wuss you are not a wuss you are not a wuss. I take a deep breath and type the URL into my browser.

I have to give our hate blogger credit for excellent design sense. She's taken our Chick Habit logo—a baby chick held in a manicured hand—and realistically severed that li'l chicken's head for her own logo. She also altered our site's purple color palate ever so slightly so that Breaking the Chick Habit looks like an angry eggplant exploded all over it. I also notice the cleverness of the name: In acronym form, it spells BTCH.

The site hasn't been updated since yesterday, so the first post at the top of the screen is still "Top 5 Things Alex Lyons Should Do Instead of Writing in Public." It's written in the manner of a Letterman Top Ten and lists, in descending order, occupations that would apparently better suit me:

5. Cleaning toilets. She thinks her shit doesn't stink, so other people's shit probably won't bother her either.

4. Hospital orderly. She's quite familiar with bile already.

3. Nursery school aide. Fits her maturity level to hang around with toddlers.

2. Garbage collector. She's used to producing trash so picking it up won't be too much of a stretch.

1. Kill herself. That's not really an occupation, it's a one-off job.

I'm so shaken by this—especially the last one—that I have to get up and pace around the ten square feet of the living room. I guess my Internet nemesis stopped at five, rather than doing the full ten, because once you suggest someone should kill herself there's really nowhere else to go. For each number on the list, the hate blogger has hyperlinked to one of my posts. If you click on "Kill herself" it goes to a particularly judgmental post I wrote about women who live-tweet their own weddings. "About to walk down the aisle!" DashingDiva79 had tweeted last month. "About to stick my head in the oven!" I had blithely written about her up-to-the-minute marriage coverage.

When I had written that post, I chuckled to myself—but I also wondered if I had crossed the line. I had used

DashingDiva79's real name in the post—Ashley Smathers—and now when you Google her, my petty post is the first thing that shows up.

I click through the other links. I've posted over a thousand times since I started this job, and yet this anonymous blogger has somehow zeroed in on the five posts that I've felt most conflicted about. I continue to pace. Should I call Peter? Cry on the phone to my mom? IM my fury to Rel? I thought the site would be upsetting, but I hoped it would be something I could laugh off. This isn't funny at all.

But rather than take some kind of action, I am compelled instead to devour the entire website in one sitting. It's only been around for a month (how did it take us so long to find it?) so the archives aren't *too* deep—it's averaging about a post a day. The post preceding the one about me is the one that calls Rel racist. "The stereotypes she perpetuates about people of color are so awful," our hate blogger wrote, "I can't believe that Tina agrees to work with her." But then she adds, "Too bad Tina's too dumb to protest."

I even make myself watch the infamous Causing Treble performance, which was posted last week, without comment. The earnestness in my little face as I head-bang to the extended bridge in "Bohemian Rhapsody" is nearly heartbreaking. I move on quickly to the photo of Tina from high school (it's not *that* bad) and see that the hate blogger has also posted an anonymous e-mail from one of Tina's ex-coworkers. Before Tina was a freelance stylist, she worked under Rosie Stevenson, one of the most famous stylists in the fashion business. You might know her from her little-seen reality show, *Ro's Guide to Style*. "When she first started working here, Tina thought that French-tipped manicures were cutting-edge. I don't know if you can sue someone for intellectual theft for stealing your style, but Ro should lawyer up."

I see the posts shaming Rel for her drug-laced past and a couple more about specific things we've written. (Our blogger does not take kindly to our blanket coverage of every *Real Housewives* iteration—"These are not the kinds of women the Chickies should be promoting with their considerable platform.") And then I see something that makes me take a sharp breath.

It's a scanned-in clipping of a Connecticut newspaper story from 1992. The article is about the local reaction to brand-new first lady Hillary Clinton. It has a photograph of me, along with a quote: "I love Hillary Clinton. I think it is super neat that she is out being a lawyer and not home baking cookies."

I was obviously parroting back something I overheard my notoriously non-cookie-baking mother say. I recall her gathering her fellow teachers in our living room to make phone calls on behalf of Bill. I helped her seal envelopes asking for campaign donations because, always the teacher, she wanted me to learn about civic involvement. I remember watching her dark hair shine under our kitchen lamp as she stayed up late decorating placards. Whatever I feel about everything that Hillary has gone through in the intervening twenty years—and I have a *lot* of feelings about that one—that has remained a fond and private memory of a special time spent with my mom.

Until now.

The headline on that post is simply "How Did This Bright Little Girl Become Such a Raging Bitch?"

It's a mindfuck to see a photograph of your vulnerable small self on the Internet, posted for the purpose of making you feel like a jerk. Furthermore, it's immediately clear to me that our hate blogger is someone who knows me personally. There's no other explanation for why she would have included such a seemingly random image—or how she would have found it.

I start trying to catalogue all the people I may have wronged in the past twenty-five years. Maybe it was that girl in college whose boyfriend I made out with on my twenty-first birthday. Or that guy who always hated me because I beat him in high school debate.

I'm on the verge of a sweaty panic attack when I realize that the little IM bar I've minimized is blinking angrily in the lower left-hand corner of my laptop screen. Moira. Shit.

MoiraPoira (11:45:01): Where are you?

MoiraPoira (11:46:32): Hello?

MoiraPoira (12:01:04): It's almost the end of the month and let's just say your traffic numbers are not what they should be. Molly is eager to write on Selena Gomez pole dancing if you're not up to the challenge of posting today.

Alex182 (12:02:56): I'm really sorry. I'm just not feeling very well. I'll get something good for you right away.

Before Moira's traffic admonition, I had considered telling her about our prolific little hater. Chick Habit is her baby, after all, so she'd probably want to do something about the site. But I'm now so nervous about finding a blockbuster post that I'm no longer in the mood to confess to Moira. She'd probably just admonish me for being a pussy and say something about needing a stiff upper lip if I want to succeed at this job. So instead I shove my concerns about BTCH down into the bottom of my churning stomach. I need to find something to write about before I can run out to the bodega and get the world's greatest hangover remedy—bacon, egg, and cheese on a roll.

I have bacon on the brain as I refresh refresh refresh my RSS feed. Nothing doing. I scroll down through Twitter to see if anyone is talking about anything post-worthy. All anyone seems to be discussing is a new Lady Gaga single, which Rel already posted about two hours ago. I turn to my Facebook wall—this is a last resort. Peter's mom has just posted photos from her bridge club's road trip to Fort Ticonderoga. There's a post from Jay, my sincere med student friend from college, who "likes" a story from the *Times* about the rising costs of health care in America. I also see that some super-lefty girl—I think from college, but I don't recognize her name—has posted a similarly useless article about the secret links between BP oil and American Apparel, or BP oil and Whole Foods, or BP oil and puppies. I don't bother clicking through to find out which it is.

Since nothing good is popping up, I decide to stall a bit by posting a quick link to a study that shows if you loved chocolate as a kid you will be more likely to be an alcoholic as an adult. You know, because of science. I file to Moira in a mere ten minutes. I realize I haven't IMed with Tina yet today, and so I decided to message her.

Alex182 (12:13:04): Hey! I finally looked at the hate site. They're pretty harsh, but I think that pic of you from high school is kind of cute :)

TheSevAbides (12:13:38): It's not.

Alex182 (12:13:44): Well compared to the other crap on there it's pretty mild.

TheSevAbides (12:14:25): I guess.

TheSevAbides (12:14:39): By the way, why did you post about the Tallahassee Ten?

Alex182 (12:15:11): I thought the video was good and I had an angle on it.

TheSevAbides (12:15:42): That was my story. I posted on it before.

Alex182 (12:16:18): Sorry. I didn't mean to step on your toes.

TheSevAbides (12:17:32): This isn't the first time this has happened. You should watch yourself.

Shit. The last thing I wanted to do was piss Tina off after our breakthrough last night. I try to change the subject back to BTCH.

Alex182 (12:18:20): I'm really sorry. It won't happen again.

Alex182 (12:18:25): Did you find out any of that IP stuff yet?

TheSevAbides (12:20:29): I'm actually super busy right now.

Alex182 (12:21:39): Sorry. Talk later.

Tina's coldness and Moira's pressure and BTCH are all adding up to an oppressive weight perched on top of my chest, and I begin to feel like I might vomit. Again.

Prettyinpink86 (12:23:19): Do you need me to help you with anything? Moira says you're having a rough time today ;)

I want to say to Molly, You shove that winky-face emoticon where the sun don't shine. Instead I type:

Alex182 (12:24:22): I'm fine, thanks for asking. I don't need any help.

What I do need is to satisfy my bacon jones. I'll feel less crazy if I eat something, I figure, since I haven't had anything to eat since my salad of the day before. And so I run across the street, clutching my iPhone.

The air inside the bodega is cool and calming. It smells like a combination of Café Bustelo and the slightly wilted dahlias sitting in buckets near the register. I am the only customer in the store, save for the deli cat that is lazily stretching in his oval bed. Manuel makes me the platonic ideal of a bacon, egg, and cheese sandwich: The egg is fluffy and glistening with oil; the bacon is freshly cooked, its fatty edges still extant; the cheese is that gorgeous neon orange color. I watch as it melts evenly into a thin layer of film over the egg. He even toasts the bun, which is not hard and stale but soft and pliable—I can *see* how pliable—in his large, latex-covered hands. I watch, nearly drooling, as he wraps the sandwich in wax paper and then again in tinfoil, then sticks it, along with about forty-five napkins, more napkins than any one girl could need, into a plastic bag. He hands the bag over to the counterman and smiles at me.

"Thanks," I say, grateful for the easy interaction. I pay for my sandwich and head back home, but the second I step outside my myriad anxieties hit me along with a blast of truck exhaust and hot air. "Shit shit shit shit shit," I chant quietly as I dart back into the street.

As quickly as possible I open the door and throw my canvas bag onto the Saarinen chair my grandparents gave us. That chair is the one nice thing in our apartment, and instead of using it to actually sit in, Peter and I have turned it into a crap receptacle. The second we enter the apartment we dump all the day's detritus directly onto the chair. I slump back onto the crusty couch and flip my laptop open again.

There's an IM waiting for me from Jane.

JaneRivera (12:47:11): Hey gurl.

* * *

Jane and I met during the second week of our freshman year at Wesleyan. A friend of hers from boarding school lived down the hall from me, and Jane came with us to a white-trash party that was being thrown by a French Canadian hockey player who lived in our dorm. We all wore gleaming white wife-beaters and multicolored bras without even coordinating. I don't remember much from that night (blame the Everclear punch) but I do recall Jane making a really viciously funny joke about our truly dumb Canuck host and his unformed "fetus face."

After that Jane and I were fast friends. We lived together the summer between our sophomore and junior years and continued to be roomies when we moved to New York. When my dad died, Jane was the one who made me get out of bed every morning even when I was plastered to the sheets with tears still crusted to my face. My mom has decreed that Jane is an honorary Lyons, and she has come home with me every Thanksgiving since we were nineteen—her family lives in Iowa so the trek was always too long and expensive to make just for a few days.

The thing about Jane is that she isn't all biting humor. She's also got a very strong sense of character. She's a social worker who works with teenage girls, and she cares about her adolescent charges with her entire being. Which is not to say she's smug or preachy about what she's doing for a living—just sincere. Since I started working at Chick Habit I've seen less of Jane than I used to—at the end of the day I'm so tired I just want to couch-melt. We try to see each other on weekends but now that she lives with her boyfriend, too, our shared tendency is to hole up in our respective apartments.

Alex182 (1:05:27): Hey, hon.

JaneRivera (1:05:33): What's going on?

Alex182 (1:05:42): Merrrrrrrrrrrrrr

JaneRivera (1:05:49): ???

Alex182 (1:06:02): http://www.breakingthechickhabit.com And that's not all! I had a huge fight with Peter this morning, which was probably my fault.

JaneRivera (1:09:21): Are you around tonight? We should hang out. I haven't seen you in forever! You can tell me all about it.

Alex182 (1:10:14): Let me check with Peter. If he's working, I definitely want to play. But if he's going to be home I should really be here with him. I need to weasel my way back into his good graces.

JaneRivera (1:11:46): K.

I am actually desperate to see Jane. My sense of self has been so altered by the BTCH, I need to see someone who has long known the real me as opposed to the virtual me. I e-mail Peter at his work address to be sure that he gets it.

To: peter.rice@polydraftergroup.com
From: alex@chickhabit.net
Subject: Tonight

Hey Love,

I'm really sorry again about last night. I never meant to worry you, I'm just having a hard time with everything that's going on.

Anyway, I was wondering if you're going to be late at work tonight. If the answer is yes, I am going to see Jane. If the answer is no, I'll cook something amazing.

Hope you're surviving at work.

xoxox A

Peter responds immediately.

To: alex@chickhabit.net
From: peter.rice@polydraftergroup.com
Subject: Re: Tonight

I am going to be here until at least 11. Go be with Jane. Don't worry about this AM. We can talk about it more later but it's nbd.

Love,
P

I sigh with relief and IM Jane as soon as I get Peter's e-mail.

Alex182 (1:21:22): Peter says it's cool—I think he's mostly forgiven me. I can't wait to see you!!!

JaneRivera (1:21:45): Yaaaay! Me too. Let's meet at the Cactus Inn.

Alex182 (1:22:31): Yessss! We haven't been there in forevs. I'll see you after I'm done with work.

JaneRivera (1:22:58): Awesome. xoxoxo

This part of the summer is notoriously slow news-wise, and there isn't even a good celebrity wedding that I can fawn over and/or mock. My RSS feed is a wasteland, same with Twitter and Facebook. As a last-ditch effort, I decide to check my inbox for tips.

The first thing I see when I click to my Chick Habit account could be spam, or it could be that big break I've been looking for. The sender's name is just a series of symbols, but the subject line has traffic landslide potential:

Daughter of "Genius Mom" Author Darleen West: Snorting Coke in Her Skivvies

Darleen West has made a mint off telling America's women that they're just not working hard enough at being good mothers. She made a huge splash last year with her book, *How to Raise a Genius, Times Four.* You see, Mrs. West has a set of quadruplet daughters, all of whom go to top-tier schools: Raina is at Yale, Rachel is at Harvard, Renata goes to Columbia, and Rebecca—who invented a new kind of robot when she was still in high school in Omaha—is the toast of MIT.

West was an executive at a big petrochemical firm until she had the quads when she was thirty-seven. It was the result of in vitro, of course (not that she would ever admit to it). When she realized that she was pregnant with four, rather than one, she figured a large brood was part of God's plan for her. Her husband, Bob, a fellow exec, kept working for the Fortune 500 company, but West decided that she was going to put all her considerable gumption into raising those four girls to be the best women they could possibly be.

In her book, Darleen outlined the countless hours she spent drilling the quads on their times tables before kindergarten and how she taught all four girls to read ancient Greek before their seventh birthday. "Rebecca fought me at first," Darleen conceded in the *New York Times* excerpt, "but eventually she came around and said, 'Mama, *eukha'ristos eimi*—thank you for making me learn.'" The problem with today's moms, Darleen has said, is that they're too lazy. Her perfectly coiffed and expertly dyed blond bob makes frequent appearances as a parenting expert on various morning shows.

Now that Darleen has become a national figure, she's decided to take her influence to the next level: She's running for state senate in Nebraska's twentieth district in a special election to fill a vacant seat. The previous state senator had to resign earlier this year because of a scandal involving improper use of funds. He was making state troopers drive his mistress to the salon and his kids to soccer games. A brief perusal of the brand-new darleen4senate.org website shows that Darleen is a Republican in a pretty red district. Her platform is the usual "yay babies, boo taxes" GOP agenda. If she can win the primary, she's got the election in the bag.

I open the e-mail to find a link inside. Is this for real? I try responding to the sender, asking that question, but my e-mail bounces back. Could it really be one of Darleen's perfect children, fucking up on the World Wide Web?

Chapter Four

I click on the link, which brings me to a password-protected YouTube URL. The e-mail informs me that the password is TheInvisibleWoman. I hesitate for a second—is this going to be a virus that infects my computer with endless porn pop-ups?—but my curiosity outweighs the fear. I click over to the site and type in the password.

A grainy image of a standard dorm room appears on my screen: two uncomfortable-looking wooden chairs and a well-made bed topped with a Laura Ashley quilt. The only light in the room appears to be coming from a kitschy lamp shaped like an owl, which is perched right next to the bed. I hear a barely post-pubertal man's voice say, "Come here, Becky. I have a surprise for you."

If this video is legit, then its star is Rebecca West, the rebellious, robot-making MIT wunderkind, and it will be Chick Habit gold. In all the press Darleen received, Rebecca was always cast as the true success story: She was not only the most accomplished but her spunkiness (she stood up to her mom sometimes!) proved that Darleen's draconian parenting tactics did not break a child's spirit.

Darleen and the four girls appeared on the *Today* show around the time *How to Raise a Genius* came out. I remember Ann Curry turning to Rebecca and asking her if she ever regretted spending so much of her childhood inside learning a dead language rather than outside playing with her sisters.

Rebecca smiled condescendingly at Ann and said, "I don't regret a thing."

Now, on-screen, a lithe, slightly gawky blonde comes into frame. The video quality is mediocre, but she does look just like the cardigan-clad girl from the *Today* show sofa. This time the prim sweater has been discarded in favor of a lacy bralette and what appear to be bathing suit bottoms. I have to smile at her ensemble. This is definitely collegiate "I haven't done laundry in two weeks" chic. But I'm also impressed with its brashness—Becky is definitely not thinking about her dear old mom or the *Today* show in this moment, prancing around half-naked in front of a camera.

Suddenly a textbook covered in tidy lines of cocaine slides onto the table in front of the camera. I try to make out the book's title. It looks like it's called *Understanding Intelligence*.

"Surprise!" the guy's voice exclaims. Becky's face lights up and she does a little victory dance. A twenty-dollar bill is pushed toward her, and she rolls it up with expert precision, her snub nose wrinkling with the effort. "You go first," she tells the guy off-screen. "You paid for it this time."

The camera is put down for a second and all I can see is the

Laura Ashley pattern up close while a deep snort reverberates. Becky's companion picks up the camera again and points it right at her delicate face as she snorts one line, then two, then three. "Hey, hey!" the guy says. "Slow down, sister. Save some for tonight."

Becky picks her face up from the textbook and looks directly at the camera. As she dabs at her nose with her fingers, I notice what a guileless face it is. She's got a wide, open expression and a smattering of freckles across that baby nose. She's so pale that even in the terrible lighting you can see the faint blue veins on her forehead, which is surrounded by fine hairs so blond they're almost white. I take a screen shot of her face, so that I can compare it with other photos later if I decide to post this.

"Fine." She sighs and puts down the rolled-up twenty.

"Since I just gave you all that sugar, how about you give me some sugar?" the guy says to her.

At this suggestion, Becky smiles a shy little grin. "Okay," she says. She stands up, so her face is out of frame. She lifts off her bra in one swift motion and walks toward the camera.

The video ends and for a minute all I can do is sit there and stare at the screen. Then I look Becky up on Facebook.

I start clicking through her photos—her settings are so lax I can see everything. At first they're staid and boring: Becky standing hand in hand with the robot she made; Becky with her arms wholesomely slung around her sisters' shoulders; Becky riding a roller coaster at the Nebraska state fair. She certainly resembles the girl in the video, but her corn-fed good looks are so generic that I need something more substantial to prove that it's really Becky blowing all those lines.

After a few more clicks, I find exactly what I'm looking for. In the background of one of the photos, clearly taken in a dorm room, is the telltale Laura Ashley bedspread. The sweet pink flowers nearly throb through my screen.

My first thought is: This is going to be the biggest page-view bonanza in the history of Chick Habit.

My second thought is: This is really going to tank Darleen's nascent political career.

My final thought is: Do I really want to ruin this poor kid's life? Becky West's only worldly significance at this point is that her mother is a fame-seeking missile. It's not her fault that Darleen has cast her as a superior being in a national morality play. Sure, she's been happy to fill that role when confronted by Ann Curry about it—but I'm sympathetic to the desire to please one's mother and to look like a princess on national TV. But it's not just her good-girl status that's at risk here. I'm no lawyer, but I wonder if she could be prosecuted for the sheer amount of coke strewn around her dorm room. I guess she could always take the Miley Cyrus route and argue it's an "herbal supplement."

When I was a kid, I would never have dreamed that I would earn my living investigating the allegedly drug-addled children of semi-celebrities in order to write about them on the Internet. For one thing, the Internet didn't really exist when I was little. And for another, I wanted to be an actress before I wanted to be a writer.

I always got the leads in the local theater productions in our small Connecticut town, but mostly because the competition wasn't especially fierce. I was Charlotte in *Charlotte's Web* in first grade because I was the only precocious kid who could memorize all the lines without faltering (though I must say, my spider dance of death at the end of the E. B. White story was worthy of Sarah Bernhardt). My being an actress was a fantasy my mother always encouraged, even though my talent was middling at best. She supported any and all of my creative pursuits. Probably because deep down she felt like she had shelved her own.

My parents moved to Stanton in the late seventies, right after grad school, where they had met. My father had finished his Ph.D. in chemistry at U Conn but hadn't fared well in the university job market. He had too much pride (and too much debt) to keep putting himself out there at the collegiate level. When he was offered a job teaching advanced chemistry at Manning prep, he took it.

Dad finished his degree before my mother did. She had already completed all her coursework toward a Ph.D. in comparative literature, so she decided to come with him to Manning to write her dissertation on the realist works of Spanish novelist Vicente Blasco Ibáñez. As my parents told it, she set up a workspace with carefully thrifted lamps and cozy fluffy chairs in the attic of the lovely old Greek revival that Manning had provided my parents.

While my father adapted to the rhythms of the school year and the excesses of his wealthy students ("Donny will not be able to take his chemistry test this week because he must visit his father at the villa in Switzerland"), my mother floundered up there in the attic. She started out on a strict schedule, writing at least a thousand words a day. But as she reached the middle of her dissertation, she became completely blocked. She would sit at the typewriter for hours and for every sentence she'd write, she'd erase two more. It got so bad that she became phobic, she's told me: She would start to shake and sweat just walking up the steps to the office she had so lovingly appointed.

My father didn't have much patience for my mother's freak-out. My mom's baseline personality is placid and bright; my dad was more of a brooder. The pattern they had set from the beginning was that my mother was the ray of sunshine that brightened up his default gloom. He couldn't understand how his cheerful wife had become such an anxious mess—all he knew was he wanted her to get control of it. In order to yank her out of her doldrums he suggested a cross-country road trip to Berkeley the summer between his first and second years at Manning.

As they rambled through Wisconsin in their beat-up 1969 Bug, my father gave my mother a bombshell ultimatum: Either finish your dissertation in the six months after we return from this trip or take a job I've secured for you in the English department at Manning. I don't know how the conversation played out after that. My parents never went into the particulars. All I know is my mother took the job at Manning. The half-finished dissertation is in a locked file cabinet in that attic office, where my mom grades papers to this day.

When my dad was still alive, my parents told this story so many times that the pathos got ironed out of it. They tried to make my mother's panic seem silly, rather than harrowing, but I never really took it that way. And yet, my mom has never seemed unhappy as a teacher—she takes pride in her work and genuine succor from the connection with her young students. But there's a palpable wistfulness about her. I suspect she always wonders what might have been if she had really pushed herself to write.

As if living out her sublimated fantasy, I wrote for the college newspaper at Wesleyan, and I took that writing very, very seriously. I didn't want my dad to feel like he'd wasted his money, and I wanted to be proud of the articles I e-mailed home to my mom. I wrote some culture pieces about a subset of girl bands I liked and referred to as clit rock. But I also wrote investigative features that I thought would really change the world—or at least change Connecticut.

I was most proud of the eight-thousand-word exposé on an underfunded Bridgeport shelter for victims of domestic violence that won me the creative-nonfiction award for advocacy journalism at the end of my senior year. I was a favorite of the English department, and several of my fellow newspaper nerds complained that I wasn't enough of an activist to deserve the award—like my piece was wasn't worthy because I'd never chained myself to the nearest Planned Parenthood.

That was around the time I started applying for jobs. I thought I would be a shoo-in for intern or assistant gigs at liberal bastions like *American Prospect* and *The Nation*. But I heard nary a peep from any of them—even *Mother Jones* wouldn't have me. Turns out that all the other earnest college kids from Vassar and Brown had already scooped up every position possible.

Then I tried to get a gig at every newspaper in the country, from Traverse City to Tarzana. I would have been happy to have covered the sanitation beat, writing about changes in street-sweeping for some tiny local daily in the hinterlands, but none of them would hire me, either—not even in an unpaid position.

After that second round of rejections, I decided to try for the gig at *Rev*. Sure, it wouldn't involve the hard-hitting reporting I wanted to be doing, but I was hardly in a position to be picky. I knew that the industry had been slowly dying for years and I would be lucky to get any kind of job. Behind my dad's back my mom secretly slipped me money for health insurance and other incidentals, since *Rev* wasn't about to give me any benefits even though I worked full-time.

I'm still paying for my own health insurance these days out of pocket—and I can't afford to lose my job. What's more, my mom would be crushed. These are the prevailing thoughts in my head when I forward the e-mail to Moira, adding a single exclamation before the link: "OMG!!!!"

Moira IMs me right away.

MoiraPoira (1:45:38): This is remarkable. Are you sure it's the real thing?

Alex182 (1:45:45): Pretty sure. I took a screen shot of that close-up of her face, and it looks just like her Facebook photos.

MoiraPoira (1:46:04): That's not enough.

Alex182 (1:46:13): Okay, how about this: The quilt on the bed in the video matches the quilt on the bed in her Facebook photos.

MoiraPoira (1:46:25): Better! I need to ask first: This girl is over 18, right?

Alex182 (1:46:57): She's 20.

MoiraPoira (1:48:35): I need to send this to our lawyer now. If he says it's kosher for us to post, you're going to have to reach out to Rebecca and Darleen for comment. Can you handle that?

Alex182 (1:48:59): I guess?

MoiraPoira (1:49:33): Guessing is not good enough. If you want this, you're going to have to reach out to them. If not, I am happy to give this scoop to Molly. But you'd have to be a fool to give this away—this post just saved your ass.

Smart Moira: She knows that I am way too competitive to allow any of the other girls—especially Molly!—to get credit for this. And she knows I need the page views. So do I.

Alex182 (1:50:01): I'll contact them as soon as we get the lawyer's okay.

Curiously, my stomach churning has disappeared. My heart is racing but my previously hungover brain feels clear and sharp. I do two posts in quick succession. One is about the tabloid treatment of Jennifer Aniston. Headline: "How Does Gorgeous

Multimillionaire Jennifer Aniston Get Called a Loser?" The other is a video of a Siamese kitten who has wedged himself into a large Mason jar. Headline: "Jar Jar Awwwwwwww."

Doing those posts takes about forty-five minutes and I then have a lull. I catch my breath after the brief frenzy of work, and it is just enough time for the shame spiral to take hold. I start thinking about the potential repercussions of publishing this video. I can't even imagine what a field day the hate blogger will have with my posting this. She'll probably Photoshop my face onto Muammar Gadhafi's corpse.

I bet the commenters will be worked into their highest self-righteous lather about this video. As much as we like to say we don't care about the commenters and we try to downplay their importance, they manage to burrow into our skulls. Rel and I have had long conversations about the most prolific ones, as if they are distant cousins we are forced to tolerate at family reunions: "Oh my god, did you see what Weathergrrrl said yesterday about our beauty Q & A? 'The world will only change through revolutionary action. Not through satisfying advertisers with stories about makeup.' She really is a lunatic," Rel once told me. "She's always e-mailing me, trying to get me to write more about 'oppressed peoples.'"

Which is not to say we're not exceedingly fond of some of them: They mention us by name in the comments, occasionally to support us or tell us we made their day better. Once I posted something more personal than I usually do; it was a thinly veiled anecdote about my relationship with Caleb, pegged to some new book about how it's a mistake for girls to try to gain acceptance from guys by aping their behavior. My favorite commenter,

MrsDarcy25, sent me a personal message, telling me about her own failure to join her boyfriend's dudely social circle. "This post made me feel less alone," she wrote. Without sounding too Hallmark about it, I was touched.

But posting something like the Becky West video will be like detonating a nuke in a crowd of readers—and I don't know if I have the thick skin to do it. I picture Becky back on that *Today* show couch, trying to explain to the new anchor, Savannah Guthrie, why she was wearing a bikini bottom for underwear while snorting coke off her robotics textbook.

Normally when I am this anxious about something work related I call Peter, but I tell myself that after our explosive morning I want to give him some space. If I'm being honest with myself, that's not the only reason I don't call. One of the pillars of Peter's self-construction is a firm moral fiber. Maybe it's the former altar boy in him, I don't know. But if I tell him that I'm nervous about making this live, I'm pretty sure he'll tell me not to post it. Even if I explain about the page-view pressure and about how horrible Darleen West is, he'll stand firm. He might launch into a jeremiad about personal privacy and media responsibility. He'll heave that deep, chesty sigh he always makes whenever he's disappointed in me.

I can hear his voice now: "Alex," he'll say, "don't do this."

Chapter Five

I need to get ready to see Jane, so I peel off the muumuu, which is starting to smell like wet dog. I put on a bra and a clean madras sundress. I pull my air-dried hair back into a ponytail. Since the Cactus Inn, where I've arranged to meet Jane, is only a ten-minute walk from my apartment, I decide to take the time to mask my under-eye circles with some expensive French concealer that Tina swears by. I slop the beige goop in the deep troughs under my eyes and the dark pigmentation on my eyelids. Now I look like I'm wearing flesh-colored swim goggles. I accept this as an improvement, spritz on some perfume, and head out the door.

Jane is sitting at a sidewalk table as I approach the Cactus Inn, and she starts waving wildly as soon as she sees me in the distance. Every time I see her, the first thing I notice is her crooked grin, and I'm reminded anew of how much I love her. The sun is shining on her face, so she has on great big Elizabeth Taylor seventies shades. Her nearly black hair is in the chic bob she's had since we moved to New York, and it looks freshly washed.

She gets up to hug me and promptly says, "You look like shit." Even underneath the enormous sunglasses I can see her zeroing in on my shoddy makeup job.

"I know. I only got a few hours of sleep last night."

"Is it because you were freaking out about that stupid hate site?"

"Kind of?" I can hear my voice swing up at the end of this sentence, as if I am asking a question. I don't really want to talk to her about the Coney Island shenanigans. Jane doesn't have a whole lot of patience for my misbehavior if she thinks I've been thoughtless about it. If I tell her the truth about my fight with Peter, she'll tell me I'm being a jerk. So I change the subject. "How are you?"

"Oh I'm fine, truly. Today that punk Janelle O'Reilly called me a Chink bitch under her breath, which is a new one. I guess in the right lighting I could pass for Chinese," Jane says. She is actually Peruvian, and Janelle is one of her favorite, and most vexing, kids. "But she's just moody because I tried to get her to talk to me about why she suddenly has scratch marks on her inner arm that she's trying to cover with about a thousand rubber bracelets. It's a challenge. Hence the margarita." Jane lifts it up, like a toast to the air.

Every time I hear about Jane's job I feel guilty about spending so much time contemplating our cultural feelings about Jennifer Aniston.

"But my stuff is boring," Jane says, setting her drink down

and looking at my face. "I want to hear more about the latest crisis."

"It's not boring," I tell her. "It's great. How's Ali?"

"He's good. He got this enormous smoker that looks like R2-D2 and now he spends most of his free time in our crack yard figuring out how to smoke the hell out of large quantities of meat." Jane and Aleister live in an apartment in the neighborhood next to ours. While they were drawn to the place because of the outdoor space, that space is a little, shall we say, rustic. It's entirely concrete, and when Jane and Ali first moved in, it was filled with broken stroller parts and beheaded Barbies that had been left behind by the previous tenant. They've cleaned it up quite a bit, but Jane still refers to it as the crack yard.

"Ah yes, men and their meat," I say. And then I can't help bringing the conversation back to what's been going on at work. "My coworker Tina is supposed to be doing some Internet recon to see if she can find out who owns the Breaking the Chick Habit domain, but I haven't heard back from her on that. But I do have one major clue about the hate blogger's identity: She's definitely someone who knows me."

"What?" Jane squeals, delighting in the gossip. "How can you tell?"

I explain about the newspaper clipping and how it has me spooked.

Jane's thoughtful for a minute. "Hmm, I guess it does sound like it's someone who knows you. Though there is the possibility that it could be a stranger who is really committed to digging up relics from your past."

"I am a nobody! Just some girl who writes for some website. I refuse to believe that someone out there who has never even met me is demented enough to do all of this: to figure out where I grew up; to travel to the local Stanton, Connecticut, library; and to copy microfiche from 1992 so they can scan it into the Internet to prove a point," I say.

"You never know. But you're probably right, so let's put our thinking caps on. Is it that girl who was dating Roger when you made out with him on your twenty-first birthday?" Jane asks.

"OMG, soul mates!" I laugh. "I thought of her, too. But I would hope that she's over something that happened one night four years ago."

"What about that weird girl who was in our French hypertextualism class? The one with the midget hands?" Jane waves her hands around for extra effect.

"She was just weirdly obsessed with those Parisian student protests in the sixties. She wasn't psychotic. And I don't think she hated me." I'm a little defensive. I already feel like so many strangers hate on me in the Chick Habit comments that the idea of a random, distant acquaintance wishing me ill makes me shift around uncomfortably, uncrossing and then recrossing my legs.

"But remember that one time you guys got into that huge argument in class about Deleuze? And when you were walking out of the room she called you a De-loser?"

"Now you're being deliberately obscure."

"I'm just trying to help! Honestly, I can't really think of anyone else you've mortally offended," Jane says.

I sigh. "Well, think on it and get back to me," I say just as our waiter arrives. He's got neck tattoos and his ears have big floppy gauges in them, but he's wearing a crisp white shirt tucked into black slacks. "A blood orange margarita, no salt, please," I tell him. He sneers at my smile, so I drop it.

"Hair of the dog?" Jane asks after he's left the table.

"Yes. I need it to deal with this latest fresh hell. Do you remember that book that came out last year, *How to Raise a Genius, Times Four?*"

Jane frowns. "Vaguely? Some fertile midwestern lady crowing about how great her kids turned out, right?"

"Basically. It's by this former executive Darleen West and it's about how well her radical parenting techniques worked on her quadruplets. I found out that one of those 'great kids' apparently loves coke, and I don't mean the soda."

"Oooh, juicy!" Jane exclaims. "How did you find out?"

"Someone sent me video of Darleen's twenty-year-old daughter snorting a ton of the stuff and taking her top off."

"Geniuses gone wild, huh?" Though I'm judgmental about my job, Jane's mostly amused by it, if not actively entertained. Like most of the girls we hung out with in college, she holds the *New Yorker* and *Us Weekly* in almost equal regard.

"Pretty much. Mostly I'm wondering if I'm going to destroy this girl's life if I post the video. I sort of enjoy the fact that we're going to prove that Darleen West is an enormous hypocrite, especially because she's shamed so many other women into thinking they're bad mothers. She's running for office in Nebraska now, so proving what a fraud she is could actually be kind of important. And it certainly won't hurt my status at work. But the kid, oy. She's going to be totally humiliated. She might also be prosecutable because of the coke. Is it worth it?"

"You're right, that is a pickle," Jane says just as the waiter returns with a snarl on his face and roughly sets down our drinks. "Uh, thanks?" Jane says as he storms off.

"Be nice," I tell her. "We come here for the dirt-cheap booze, not the service."

"Maybe," she says. "But doesn't he rely on our tips to pay for all those Magritte tattoos?"

"True, true." I laugh. But I don't want the conversation to get away from my dilemma. "So what do you think I should do?" I ask, pushing.

She considers it for another moment and then says, "If the lawyers are okay with it, I think you should post it."

"Really?" I thought she would probably take the high road on this one because she works with teenagers.

"Yes. That girl was stupid enough to record it. It'll be a hard pill for her to swallow but I don't think you're responsible for her bad decisions."

"I'm surprised you're on board with this."

"Why?" Jane says, her face unmoving, almost hard.

"Well, I thought maybe because the girl is only twenty, you'd be against my posting the video. That's not so much older than your kids . . ." My voice trails off a little at the end.

"Those girls are nothing like my kids," Jane says sharply, taking a big swig of her drink. "Most of the kids I counsel will barely graduate from high school. Nobody's writing bestsellers about how great *they* are. You're high if you think a cute rich girl like this is going to go to jail because of this video. This little brat deserves to be taken down a peg."

"Way harsh, Jane." While I hold only contempt for Darleen, my whole problem is that I'm sympathetic to Becky. I can imagine being in Becky's shoes—but I guess the always-pragmatic Jane can't. Or maybe she just doesn't want to.

"Real talk, Alex."

"I guess you have a point," I say, conceding.

"Just do me a favor?" Jane says as she sucks down the rest of her margarita.

"Shoot."

"Do not mindfuck this to death. If you decide to do it, do it and just move on with your life. Do not endlessly obsess about it afterward."

"Um, do you know me? In the seven years we've known each other, have I been able to 'just move on' without obsessing about *anything*?" I smile at Jane across the table.

Jane smiles right back at me. "No. But a girl can dream, can't she?"

The waiter finally comes back to our table and Jane orders a second margarita while I opt for a club soda. I get up to go to the bathroom and as I'm walking toward the back of the restaurant, dodging the fake palm trees, I see a girl about my age who looks really familiar. She's got curly brown hair, the kind of perfect sproingy curls that you see in photographs of children from the thirties. Her nose is small and inoffensive; her standout characteristic has to be the dimples in her cheeks. You could fit dimes in those suckers. I'm about to walk past the table where she's having a muted conversation with another, slightly older, woman when I place her: It's Molly!

I do the mature thing: I turn my face away from her and rush toward the bathroom.

In the bathroom I lock myself in a stall and sit for a while, trying to decide what to do. I really don't feel like exchanging fake pleasantries with Molly.

I get up to splash some water on my face. I look at my reflection in the bathroom mirror. I tell mature mirror Alex, You are older and wiser than Molly is—a whole two years older. You should go over and introduce yourself, which is the polite, adult thing to do. This girl has been nothing but nice to you, and you shouldn't resent her for being a hard worker.

Also, if I go over and show my face, I can say something just a tad menacing so she will get the message that she needs to step off my beat.

I check to make sure my ponytail is high and proud, leave the bathroom, and stride confidently over to Molly's table, where she's still chatting quietly and intently with her friend.

"Molly?" She looks startled when I say her name, and since I'm standing over her, I feel powerful for a second, like I could take my hand and smush her curls into oblivion if I needed to. "I'm Alex Lyons. I recognized you from your Twitter photo."

Her dimples start flashing when she realizes who I am. *"Oh my God hiiiiii!"* she says, and before I have a chance to appear threatening, she gives me a bear hug. I can feel a dampness from her armpits on my shoulders, and she smells like Clinique

Happy perfume, which is what I wore in the sixth grade. I hug back limply. "It is so amazing to finally meet you in person!"

"It's good to meet you in person, too." I stand there awkwardly. Now that my plan to be cool toward her has been foiled, I don't know what to say. Molly doesn't introduce me to the woman sitting across from her, but I do get a good look at her. She's wearing an expensive-looking dress and some worn-in Louboutins; the signature red heels are pretty scuffed. I'm not getting a vibe that she cares to say hello. She's already taken out her iPhone, which has a bright pink vinyl cover, and appears to be playing Angry Birds.

I ask Molly the only question that I can think of, which makes me sound like a wizened barfly: "So, do you come here often?"

"I live in Fort Greene, so it's not too far for me, and the drinks are so cheap!" Molly chirps.

We stand in uncomfortable silence for another moment before I say, "Well, I should get back to my table." Molly is still quite close to me, smiling so widely that it's starting to creep me out. I take a step away from her.

"Okey doke! Hey, I am sorry about that Breaking the Chick Habit site. What an old meanie that person must be!"

"Wait, what? How do you know about that site?" Whatever feelings of strength I had before have completely dissipated. Obviously I know that anyone with Internet access can see the BTCH site, but as long as I was only talking about it with Tina and Rel, I could fool myself into thinking that we were the only ones who had read it.

"Tina told me! Doi! I barely read it, it was too mean for my blood," Molly says, shaking her perky little head, while still smiling.

I'm not sure how to respond to this. Is she trying to make me feel bad by bringing up BTCH? Is she going to mention my blasted a cappella performance? Is she really just trying to sympathize? While I'm attempting to figure this out I realize I haven't said anything for an uncomfortably long time. "I have to get back to my friend," I finally blurt out.

Molly doesn't appear to notice how weird I've gotten. "Okay! I am so glad you came over! We should come here and drink margs together ASAP."

"Sure," I tell her, knowing I would rather drink lighter fluid. But before I can turn around to leave, Molly leaps up and hugs me again.

"Can't wait to see you online tomorrow, Alex!" I can't even manage to respond to this, and so I just start backing away slowly.

I head outside to my table, feeling off-kilter. Why was Molly so dementedly friendly? Is it because knows something about BTCH that I don't? And furthermore, who was that woman Molly was with? Was she just some friend who didn't feel like feigning interest in a stranger? Now that I think of it, she looked sort of familiar. I feel like I've seen her ombré dye job before.

"What's wrong?" Jane says. "You look constipated."

I don't feel like going into my weird exchange with Molly. I don't want to sound like a complete nut job by telling her that I think my coworker is trying to gaslight me because she gave me a really big hug.

"You got me. I have not pooped for like four days," I tell her.

Jane orders a third margarita, and I get another club soda, mindful of the hangover I'm still nursing. I also want to be sober when I get home. We linger outside the Cactus Inn for another hour gossiping about our mutual acquaintances (apparently two of our guy friends from college have swapped girlfriends, after a particularly poignant orgy).

Finally, we each put $10 on the table and stand to leave.

"Promise you'll tell me what happens with the video and this hater website?" Jane asks.

"I promise."

"If it turns out that we do know your hate blogger, I will go pee on her doorstep."

"You're a real pal," I tell her.

The ten-minute walk home feels longer than usual. It's not even eight P.M. yet and so the temperature's still hovering near ninety. Small half circles of sweat stain my once-fresh dress, and I wish that I had brought my iPod so I could drown out the worries that are crowding back into my brain. Talking to Jane was cathartic but despite her go-ahead to post the Becky video I'm still anxious about it. I'm also slightly freaked out by running into Molly. I resolve not to look at my e-mail until I get home, just to ward off the anxiety for a few minutes more.

The apartment is empty when I get there, and I take off my sundress and put on some of Peter's old boxers and a white T-shirt. Finally I do check my phone—no word from the lawyers yet, and no further communication from the video leaker. I must admit I'm relieved. I do have a text from Peter, though.

Peter Rice (7:55 PM): I'll be home in an hour, can't wait to see you!

I flop onto the couch to await his return. I decide to put on the TV and flip until I find something that will take my mind off my predicament. Oxygen is airing their perpetual reruns of *America's Next Top Model,* and I'm delighted to discover that Amber's cycle is on tonight. The models have been flown to Madrid for the last leg of the competition, and Amber accuses another girl of stealing her rice cakes. Weaves are pulled; threats are made. Amber utters that well-worn reality TV cliché about not making friends. "I came here to win, I didn't come here to make friends . . . or share my rice cakes," Amber says.

I don't remember who was kicked off at the end of that episode, and I don't get to be reminded, because I fall asleep before the judging panel begins.

WEDNESDAY

Chapter Six

"Hey, babe." Peter's hovering over me in the early morning light.

"What time is it?" I ask. I notice that he's fully awake already and fear that I'm starting off yet another morning on Moira's shit list. As soon as my eyes focus I try to locate my iPhone. Maybe there's an e-mail waiting for me from one of our lawyers telling me I can't post the Becky West video—thereby rendering all my dithering moot.

"Don't worry, it's only six fifteen. You fell asleep on the couch before I got home."

"Ooof. I'm sorry, I wanted to hang out last night."

"It's really okay. I was beat by the time I got back here at eleven. This report on Omnitown is killing me." This is the deal he's been working on for at least a week. I know that Omnitown is trying to acquire a media company and Peter's advising them on it, but that's about the extent of my understanding.

"Are you sure?"

"Absolutely. We'll have time together this weekend. Besides, you looked so cute all tuckered out on the couch, I didn't want to disturb you."

I smile up at him. I don't have the heart to ruin this moment with my agita over the Rebecca West exposé.

He smiles back. "I gotta hop in the shower."

Peter has already made the coffee, so I pour myself a cup and sit down at our small kitchen table. I want to fully wake up for once before I make the commute to the couch. There's a binder taking up most of our tiny Ikea table, and before I move it I open it to see what's inside.

I realize immediately that it's a PowerPoint presentation from Peter's work and my eyes glaze over as they see foreign jargon like "Significant synergies create value" and terminology like "double-digit IRRs." I'm about to shove it away and get to my laptop when my eyes focus in on the name Tyson Collins—a.k.a. the big boss man, owner of the media conglomerate that owns Chick Habit.

Peter's singing an off-key rendition of "Gigantic" by the Pixies in the shower. He generally starts vocalizing halfway through, so I know he's got a few more minutes in there. I read the report as quickly as I possibly can, stumbling over the business-speak and trying to make sense of the numerous graphs and earnings projections. Maybe the inclusion of Collins's name is innocuous; maybe he's just an investor in Omnitown or he's on the corporate board.

But then I reach a slide called "Strategic Rationale: acquisition creates substantial value for shareholders" that I can understand. It's about how Omnitown can purchase Collins Media's stable of websites, and its implications make me want to yack up that coffee: "A combination is expected to generate annualized adjusted EBITDA benefits of at least 33 percent, primarily through a targeted 10–20 percent reduction in headcount."

I feel my stomach plummet. If the sale of Collins Media goes through, our staff is going to be reduced by as much as 20 percent. Moira's recent page view pressure now makes a whole lot more sense: If I don't get my traffic stats up as quickly as possible, my head will be the first one on the chopping block.

I hear the water go off in the bathroom and quickly shut the binder before I get to the end of the report. I know I shouldn't have even started reading the thing—it's proprietary information—but still, how could Peter be working on this deal? He knows that if it goes through I might lose my job. Does he think his work is somehow more important than mine is, just because he makes more money? How can he be singing in the shower right now when he knows that this is happening? Suddenly I feel a whole lot less guilty about being an absent girlfriend this week.

I chug the rest of my coffee and hustle over to power up my laptop. I don't want Moira to be pissed at me for being late again, especially now that my employment status is even more precarious than I thought it was. Luckily, when I get online Moira's not even there yet. I start looking through my RSS feed for something to post on.

I'm scrolling through last night's stories when Peter emerges with a towel wrapped around his slim waist. I can't even look at him directly, even though out of the corner of my eye I can see him smiling. Fuck him for looking so cheerful right now!

Moira comes online as I hear the sound of drawers closing and opening and then the distinct scrape of Peter's wingtip shoes against our hardwood floors. He comes back into the living room before she IMs me.

"What's on your mind?" Peter asks, straightening his tie with one hand while he holds the incriminating report in the other.

"Nothing's on my mind." I stand to hug him. I don't want him to know anything is amiss just yet—if I don't show him some affection before he leaves he'll know something's off. "Just sleepy."

"All right. I gotta take off. Seven thirty meeting. But let's talk tonight, for real."

"Okay, see you tonight."

I turn back to my computer and listen as the door closes behind him. I don't want to look at him longer than I have to because I'm so churned up. I'm feeling so low at this point that I can't help but navigate back to Breaking the Chick Habit before Moira sends me my marching orders. It's been updated since I checked it yesterday. The latest post has the headline "Alex Lyons Cares About the Important Issues," and the text beneath it is a complete reproduction of the post I did about the meowing Siamese trapped in the jar. I'm both relieved that this is as mean as the site's gotten today and also, weirdly, a critical reader. The dig seems slightly beneath BTCH. Her insults usually cut closer to the bone.

Finally, an IM from Moira pops onto my screen.

MoiraPoira (6:40:14): Glad to see you're on early today.

Alex182 (6:40:43): Sorry again about yesterday.

MoiraPoira (6:41:02): Let's not dwell on it.

Alex182 (6:42:42): Any word from the lawyer yet?

MoiraPoira (6:43:56): He hasn't given me solid approval yet, but it's looking good. He says he'll let me know sometime this morning.

Alex182 (6:44:12): Word.

MoiraPoira (6:45:21): Pickings are slim today, but there's yet another study debunking the link between autism and vaccines. That's always good for a commenter brawl.

Alex182 (6:46:45): Sure thing.

Moira sends me the link to the study, and I write 312 words about how parents who don't vaccinate their children—especially if they're doing it because anti-vaccine bobblehead Jenny McCarthy told them to—should probably be sterilized. "If you're letting a washed-up, fake-titted former MTV hostess give you medical advice, you don't deserve to have children," I write.

This is even more aggressive than I usually am, but I'm strangely emboldened by the hate blogger. If she's going to rag on me for writing about kittens, for God's sake, I'll give her something to *really* complain about. Plus being provocative gets me comments, and comments get me page views.

I also see this as self-training for posting the Rebecca video.

If I can handle this small controversy, maybe the bigger one won't be so bad. I resolve not to read any of the comments on this post—or any post I write for the rest of the morning. I'm not letting anything break my stride. It's a free country, I tell myself. I should be allowed to state my opinion without being attacked by the judgment police every goddamn second.

I file to Moira.

MoiraPoira (7:41:16): The first lady is about to be on the telly. Why don't you check that out on your beloved Today show.

Alex182 (7:41:38): kk

I have a moment of Zen watching Michelle Obama gracefully answer Savannah Guthrie's questions. She's wearing a black-and-white patterned dress with bold geometric shapes and a fuchsia belt. I bliss out on her bright voice without really paying that much attention to what she's saying. Child obesity something something. I know I'm going to have to rewind this portion if I'm going to write about it, but for this minute I am enjoying Michelle's ultimate composure. I could use some of that myself today. In the midst of this calm, I get an IM from Tina.

TheSevAbides (8:23:29): So I had time to look into our hate blogger's identity.

Alex182 (8:23:49): And??

TheSevAbides (8:24:15): As I suspected, our hater registered the site to a dummy company—Breaking the Chick Habit LLC—with only a PO box attached.

Alex182 (8:24:50): Bummer.

TheSevAbides (8:25:13): But I was able to see that her IP address is from Greenpoint, so at least we know she's local.

Alex182 (8:27:34): I have this suspicion that our hate blogger is someone I know.

TheSevAbides (8:27:55): How's that?

Alex182 (8:28:12): She's been writing mainly about me lately, and she posted this thing from my hometown newspaper from when I was a kid. There's no way she would have been able to find that unless she knew me.

TheSevAbides (8:29:32): Hmm, I don't know about all that. Maybe the hate blogger just figured out where you were from through clever Googling and maybe the newspaper recently digitized their archives. I mean, how do you explain how she got the photo of me from high school?

Alex182 (8:30:23): I guess.

Now Tina's just making me feel like a paranoid loon. Maybe the sleepless night and all the stress of this job have turned me into exactly that. Still, I wish I could get back to the closeness I felt toward her on Monday night (we sang on the subway together!). It's supposed to be us against them, isn't it? Maybe she'd feel just as worked up as I do if she knew that some of us might be about to lose our jobs. Not that I'm in the mood to share that with her.

Alex182 (8:31:24): Whatever, I need to get back to posting.

I rewatch the clip of the First Lady so that I can accurately transcribe some of what she's saying and eke out an angle, but as I'm watching I notice that Savannah Guthrie cannot stop giggling dorkily at everything MObama says. "I think that our parents have a right to expect that their kids will not be served pizza and Cheetos at every lunch," Michelle says, to which Savannah guffaws. Then Michelle says something about fresh produce at schools, and Savannah, absurdly, giggles. I clip together every chuckle and gasp into one big Savannah Guthrie laughing supercut, and post that with the title "Savannah Guthrie Takes Michelle Obama Super Seriously." I file this to Moira at around nine forty-five.

MoiraPoira (9:46:22): You're on a roll today. I love your vigour!

Alex182 (9:47:24): Thanks!

MoiraPoira (9:47:59): I guess you took my advice to grow a pair. This is good to know, because I just got word back from our lawyer.

Alex182 (9:48:34): And???

MoiraPoira (9:49:12): You're clear to post the video. He says it's fair use. You just need to be sure to word the post and the headline in a vague enough way so that we don't sound like we're asserting the video's of Rebecca—we're just alleging it. I still want you to contact Rebecca and Darleen for comment, of course.

Alex182 (9:50:03): OK. How long should I give them to respond before I publish it?

MoiraPoira (9:51:23): Reach out to them now and then start writing the post. Send it to me when you're done with it so that I can go over it with the lawyer. We'll include their responses if they do get back to you quickly, but even if they don't we're publishing that sucker at 1 PM. I've already loaded the video into our player.

Alex182 (9:53:02): Gotcha. Wow.

My early morning ferocity is slightly diminished by the prospect of actually confronting the intense Darleen West about her daughter's drug-addled antics. But something inside me has shifted today, and I know I have to publish the video. I could be unemployed by the end of the quarter. My mom will be crestfallen if I lose this job.

I go to the Darleen4Senate website and locate the "Contact Me" tab. The site's layout is clean and bright, with flashy blue lettering and Darleen's tight smile adorning the front page. I click on an envelope icon. She's got it rigged up so the page announces, "You've got mail!" as soon as I hover over the envelope. I quickly type an e-mail:

To: darleen@darleen4senate.org
From: alex@chickhabit.net
Subject: Looking for Comment: Video of your daughter Rebecca

Dear Darleen:

I'm a writer for a website for women called Chick Habit. We've received a video that we believe is of your daughter Rebecca. It shows her snorting cocaine and taking her shirt off. You can watch the video here: https://www.chickhabit.net/rebeccawestvideo.

We have not yet released this link, but we plan to this afternoon.

Given your status as a celebrity parenting expert and political hopeful, how do you respond to the existence of this video? I am on deadline so I need your reply as soon as possible.

Best,
Alex Lyons
Associate Editor, Chick Habit

I can reach Rebecca through Facebook. I waste no time crafting a similar, but shorter, missive to her:

Dear Rebecca,

I work at a website called Chick Habit. We received a video that we believe is of you:

https://www.chickhabit.net/rebeccawestvideo

What would your mom think of this behavior?

This link is still private but will be made public this afternoon. I need your response ASAP.

—Alex Lyons, associate editor

Hitting send on that Facebook message causes adrenaline to surge into my fingertips. I start writing the post with shaking hands:

> Omaha über-mom Darleen West has made millions of dollars from her image as the ideal parent, and now she's trying to parlay that image into tangible power: She's running for state senate in Nebraska. In her bestseller *How to Raise a Genius, Times Four*, the mom of fraternal quadruplets Raina, Rachel, Renata, and Rebecca told the world that her take-no-prisoners parenting method is the key to her children's success. And successful they are: All four girls attend top-tier universities and Rebecca, the apple of her mother's eye, even invented a new kind of robot while she was still in high school. "Rebecca's drive is what I admire most about her," Darleen writes on her website The Genius Method.
>
> Here's something Darleen—and her potential constituents—probably doesn't find so admirable: This video of a young woman who appears to be Rebecca West blowing rails in her underwear (NSFW):

I click off the post to embed the video in the page. I've been sure to include enough wiggle language so that we can't be sued if the girl in the video turns out not to be Becky. I check my e-mail and I see that Darleen West has already responded to me.

To: alex@chickhabit.net

From: darleen@darleen4senate.org

Subject: Re: Looking for Comment: Video of your daughter Rebecca

I will not dignify this trash with a response. You will be hearing from my lawyers. If you publish this, so help me God, I will ruin you.

I forward this to Moira and cc the lawyer—I'm sure they were already expecting this sort of thing.

MoiraPoira (11:35:29): Don't let that bag of Botox intimidate you.

Alex182 (11:36:32): I won't.

I want to give Rebecca some time to respond before I write the second half of the post, so I decide to go outside for a minute or two. I chuck off Peter's boxers and my now-limp T-shirt and pick the eyelet muumuu back off the floor. I give it a good shake and the last grains of sand fly off, landing directly on our already-icky area rug. Good thing it's made of sisal, so the sand is imperceptible. I give the muumuu a sniff, and the wet-dog scent seems to have faded enough for me to throw it back on again. I grab some flip-flops from my closet and thrust my aviator sunglasses onto my face so I can head out into the bright sunlight.

I walk to the bodega to get my customary sad desk salad,

where I ask Manuel for extra beets—it is a special occasion and I deserve a treat. My general reaction to Internet-based confrontation is to cower in a darkened corner. But today I am standing proud, almost morally superior.

In February I posted about a clip of Darleen's. She hosts a recurring segment on *Headline News* in which she gives advice to parents who are struggling with the misbehavior of their children. This particular segment was with a sweet-faced woman named Pam and her burly husband, Bill. Their son Dylan was hitting the bong instead of the books, and Darleen turned to Pam with an insincere smirk and said, "Maybe if Dylan hadn't been a latchkey kid in those formative tween years, you wouldn't be sitting here today." Pam's eyes began to well up right before they cut to commercial.

When I was writing the post I pictured my own mom up there, under the hot studio lights, being questioned about the fact that I was often home all by myself as a kid. She and my dad both stayed after school hours to pitch in with extracurriculars when I was in high school (Dad helmed the science club; Mom ran the yearbook). If I had rebelled by doing whippets in the woods rather than reading in my room, would it have been because my mom wasn't home to open the front door for me every day of her damn life?

Who is Darleen West anyway, to tell people that they're bad parents? Now that she's running for office, she has the potential to have even more influence on American women than she already does. Exposing her for the two-faced clown she's always been is basically a public service. Sure, Rebecca West is getting the short end of the deal here, with her private drug habits about to be blared out into the universe. But the collateral damage is worth it for the larger social point. Isn't it?

I almost consider calling my mom to ask her what she thinks. She's cool-headed and wise and I'm feeling pretty emotional right now. But I don't want her to worry about me, either.

Manuel tells me that my salad is ready.

"Thank you so much," I say, looking at him for some kind of sign that I'm doing the right thing. He just smiles and hands over the greens.

By the time I settle back in at home, it's twelve fifteen. Still no word from Rebecca. I keep refreshing Facebook to make sure I'm not missing any response from her. I try to find a phone number for her, but nothing comes up in a public records search. I have to write the second half of the post now so I can send it to Moira and the lawyer for approval before the one P.M. deadline.

> We are fairly certain it's Rebecca West in that video for several reasons. One, an anonymous tipster sent us the above video, identifying her. Two, we cross-checked Rebecca's Facebook photos with the video, and the likeness is striking. Check out this side-by-side screen shot of the video's heroine and this photo of Rebecca:

I load up the screen shot from the video that's a close-up of Becky's face and put it right next to a tight shot I cropped out of her Facebook photo with the robot.

Three, the floral bedspread that appears in the video is identical to the one in this photo, also from Rebecca West's Facebook profile:

Here's where I put the screen shot of the Laura Ashley bedspread next to Becky's dorm room photo.

Finally, we reached out to Darleen and Rebecca West for comment. Darleen would not go on the record about this video, but she did not deny that it was her daughter up in there, snorting a ton of the white stuff. As of press time, Rebecca has not responded to our queries. We will update you if she does.

You might wonder why this is newsworthy, why we are publishing this video of someone who is essentially a private citizen. It's because Darleen uses her platform as a parenting expert to shame other women. She's trying to use this message to get into state government, where she can wield even greater influence. She puts herself out there as the perfect mom with the perfect children. We believe in truth in advertising. Darleen West isn't perfect, and you don't have to be, either.

I file this to Moira at 12:46, and my heart's still racing. The entire back of my muumuu is soaked from nervous sweat and my fingers tremble over the keyboard. My salad sits next to me on the old brown couch, untouched and wilting. While I'm waiting for Moira's response, I keep refreshing Facebook. I continue to toggle back to Rebecca West's page; I look at that innocent little nose and try to keep my resolve. *You're doing the right thing,* I keep repeating to myself. *You can't afford to lose this job.* Rebecca is still not writing back, and we're running out of time.

Moira IMs me at 12:59.

MoiraPoira (12:59:17): This is brilliant. I looked it over, but as usual your copy is quite clean. The lawyer has seen it and he approves. It's good to go. Are you ready?

Alex182 (12:59:44): I was born ready.

I stare at the clock on my computer until it turns to one.

Chapter Seven

I refresh the site until the post goes live. I ended up going with a headline that was nearly identical to the original e-mail that the tipster had sent me: "Rebecca West, Daughter of 'Genius Mom' Darleen West: Snorting Coke in Her Skivvies?" The question mark was inserted at legal's request, just in case the comely cokehead in the video turned out to be a Becky West doppelgänger. I also send the following Facebook message to Becky, letting her know the post is live, so she has a chance to respond after the fact:

---

http://chickhabit.net/rebecca-west-daughter-of-genius-mom-darleen-west-snorting-coke-in-her-skivvies

---

Though I had been shaky and sweat-stained before the post went live, now that I can see it sitting there atop the Chick

Habit homepage, I am still and dry. In the minute or two after publication, before any page views or comments have registered in the lavender-hued boxes to the right of the post, it's like the world—or at least the Internet—is suspended. It's so quiet in the apartment I can hear the soft sigh of my laptop's hard drive.

And then I refresh the page once more. The commenters are, as usual, out of control:

CrazyBananas42 (1:01:45): Holy shit, this is awesome! This is the best fuck-you to a mom I have ever seen. I always knew that lady's genius mom routine was crap. Her perfect girl is sure going to town on that pile of yay!

Fuckerpunch (1:02:56): Are you kidding? It is so not awesome. I love how Alex ties herself in knots to justify posting this. It's a violation of Rebecca West's privacy, pure and simple.

Weathergrrrl (1:04:29): I fully agree with @Fucker-punch. Also, like the chickies didn't do their fare share of blow in college? I bet they wouldn't be so syched if someone else posted a video of their drug use online without their consent and she's naked in part of it! This is basically digital rape.

TiptoeTulip (1:06:15): I had a mother just like Darleen West and I acted out like this in college, too. I spent 8 years in therapy trying to undo the damage she inflicted on me in my teen years. My heart weeps for Rebecca West and I hope she gets the help she so clearly needs.

Libertard (1:07:22): @Fuckerpunch @Weathergrrrl @ TiptoeTulip Pull the sticks out of your asses.

My bitchface training from this morning seems to have paid off. Just a few days ago that "digital rape" comment would have inspired several sniveling IMs to Moira and/or Jane about whether or not I had gone too far. If I had really been having a rough day that comment might have spooked me far into the evening, until Peter came home, when I would be near tears by the time he walked through our midget door. But I can't ask for Peter's attention right now; when I think about what he might be keeping from me, it feels like a small, sharp object poking me in the gut.

I refresh the page again. It's been ten minutes since the post went up and already there are thirty thousand page views.

Prettyinpink86 (1:14:20): :) That Becky West video is so crazy!!

Alex182 (1:15:02): Yeah, I know.

Prettyinpink86 (1:15:44): The traffic is already really high.

Alex182 (1:16:08): Thanks.

I can't tell if Molly is genuinely being supportive with that emoticon or if she's jealous of my stats, and I don't feel like conversing with her long enough to figure it out. But the enthusiasm of her IMs reminds me to link to all my earlier posts about Darleen West so that I can get additional traffic back to them. There was that clip of her on *Headline News* condescending to poor Dylan's mom with her weed-brained son (headline: "Darleen West Takes Mother Superior Act to Basic Cable"). Then there was the time she wrote a guest op-ed for the *National Review* about how dangerous day care really is, and how the liberal media has covered up its risks. ("'Genius Mom' to Working Moms: Piss Off.") And finally, when Rebecca's sister Rachel won a prize at Harvard for a paper she had written on themes of motherhood in Virginia Woolf's books, I wrote a post called "Darleen West's Daughter Longs for a Womb of One's Own."

MoiraPoira (1:26:35): My darling girl! Your post got linked to from the homepage of Yahoo 10 minutes ago—you know that guarantees a traffic tsunami.

Alex182 (1:28:11): Amazing!

MoiraPoira (1:28:44): I've never seen a post get this popular this fast. It's brilliant! And for the first time in Chick Habit history, I got a call from Tyson Collins.

Alex182 (1:29:42): The big boss took time from his busy duck-hunting schedule to phone li'l ol' you?

MoiraPoira (1:30:12): He sure did. One of his 14 assistants told him that our servers were working on overdrive because of the massive surge. He took a look at the site and saw the post, and he told me, "I never did like that Darleen West. Met her at the Aspen Ideas Festival and she looked like someone who needed a good screw and a good steak."

Alex182 (1:31:44): He did NOT say that!

MoiraPoira (1:32:12): Screw and steak, in that order.

That makes me laugh even though I know Tyson Collins's desire to restructure his conglomerate might make me a casualty in just a few short weeks. I decide to take advantage of one of Moira's rare good moods.

Alex182 (1:33:14): If it's okay with you I'm gonna take a shower now.

MoiraPoira (1:34:45): Do it!

I go into our bathroom and toss the musty muumuu onto the tile floor. I turn the water on and stick a hand under the weak stream. That's the trade-off you make when you live in a brownstone instead of a new apartment—quaint prewar details, but no hot, strong showers. As a result I rarely feel truly clean even after a shower.

Adding to that feeling of grossness is the disgusting but true fact that Peter and I have been playing an elaborate game of bathroom chicken for a few months. Nothing—not the shower, not the mirror, not the toilet—has been thoroughly scrubbed since St. Patrick's Day. For all his togetherness, Peter has an astoundingly high tolerance for dirt, and I'm just as sloppy as he is. Most of the time we live in barely postcollegiate squalor.

Jane has this grand theory of relationships that certainly holds true for Peter and me. In every union there is one better half. When fights occur, it's usually because the worse half has done something cheeky and/or selfish (like going out to Coney Island on a Monday night without calling her boyfriend to check in). The better half gets to be sanctimonious and disapproving, but is also held to a higher standard of behavior. In turn, the worse half gets to be resentful of the better half's prissiness, but he or she also gets to be the fuckup.

However, these dynamics are relationship specific, which is to say, just because you're the better half in one relationship doesn't mean you can't be the worse half in another. When I was with Caleb, I was definitely the better half.

Caleb and I met during our last week of college, at a huge lawn party after all the art majors showed their thesis projects. I skipped the thesis showing (I really didn't need to see another sculpture made from somebody's earwax) but made it in time for the first sarcastic keg stand.

I was a regular at the art department parties because I had a thing for guys who thought of themselves as artists. I read a lot of biographies of Sylvia Plath at a tender age, and in college I was overly moved by her relationship with her poet-husband, Ted

Hughes: On their first meeting they were so animally attracted to each other that he pulled off her headband and she bit him on the face. After that their bond was not only physical but also creative. They informed and inspired each other's work.

I wanted that for myself (sans the whole putting-your-head-in-the-oven part at the end, which I always conveniently ignored) and so I gravitated to fine artists. Jane suggested a few times I try dating a writer, but I'm so competitive I thought I would fight with a fellow scribe. Also the art boys tended to be much, much better looking.

So when I got to that fateful art department party, Jane was talking to a circle of guys. I noticed Caleb straightaway because, well, he fit my stereotype: He was hot. He had shaggy blond hair and the greenest eyes I'd ever seen. He was also muscular without being bulky and had a perfectly proportioned tall frame. I was a little drunk already by the time I got there—pre-graduation week was basically a seven-day bacchanal—and so instead of hanging back and waiting for him to talk to me, like I normally would have, I marched right up to him.

"I'm Alex," I said, sticking my hand out firmly toward him.

"Caleb," he replied in that slow Southern drawl of his.

After that, things get a little fuzzy. I have a fractured memory of bantering about *Twin Peaks,* of which I had only seen one episode but fronted as if I had seen the entire series. I have a fairly distinct memory of going back to his dorm room that night—which was strewn with a deconstructed bed and filled with packing boxes—and boffing his brains out.

This was atypical behavior for me. Sure, I had hooked up with guys before without a commitment, but at that point I had never had *actual* sex with a virtual stranger. I could barely sleep that night, though I shut my eyes and feigned slumber while he breathed deeply next to me. I figured that it was going to be a onetime thing. It was the last week of college, and anyway, he was much too good-looking and cool to want to be with me. My guess was that when we woke up, he'd make some excuse about the grad party he had to dash off to.

But the next morning he stirred, slung his arm around my waist, pulled me to him, and said, "Mornin'."

"Hi." I scooched slightly away from him, afraid he could smell my morning breath.

"What say you and me find some grub around here?"

"Okay," I said, attempting to tamp down my delight.

That morning he drove me to breakfast at Friendly's in his vintage Mercedes, and we split a Fribble and talked about our post-graduation plans. He was moving to New York straightaway to pursue his art. He might take a part-time job at a gallery but he didn't want anything to take away from his work. I read between the lines that work was optional for him, but I didn't learn about the extent of his family's wealth until much later.

I told him my plans were up in the air and then we went back to his room and went at it again. After a few more hours of that I returned to my room and checked my e-mail. *Rev* had offered me an assistant gig at their new website, starting as soon as I could move to New York.

Caleb and I were completely inseparable the last week of school, and when we moved to New York I stayed with him at the Williamsburg loft his parents were funding until I could afford a place of my own. My assistant gig paid so little, and I needed to save up so that I could afford the first month's rent and a security deposit on my own hovel.

The first months of our relationship were probably the most fun I've ever had in my life. We had sex incessantly. My job at *Rev* required me to go to indie rock shows almost every night of the week, so I brought Caleb along for companionship and, if I'm honest, booze money. The VIP section of the Bowery Ballroom doesn't come with free drinks, and I always hated being the only sober person at shows. I never quite felt polished enough to be there—not only at the shows but with Caleb—and drinking and the occasional recreational coke sniff helped me feel like I belonged.

I didn't have to get into *Rev*'s offices until eleven A.M. anyway (rock 'n' roll hours!) so having a perpetual hangover didn't really matter. *Rev* was perfectly happy to have a twenty-two-year-old with no real experience write their entire website. I was closer to their target audience than the senior staffers, who had seen Pavement play in their original incarnation—not on their reunion tour. I had no deadlines and no quotas. An assistant editor would briefly glance at my posts before they went live, but that's about the only guidance I got. The DJing gigs I was doing around town padded out my meager income, at least a little—and they were fun.

But twenty-two turned into twenty-three, and my relationship with Caleb and my job at *Rev* both started to seem juvenile and unhealthy. I felt like I needed to progress in my career, and fast: My mother could only hide the health insurance cash and the winter coats she shipped me for so long. And I really wanted to show her that I could make a go of being a professional writer.

Plus, after that raucous first year together, Caleb and I started fighting. At first I secretly thought it was sort of fun. Our love was so strong that it was violent! We couldn't help but clash! But then it just became tedious. Our fights were almost always about his behavior; he would disappear for days and I wouldn't know where he was. I was pretty sure he was cheating on me, specifically with this woman Stacia who ran a hot local gallery and whom Caleb always described as "really centered." He began sharing with me, constantly, health tips that she had passed along. "Stacia says that I should really be using agave, not sugar," he told me one morning as I poured him coffee. "That way I can avoid the jagged highs and lows of a sugar crash. It's really going to be better for my creative process." I pulled a face and said, "Great."

When he would emerge from his days-long disappearances, he would just say that he had been working on his art, and if I were a *real* artist, and not some blogger monkey banging out meaningless words, I would understand that.

"Sorry I haven't been keeping up with your writing," he told me on one of those occasions. "I don't really believe in the Internet."

"What do you mean, you 'don't believe in the Internet'?" I snapped. "I remember you spending a whole lotta time posting to your blog and watching YouTube videos of dancing babies just last month."

"That was then. Now I've evolved beyond it. I'm at the point in my work where I really need to focus on my process, and the little things that go on in real time just don't affect me anymore. No offense."

I rolled my eyes and fired back something about how *some* of us didn't have the luxury of disappearing for days to make "art" and that *some* of us liked being blogger monkeys, so fuck off.

The last straw was when my dad died and Caleb refused to attend the funeral with me. That's not quite accurate: I didn't know where he was that week, so I couldn't tell him the sad news in the first place. When he resurfaced a week later, I wouldn't answer the phone. I made Jane tell him what had happened, and though he tried sending flowers and writing soppy love notes, I stopped speaking to him entirely.

So, Caleb: definitively the worse half. In her relationship with Ali, Jane says they trade off being the better half. Maybe this is why Peter isn't telling me about the Omnitown deal: He wants to remain the better half forever.

As the tepid water sluices down the sides of my face, the high of Moira's praise for the page views and my pioneering spirit wash off. I can't shake the upset I feel over Peter's sin of omission. From everything he's shown me over the past year and a half, he's a genuinely good person, which is one of the things I love best about him. When we moved in together, but before I started working at Chick Habit, we had fallen into what I remember as a blissful weekday routine. If it was really nice out we'd walk several miles home over the Brooklyn Bridge. I would stop by his office at lunch and bring him treats that I had snagged from *Rev*: a signed Spoon CD or a few tickets to a show his friends might like. Work was just work—someplace I spent eight hours a day so I could pay my rent.

I was still piecing my inner self back together after Dad died, but I knew I could always count on Peter. He wasn't overbearing about his support; he just made himself available whenever I wanted to talk. If I went silent and wet-eyed, he'd reach out and hold my hand.

My schedule got more stressful almost immediately once I started working at Chick Habit—but at least it gave me something other than worrying about my mom to obsess about. It wasn't just the punishing pace, Moira's IM tantrums, or the early morning hours that got to me. I was totally unprepared for the sheer number of commenters—Chick Habit has four hundred thousand daily readers and about 10 percent of them are frequent commenters—and how vicious they'd be. Within the first thirty-six hours of being a Chickie, I'd been called "bitch," "idiot," "moron," "retard," and "bloody fool" (we have a lot of British commenters).

After my first week I spent the entire weekend curled up in a ball, wondering if I had made a huge mistake. Peter convinced me that I hadn't. Despite the frequent emotional thunderstorms that I've been having since that first week, his support for me and my work is unflagging. At the end of a long day he always wraps me in his arms and says some version of the same thing: "You know how much I believe in you, and how talented and smart I think you are. This is a stepping-stone to someplace else, eventually. You will survive this."

I decide I will call Peter the second I get out of the shower. I've been keeping my phone off on purpose so that I could avoid speaking to him, and just surfacing thoughts of my deception and his potential betrayal makes me so anxious that I start shifting my weight from foot to foot. We need to have a real conversation—rather than a series of near misses—so that we can clear everything up.

Even though the Rebecca West video is going viral right now, it's unlikely that Peter will have seen it. Any site that's remotely entertaining is blocked by Polydrafter's notoriously tough IT guys. I've never met them, but I've heard enough about them that the picture in my head is of an army of movie-ready dorks with pocket protectors, wire-rimmed glasses, and ill-fitting pants. If they found him watching a video of some barely legal girl snorting drugs and going shirtless, he'd probably get fired. So there's still time to unburden myself without seeming too squirrely.

I turn off the water and grope around for a towel, which I wrap around my hair. I pat myself dry with another towel and, in the interest of time, step back into the black muumuu of death. I scoot back into the bedroom and—in an attempt to maintain a shred of decorum—I put on a fresh pair of underwear. The dress has become something of a security blanket: Even though it's salty and ripe smelling, it makes me more comfortable and puts me in work mode. Besides, I don't have any other waistless pieces of clothing that are easily accessible.

The phone is next to my computer, so I head back to the couch to do the hard but correct thing.

Before I reach for the phone I notice a blinking instant message from Rel on my laptop screen and decide to attend to that first. I bet she's writing to congratulate me about my big, juicy scoop. Despite my reservations about the video, I'm excited that Rel will see that I've finally done something truly audacious. I have spent a lot of time trying to sound like more of a badass than I actually am in order to impress her—telling her largely exaggerated tales about nights partying when I worked at *Rev*, about the super-hot guys, plural, I would go home with, when actually there was just one guy, singular (Adrian). I did not, of course, mention the part where my one-night wonder patted me awkwardly on the back while I sobbed in huge, gasping breaths—or the vomiting portion of the evening.

Wienerdog (1:55:23): Dude.

Alex182 (1:56:17): Afternoon!

Wienerdog (1:56:54): What is the deal with that video you posted?

Alex182 (1:57:29): The Rebecca West thing?

Wienerdog (1:57:44): Yeah.

Alex182 (1:58:58): What do you mean, what's the deal? It's pretty straightforward, no?

Wienerdog (1:59:25): I mean, where do you get off posting something like that? I think it's a pretty fucked-up thing to do.

Alex182 (2:02:12): Oh come on, don't be so uptight. You're starting to sound like the commenters.

She doesn't respond to that for several minutes. I can't believe that Rel—of all people!—is reacting this way. This from a girl who posted a video of herself getting her nipples pierced, replete with an extreme close-up of the needle going into her tender bits? Where does she get off judging me for posting something that is arguably way less graphic? Part of me is pissed that she's not more supportive, and the other part is worried that if no-boundaries Rel thinks I messed up, I must have done something morally repugnant. I want to understand what her damage is, so I decide to ask her, flat-out.

Alex182 (2:10:44): What's your damage?

Wienerdog (2:11:15): You know, I might put up a lot of intense stuff. But it's about ME, not about other people. This is that Becky chick's private shit and I just think putting it up is a really messed-up thing to do.

Alex182 (2:12:09): You didn't seem all that concerned about other peoples' privacy when you published that jerky e-mail from your ex-boyfriend last month.

Wienerdog (2:13:14): First of all, I didn't use his name. Secondly, he was an abusive shit who deserved it. What did this Becky ever do to you?

Alex182 (2:13:47): Nothing. It's not like that. It's not personal! But I don't think there's that much of a difference between what you did and what I did.

Wienerdog (2:14:14): You're wrong.

My face prickles and I close my computer to get away from the heated conversation. When I think about it, Rel's reaction shouldn't be a surprise to me. She's always had her own set of Internet ethics. Once she went nuts on one of our most frequent commenters, SelmaBouvier. In the comments of that post about Rel's ex-boyfriend ("Douchebag Dearest," pubbed on Valentine's Day), Selma posted a photo of *her* ex-boyfriend with his bare ass hanging out of a pair of truly unattractive cargo shorts. The context was one of sisterly bonding: "Hey, look," that winking bottom was saying, "I used to date a loser, too."

The problem was that you could see the guy's face, which wasn't blurred out. Rel thought that it was a violation of his privacy and messaged Selma to tell her that she'd better take the pic down or Rel would have her booted from the site. I believe her words were: "Take that fucking thing off our website or I will make sure you never get to comment again." Selma told Rel that she was a major cunt for threatening to cut her off from Chick Habit, which she described as a "lifeline" for her. But she took the photo down anyway.

I wish that I could take back that IM conversation with Rel, but it's too late. Now I just need to wait until she's cooled down a bit before I initiate any further contact, virtual or otherwise.

But Rel's condemnation has left me too shaken to call Peter. If she disapproves, what will he say? Instead, I decide to rub salt into the wound: I reopen my laptop and type breakingthechick habit.com into my browser to see what my Becky exclusive has wrought.

The site is taking forever to load, and when the severed head of that chickie finally appears, I realize that BTCH hasn't updated yet. That post making fun of me for posting about the cat video is still right below the banner. This is mildly heartening: If the hate blogger—my harshest critic—hasn't even commented on the Becky West post, it must not be that bad, right?

MoiraPoira (2:30:15): Little miss, don't let this traffic go to your head. It's been 90 minutes since your last post and I have barely heard a peep from you! Molly has already done three posts since your last one.

Alex182 (2:31:23): Sorry, I got distracted.

MoiraPoira (2:32:04): I'm not interested in the excuses.

Alex182 (2:32:44): Of course.

MoiraPoira (2:33:02): Not much going on today. All I've got for you is that some Tea Party governor just confused the Civil War with the Revolutionary War while speaking at Gettysburg.

Alex182 (2:34:11): Meh. I'm over her.

MoiraPoira (2:35:02): Yeah, me too. Listen, since Molly's been so on the ball, I've got stuff scheduled for the next 45 minutes. You've got some breathing room to find something else. You got lucky this time.

Alex182 (2:36:10): OK, I'll do some poking around.

It's so rare that I get forty-five minutes on anything in the middle of the day that I am determined to find something great. I head to my RSS feed and only have to scroll through about a hundred headlines before I find a gimme: an article in *Ad Age* about how a sanitary napkin brand is coming out with a line of printed maxi pads. There's a contest where pad users can come up with new designs, and visitors to the manufacturer's website can vote on their favorites—the top three of which will be created and sold in a drugstore near you. The front-runner is currently a gauzy watercolor of *Twilight* star Robert Pattinson. The headline is obvious: "Would You Pay to Have Robert Pattinson's Face Between Your Legs?" I write three hundred words summarizing the *Ad Age* article and asking our readers what other stars they'd enjoy bleeding on.

I file to Moira a little after three.

MoiraPoira (3:12:11): This is terrific. You should art it with some Photoshopped magic—take R. Patz and make him look like he was painted by a swoony 15-year-old.

Alex182 (3:13:22): Maybe even with a few artfully placed red splatters??

MoiraPoira (3:13:50): ahahahahahaha

Alex182 (3:14:33): I love this idea! Will do.

MoiraPoira (3:15:06): I'll have Molly do it. Your reward for the traffic that your Becky West exclusive is getting is that you can just do your gossip roundup and then take off for the day.

Alex182 (3:15:48): Oh, OK, sounds good.

Except that this is the one day that I don't want to take off early. Truthfully, mocking up a red-spotted Robert Pattinson would be a welcome distraction from my fight with Rel, the hate-blogger drama, and dealing with Peter. Still, I tell myself firmly that I made my decision to run the Becky West video, and I need to stand by it no matter what the consequences are. Yet I can't resist peeking at the comments again to see if our readers think the Becky West exposé is as scummy as Rel seems to. There are now over nine hundred comments on the post, and when I take a look at the latest ones, I realize that it's at the point in a commenter pileup where they're no longer even posting about the original content. Instead, they've turned on each other:

VIVisection (4:45:22): @Mamacita79 I can't believe you think you're a good parent because you've read every one of Darleen West's books. She's a snake oil salesman and you're a moron.

Mamacita79 (4:46:31): @VIVisection You sound like one of those women who can't find a man to have kids with. I feel sorry for you, but you don't have to be so prejudiced against mothers because of your own bad luck.

The internecine commenter strife fails to make me feel any better about the post, so I turn back to my final duties for the day. As I'm reading about how much Sandra Bullock's new boyfriend is bonding with her adopted baby, Louis, I realize I should probably check my Chick Habit e-mail account. With all the other things going on, I haven't really scrutinized my inbox—I found enough fodder without it, and I didn't want to read a bunch of angry missives sent by our more sensitive commenters and/or Darleen West's lawyers.

But I also want to see if Rebecca West has surfaced. She hasn't responded to my Facebook message from a few hours ago. I click over to my mailbox. I don't see any word from her, which seems strange—you'd think that she'd want to get her story out there, to counter what seems to be going on in the video. Is it possible she doesn't know about it yet?

Then my eye catches on a familiar-looking name.

From: Breaking the Chick Habit
To: alex@chickhabit.net
Subject: Now You've Done It

I knew that the hate blogger wouldn't be able to resist the Becky West bait, but I didn't expect her to break the fourth wall and contact me. There are single-subject hate blogs littering the Internet, and BTCH, for all that I find it upsetting, really isn't any worse than many others. It's certainly not as bad as the response I saw to the blog of a fourteen-year-old girl named Dakota who had been writing about her cancer treatment in chipper posts with titles like "Chemo Was Rough but It Won't Get Me Down!!!" accompanied by photos of her shrunken self in a hospital bed—she always had a wan smile on her face and was often giving the camera a thumbs-up. That girl's hate blogger would copy every single post she wrote and write a snide and unoriginal comment at the top of it (for example, "nice hairdo, Mr. Clean," after Dakota lost all of her hair). The hater, who was eventually unmasked by a TV newsmagazine—it turned out to be the disturbed mother of someone Dakota had snubbed in middle school—kept this up until the girl died, just shy of her fifteenth birthday.

So BTCH, comparatively, is child's play. I can almost pretend that whoever is behind it never intended for me to see it—she's just been using it to vent about sometimes-legitimate criticisms of a site that she feels strongly about. Because of the conversational tone we Chickies take and because of the emotionally charged subjects we tend to discuss (say, water birth), our readers often see posts they disagree with as a personal affront (hence the common comment "I thought this site was supposed to be supportive of women and their choices").

But now BTCH is trying to contact me. This e-mail she intends me to see.

Dear Alex,

As you probably know already, I've been following your writing closely. When you were first hired at

Chick Habit I had high hopes for your work. But as the months have gone on, you have disappointed me time and again. I thought that your unsympathetic item about the plight of displaced sex workers in Reykjavik was the lowest you would go. I was wrong. With this Becky West piece, you've posted the private video of a successful young woman—and probably ruined her life—just to whore for some page views.

Don't you think you deserve some comeuppance for your casual cruelty?

I do. But I am a fair-minded individual, so I'm going to give you until eleven a.m. on Friday to make things right. If you don't take down the Rebecca West video and publish, in its place, a sincere mea culpa, I'm going to release the incriminating materials I have about *you.*

What are these materials, you might wonder. They're pretty remarkable. I just wanted to say what a lovely tramp stamp you have, my dear. Some people might find a bright pink smiley face so near your ass crack to be tacky, but I think it's just adorable.

There's still time to do the right thing, Alex.

Stay Sweet,
BTCH

I instinctively look around the room—it's like I can feel her watching me. The small, paranoid voice inside wonders if BTCH has somehow planted a camera in my apartment, though the rational rest of me realizes that that is insane.

My brain immediately shifts into high gear. I go back through the BTCH archives one more time to see if I can dig up any clues to either the blogger's identity or the dirt she has on me. As I'm scrolling through I notice that the site began dissing Ariel, Tina, and me in equal measure, but in the past two weeks almost every single post has been attacking me alone. This lends some support to my theory that I know the bitch behind BTCH.

I know I can't comply with BTCH's demand to have the video taken down. Moira would never delete the Becky West exclusive now that it's live and skyrocketing. I know from experience. I freaked out once about an unnecessarily nasty post I had written about Vince Vaughn's bloated carb face that had engendered tons of hate mail. Now I can laugh about the number of people who really, really care about Vince Vaughn, but back then I wanted to make it all go away and I asked Moira to remove the post. Moira said that unless something is factually incorrect our company policy states that we do not recant anything that has been published, and then she added that there are no exceptions for writers with an overdeveloped sense of guilt. That same no-exception policy would apply, I'm sure, to writers being threatened by Internet vigilantes—and, besides, even if that were reason for Moira to consider taking down the Becky West piece, the fact that the post already has five hundred thousand page views and counting is an even stronger reason not to.

Suddenly I couldn't care less that I'm halfway to making a bonus.

I assume by "incriminating materials" that the hate blogger means that sex tape I made with my college boyfriend, Adam—the one where he filmed me from behind. I thought I had been prudent because I hadn't shown my face to the camera, but I forgot about my idiot tramp stamp, the one I got on spring break in Fort Lauderdale when I was eighteen. Since I never see that damned tattoo—and I periodically toy with the idea of getting it removed—I mostly forget that it's there.

How could Adam do this to me? I thought we were friends. Or at least benign acquaintances. Our split was pretty bloodless considering how long we had been together (eighteen months of college time is at least five years of grown-person time).

Adam and I started dating at the end of freshman year. I wasn't head over heels for him, even at the beginning. We had almost nothing in common—Adam was a stoner-slash-scientist who spent most of his time trying to figure out a better way to grow weed in his dorm room while studying for organic chem. But he was sweet enough, and I desperately wanted a real boyfriend. So after one night of heavy petting—the only moment I remember from that first interlude is when he said, "Your boobs are much bigger than I thought they were"—I asked him if he wanted to be exclusive. He said, "Okay."

My father loved him—they were both science guys and they would stand in a room together and stare at their shoes in precisely the same way. This made my dad comfortable, and he would always say, "That Adam fellow has a good head on his shoulders." My mom was not so enthused. She never said so aloud, but I know she thought I was settling for him. Whenever I asked her what she thought about him, she'd say, "As long as he makes you happy, he's fine by me."

At the end of sophomore year I decided to come home for the summer and work at the day camp that was run on Manning's campus, while Adam traveled around the country working on organic farms. My mother was thrilled to have me back home for a few months, and she gently encouraged the space that was already growing between Adam and me. "You should immerse yourself in the kids!" she would tell me whenever I would say I missed him.

We stayed together for another six months out of collective inertia and then remained friendly enough for the rest of college. After graduation he moved to rural Argentina to teach English and perfect his miracle grow technique. The last I heard of him, which has to be a year ago, he was living in a yurt on the Pampas.

I pause for a second, my panic abating slightly as a logistical question occurs to me: *How* could Adam do this to me? Since when do South American yurts have high-speed Internet hookups?

I have no idea whether Adam can get Facebook messages—if he's still in the most desolate part of Argentina, he probably won't—but I need to at least reach out to him.

Hey, Adam,

I hope you're well. Julia told me that you're in Argentina working as a farmhand on a sheep ranch. I know this seems out of the blue, but I have a question for you about that video we made. You know the one. If you get this please write back as soon as you get it.

Alex

Somehow I then manage to focus on the last post of the day, my gossip roundup. I make a hack-y joke about Meg Ryan's trout lips and write about some washed-up star's house foreclosure in Orange County and file to Moira so that I can properly freak out.

MoiraPoira (4:10:22): Off with you

Alex182 (4:11:04): Great

MoiraPoira (4:11:33): I've been getting tons of media requests for you today, so I may be in touch tonight about changes to your schedule tomorrow.

Alex182 (4:12:20): What do you mean, media requests?

MoiraPoira (4:13:32): You know, TV appearances, radio interviews, that sort of thing. The whole world wants to talk to you about Rebecca West. She and Darleen are still refusing to comment on the scandal, so you're the media's best bet. I need to coordinate with Tyson Collins's people, since they need to sign off on any appearances before you do them.

Alex182 (4:14:59): Um, OK.

MoiraPoira (4:15:30): Don't worry, darling, you'll be fabulous! This is all good news!

Alex182 (4:15:59): Yay?

MoiraPoira (4:16:48): That's the spirit.

Fuck! Will the hate blogger renege on her promise to hold off on posting whatever she has on me if she sees me crowing about my exclusive? What do I tell Peter about all this? What if Adam doesn't write back? I have so many questions bursting out of my skull that I start feeling claustrophobic in our dank basement lair. I have to get out of here.

I finally turn on my phone and call Jane. She's certainly home from school now and she's the only one I can trust with the whole story, with all its messiness—even with my honesty about how culpable I really am.

Chapter Eight

Jane picks up on the first ring.

"Alex? Is that you? What's the matter? All I hear is hyperventilating."

I try to speak, but hearing her voice makes me even more upset than I thought I was. Finally, I stutter out, "Ye . . . ye . . . yes it's mmmmeee."

"Is this about that hate blog?"

"S . . . sssort of." I can hear myself panting into the phone even as I try to take deep, calming breaths.

"Listen, I'm here at home, and I have many paper bags that you can breathe into. Come here immediately and you can tell me everything."

"Oh . . . ohkay." I'm so relieved I have someplace to go and someone to talk to, since I can't stay here and rely on Peter. I turn my phone off after I hear silence at the other end. I don't want anyone to be able to reach me.

I grope around the bedroom for my canvas bag and somehow

make it outside into the light. The sun blazes onto my indoor skin and I paw around in my bag for my oversized sunglasses. I stumble the mile over to Jane's, trying to understand how my life has been completely upended since I started work this week.

It's only Wednesday.

Jane lives on the parlor floor of a brownstone that's similar to the apartment Peter and I share. Her bedroom faces the street, just as ours does, and as I approach I can see her little face poking out of the curtains, looking for me. I give her a weak wave from the stoop, and I can hear her footsteps approach the door.

Jane takes one look at my face, says, "Oh, honey!" and wraps me in her arms, and before I can help myself I start to cry. She ushers me quickly into her apartment, practically pushes me onto the pillow-strewn futon in her living room, and sits down next to me, rubbing my back in circular motions.

Finally I'm calm enough to speak. I run through my whole dramatic day, ending with the sex tape and my fears about Adam: "How could Adam do this to me? Isn't this against the stoner code of ethics or something?"

"I don't think Jah Rastafari would approve, no," Jane says. "But you still can't be sure that it's something that Adam sent."

"I think I would remember if I had made a sex tape with someone else," I tell her.

"I know, honey. But I just don't believe Adam would do something like this." Jane pauses and then says gently, "Do you think he might have shared it with anyone else?"

"Oh God," I say, a fresh wave of panic washing over me. Could Adam have sent the video to a bunch of his dumbass, Phishobsessed friends? Did one of those thoughtless hippies send the video to BTCH? Just how many people have seen my smiley-face tattoo? And how many more might? What if it's already out there on the Internet? What if this story makes my anonymous sex tape an Internet sensation like David After Dentist, but, you know, porny? I curl up into the fetal position around one of Jane's Indian-inspired shams.

Jane gets up and goes into her bedroom. "I hoped it wouldn't come to this," she calls back. "But before you came over I found something to give you in case of a total meltdown."

I look up from the couch and Jane is miraculously already sitting next to me again, holding a white pill in her tan hand. "Take it."

"What is it?" I say.

"It's a Xanax, the highest possible dose. I'm supposed to use them for my fear of flying but I think this is an even better purpose."

I snatch the pill from Jane's hand and swallow it dry. The pill leaves a bitter, chalky trail down my tongue and throat and I grimace. Jane gets up again and returns this time with a glass of water, and I wash the whiteness down into my belly.

I don't know if it's a placebo effect or if the drug hits me fast because I've barely eaten anything today. But I feel more relaxed immediately, like my fallen, conflicted self has risen up out of my tired body and is hovering over the two of us.

"I'm going to put you to bed," Jane says. "I wish you could appreciate the irony of this situation. You put out a revealing video of someone on the Internet, and now you're losing your mind about someone doing the same thing to you."

"I appreciate it. I'm just not enjoying it." In fact, the internal contradiction is tearing me apart. But that stress feels very far away now that the sedatives are kicking in.

"That's fair," she says as she brings me a blanket and helps me arrange myself on the futon.

"Were you waiting until I was on chill pills to say that to me?"

"Maybe," Jane says, grinning.

I try to come up with a pithy response, but it's too much work. My eyes close involuntarily.

The first things I see when I open my eyes are Jane's long, clean fingers gliding across the keyboard of her laptop. She's sitting across from me in an overstuffed chair, wearing her reading glasses and looking very tidy and wise.

"Hi," I mutter.

"Hey, sleepyhead. Feeling any better?"

"Sort of. My head's pretty fuzzy. What time is it?" I look around, my lashes still crusted with sleep, to see if it's still light out. I can see a sliver of dark through Jane's back window.

"Around nine. You were out cold for quite a while."

"Jeez. Thanks for the Xanax, by the way." I sit up too quickly and feel woozy. I remember instantly why I'm at Jane's, but the little white pill is allowing me to accept the situation without another freak-out for now.

"Anytime. And I have one bit of good news," Jane says, taking her glasses off and putting them on the fluffed-up arm of her chair. "I did some serious Googling and there's no sex tape of you anywhere on the Internet."

"Thank God," I say, allowing a small bit of hope to grow in

my chest. "But that's a *yet*. No sex tape on the Internet *yet*." Deflating again.

"But you have until Friday to nip this in the bud, so that's good, right?" Jane says brightly.

"I guess?"

"So that means you have some time to track down this hate blogger and talk some sense into her."

"How would I even begin to do that?" I'm grateful for Jane's deep Google but forty hours is hardly a lot of time to find the hate blogger and somehow convince her to spare me the embarrassment.

"I've got someone we can trust on the case."

"Who?"

"My little cousin Leon." Jane's grinning uncontrollably when she says this, as if she's solved a particularly vexing crossword puzzle. I'm not so thrilled.

"What? He's a seventeen-year-old boy! What did you tell him?"

"Contain yourself. Leon's a good kid, and he's a web genius. And besides, he's got no interest in sex tapes of you or any other soul of the female persuasion."

"Oh." This is only mildly soothing. And sort of surprising—it never occurred to me that Leon was gay, but then I try not to think about the sexual lives of minors.

"Don't worry. I told him you were my friend and that this blogger was bullying you. After his hellish middle school experience he hates bullies more than anything. He loves me because I let him get drunk on expensive wine the last time he came to visit, and I didn't tell his mom that he barfed on the patio." Jane gestures vaguely to the back of her house, as if to point out the precise place where the barfing occurred.

"Okay," I say uneasily. This is the closest thing I've got to good news right now, so I guess I'll have to take it.

"I also heard from Peter." Jane's voice is neutral when she says this. I can tell she's trying to be fair. It's infuriating (shouldn't she be on team Alex right now?) but sweet at the same time. She genuinely likes Peter. She also likes meddling.

"I don't want to talk to him. I don't even feel like I know what to think about him right now." I sink back into a horizontal line, like my spine has lost all strength.

"He was worried about you because your phone was off all day. I told him you had a bad day at work and were napping at my apartment," she says crisply.

"What did he say?" I ask, sitting up and leaning toward Jane. I'm still mad, but I'm not ready to write the guy off entirely.

"He said that he really wanted to talk to you. He sounded very upset, Al."

"I know."

"You should call him and try to clear things up. You don't know the whole story on Omnitown, just what you think you read." I know she's right, and I sigh deeply, looking away from her.

"I will, I swear. Just not this second."

"A good man is hard to find, and I don't mean that in the Flannery O'Connor sort of way," Jane says, and she reaches out to pat my hand.

I know what Jane's face looks like without even glancing at it. Her lips will be a straight red line, and her eyes will be squinting at me in disapproval. She used to give me a version of this look when we lived together and I forgot to replace a spent toilet paper roll with a new one. That was disapproval face level 1. I bet she has disapproval face level 3 or 4 out now, which means her mouth is even tighter and her eyes even smaller.

Miraculously, and perhaps because she thinks I've been through enough today already, Jane changes the subject, sparing me a real confrontation. "I promised Cheyenne that I would go to her show tonight."

"Ughhhhhhh." I bury my face into the futon cushion. Another night spent in the bowels of Bushwick listening to Chey, our friend from Wesleyan, yowl like a freshly neutered cat. She's the front woman of a noise-rock band called Barbizon, which released an EP called *Mitzi Kills* on an Internet-only label last month. I believe there are currently four hundred copies floating around on iPods in the greater north Brooklyn region.

"If you want to stay here and take another Xanax you are more than welcome to," Jane says firmly. "Or if you want to go home and see your good man, that's another option."

"I'll come with you to see Chey," I grumble. I'm not ready to face Peter yet.

"Okay, cool. We'll have fun and it will take your mind off things. Especially if you change out of that disgusting sack you're wearing."

"Hey!" I know the muumuu is nasty, but somehow it's a shock to realize that everyone else thinks I'm foul, too. I really thought I was covering the stank with the green tea perfume. Guess not.

"Real talk, girl. That thing you call a dress makes you look like a hobo."

"Fine. Will you let me borrow something?"

"Always."

I get off the couch and pad over to Jane's overflowing closet. We settle on a striped, seventies-inspired top that has thin straps, and a pair of wide-legged, almost sailor-style jeans. She gives me nude espadrille wedges and a pair of big hoop earrings, and sits me down on the bed so she can do my makeup. The gentle feeling of the big round blush brush on my cheeks is so soothing that I almost fall asleep again.

"There!" Jane says, startling me awake. "Much better."

She looks pleased with her dress-me-up Alex, and I get up to check myself out in the mirror. She's right; I do look better. I smile at her, because I also feel better now that I look presentable. Perhaps if I took the time to bathe and clothe myself appropriately on the regular, my workdays wouldn't seem so dire. Sharing clothes with Jane reminds me of college, before Chick Habit took over my life, before we had serious boyfriends and full sets of cutlery. When we used to stay out late and drink more than we should and go to class with evil, pounding hangovers. When my dad was still alive and I thought I would live forever, too.

On some level, I know that I need to face the present, that I need to stand by my decision to publish the Rebecca West video, even if it means dealing with unpleasant consequences. But right now I want desperately to turn back the clock approximately four years, just for the night.

I look over at Jane, who is wearing a floral romper that would look ridiculous on nine-tenths of the population but somehow is adorable on her. "Thank you for all of this. I don't know what I'd do without you," I say, my eyes welling up ever so slightly.

Jane finishes fastening the last tiny buckle on her fringed sandal, looks at me, and starts making barfing noises.

I laugh. "Come on, I was trying to have a moment!"

"Don't be maudlin. Of course I'm always here for you." She walks over to the bathroom and returns with another Xanax in her small hand. "Here, take one for the road. Now let's blow this Popsicle stand."

I put the Xanax in my purse along with the crumpled-up muumuu and we walk out the door and onto the first of three subways we will need to get out to the boonies of Bushwick. The entire trip takes us nearly an hour, and Jane distracts me from my solipsism by telling me an involved story about her creepy, sexist landlord. She's convinced he's spying on her because one time she left her snow boots in the vestibule and Ali got a phone call about it within fifteen minutes. She's convinced he's a pig because once, when Ali changed his phone number, Jane got a call from the landlord asking for his new contact information. Jane gave it to him, and he told her, "Thanks, sweetheart. You know I really prefer to speak to the man of the house."

I can step outside myself enough to let Jane rage and make appropriate comments like "Oh no he didn't!" at the proper intervals. Just as we're pulling up to the Myrtle Avenue stop on the J train, Jane turns to me and says, "Hey, I need to tell you something."

"What?"

"I think Caleb is going to be there tonight. I heard he lives in the space where Barbizon's performing."

"Christ, Jane, why didn't you tell me before I trekked all the way out here with you?" This unexpected curve scares me. I don't think I can take any more upheaval today, and my heart starts beating faster.

"Because if I told you, you would have stayed on my futon zonked out on Xanax. I think this is a better option."

I haven't seen Caleb since we broke up. Jane's right—I would have stayed at her place in a sedated fog if she had told me the truth. But that doesn't mean I'm ready to face him, especially not after everything that's been going on.

Caleb's always had the remarkable ability to manufacture insecurities in me where they didn't previously exist. For instance: I never thought about the fact that I didn't shave the backs of my thighs until he pointed out how hairy they were. I believe he told me I had "monkey legs." When I got offended, he pretended to be shocked. "But they're so cute and fuzzy!" he protested.

It's impossible for me to back out now—home is at least an hour away—so I just pull a sour face as I follow Jane to our destination: a freestanding Victorian mansion surrounded by two empty lots. The building's façade could charitably be described as sweetly distressed, or uncharitably called a dump. The overwrought gables are in disrepair, the porch has at least two broken steps, and the house looks like it hasn't been painted since the Watergate hearings. We can hear the first song off *Mitzi Kills*, "Room 69," as we approach the unlocked front door.

The narrow entryway opens up to a big dark space. There are Christmas tree lights taped haphazardly to the walls, and the only other light source is coming from a small platform stage where Barbizon is performing. Chey and her bandmates look like fem-bot factory rejects: They're clad in metallic silver dresses so tight you can see every granny-panty-fabric bump.

Chey's done her hair up in a sixties bouffant and is wearing black-framed glasses. She's grasping the mic so hard her knuckles are white, and there's a small crowd of mostly boys staring up at her adoringly while she screeches. I take a quick, furtive look around. Caleb is nowhere to be seen.

Jane and I move in behind the scrum. I check my phone to see if Adam has e-mailed, but no luck. After a few minutes I can't take the din anymore.

"I'm going to find the booze," I shout to Jane.

"Okay," she says. "I want to hear the rest of their set." I walk back past the raised platform into the kitchen.

The kitchen is full of people hiding from the onslaught of noise. I spot another friend, Julia, and sidle up to her. She's talking to two girls who look vaguely familiar.

"Hey!" Julia gives me a big hug. "I haven't seen you in months!"

"I know, I've been hibernating."

"I've been reading your stuff on Chick Habit. It's so much fun!" Julia is an assistant at an anarchist publishing house that seems to exclusively print books about new JFK conspiracy theories. She's got a very well-maintained blond pageboy haircut and gravitates toward gamine French fashions. Tonight she's wearing a striped boatneck shirt and black cigarette pants. We know each other because we worked at the Wesleyan newspaper together as editors.

"Hey, thanks, that means a lot. It's been sort of rough lately." Julia doesn't respond—it's loud in the kitchen so she might not have heard me—plus I don't really want to talk about Chick Habit right now, so I turn to the two girls she's talking to.

The girl to Julia's left is cheerful looking, with a mess of shaggy blond hair. She's wearing a simple denim dress and orthopedic sandals and she's about my height but is shaped like a thick square. The other girl is tiny and sourpussed. I have at least half a foot on her, and she's so skinny that her shapeless black dress hangs off her body. She's wearing big, thick glasses with Lucite frames, which look German and expensive.

I can't place these girls. I'm pretty sure we went to Wesleyan together and that I should know their names, but I don't. The little one worked at the paper with me, I'm almost positive about that, which makes it even worse that I don't remember her. I realize I need to get out of this conversation as quickly as possible and reach for my phone, but then I remember that it's still off and I can't fake an urgent e-mail or text. How did people get out of awkward moments before smart phones? I spot a table laden with half-filled plastic bottles of cut-rate hard liquor and there's my answer.

"I need to get a drink. Does anyone want anything?" I chirp.

"No, thanks," Julia says.

"I'm good," says the square. Sourpuss doesn't respond.

"Be right back!" I say.

As soon as I turn away I walk right into Caleb.

"Oh, hi," I say before I can think of something more clever.

"Hey," he says. "It's good to see you."

"It's good to see you, too," I say, and unfortunately I mean it. I have to admit, he looks amazing. He's wearing a vintage Wrangler shirt that I bought him three years ago, which hugs his lean, muscular torso. His blond five o'clock shadow gives his face depth that it doesn't have when he's clean-shaven. His hair is perfectly mussed. My solar plexus is already jumping, like there are small frogs hopping inside me. Why does he still have this effect on me?

"You look great," he says. "That outfit looks like something from *Soul Train*."

As usual I can't tell if this is a compliment or an insult. He was smirking when he said it, but he's always smirking.

"Thanks?" I say. Feeling off-kilter, I quickly add, "I was just going to get a drink," hoping he'll take the hint and leave me alone.

To my dismay, he says, "Me, too. I'll pour one for you." We walk over to the table and he pours us Jim Beam out of a plastic bottle into two red keg cups. "I don't think there's any ice," he says, handing me one.

"That's okay," I tell him.

I take a sip of bourbon. I don't know what else to say, because I don't know how to behave. As unsupportive and dickish as Caleb was toward me, there was always a certain electricity coming off his limbs that I can still feel, a certain cockiness that I have to admire. I know that I should just walk away from the booze and from him. But I can't help it. I don't know what to think about Peter right now—maybe he's just as selfish as Caleb is, but he hides it better. Perhaps that's worse in the end. At least with Caleb, what you see is what you get.

Besides, Caleb would never get on some high horse about my publishing the Rebecca West video. He doesn't believe in privacy in the first place. I know because one night early on in our relationship the condom broke. I wasn't that worried about it until three weeks later, when my period was late. I marched, crying, over to a Duane Reade on Seventh Avenue near my apartment and bought the most expensive pregnancy test they had. That was when I was making $10 an hour at *Rev*, but my theory was—and still is—you don't skimp on pregnancy tests or tattoo artists. I learned that the hard way.

Caleb held my hand, which I had stuck outside the door of his tiny bathroom, while I took the test (which, thank God, was negative). Two weeks later, I visited him at his studio and saw a digital C print of my discarded pregnancy test on glossy paper. In old-fashioned printer's-block letters the words ALEX IS NEGATIVE were written at the bottom of the print. I was furious—partly for the invasion of my privacy, and partly for the wordplay: Caleb was always telling me to stop being such a Negative Nellie, when I thought I was only being my realist self. "That was my test! " I hissed at him.

He responded, "It's not yours if I've created something entirely new out of it."

Later, he showed that piece at an up-and-coming Williamsburg gallery.

The memory makes me cringe and I down the bourbon left in my cup.

"I thought you were domesticated," Caleb says. "But it looks like you're back to your old tricks." He takes my cup and pours me another shot. "So how have you been?"

"Okay, I guess. I've got some weird shit going on at work." The sensible angel on my shoulder tells me I should get out of this conversation and find Jane, but there's something keeping me planted in this spot. I didn't realize it until I started awkwardly chatting with Caleb, but there's a latent sliver of me that missed feeling emotionally askew in this specific way. He kicks up rocks inside me.

"Where are you working now? Some website? Girlie Town?"

His condescension irritates me and gives me a little more backbone. "It's called Chick Habit," I tell him, giving him my meanest expression. To my pleasant surprise he looks sincerely wounded.

"Alex," he says, catching my hand and forcing eye contact. "I'm really sorry about your dad. You never let me say that."

I'm surprised into silence—I never expected to get an admission of wrongdoing from Caleb about anything. Sure, he still hasn't apologized for being a crap boyfriend, but it's a start. I avert my eyes because I don't know what to say and see that Jane's come into the kitchen. Chey's screams have been replaced with the Arcade Fire's funereal dirges. Jane is talking to Julia and those two girls, and I can tell she's trying to catch my eye.

"I want to show you my latest piece," Caleb says. "It's on my computer upstairs. You might not believe me but you really inspired me. It would mean a lot if you came up and looked at it." I look right at Caleb, trying to discern whether he's being genuine. I know I shouldn't be tempted by his offer but playing the muse again, if only for a few minutes, is highly seductive.

Before I can say anything, Jane appears by my side. "Can I steal Alex for a second?" she asks, and instead of waiting for a response she yanks me by the arm into a small alcove off of the kitchen.

"What are you doing?" Her face is at disappointment level 10 now.

"I'm just talking to him!" I say defensively, even though I'm not sure if it was more than that.

"You are *not* just talking to him. You are giving him fuck-me eyes, and may I remind you that you have a very nice boyfriend at home who is worried sick about you!" Jane's nostrils are flaring with rage. She's in overprotective mama grizzly mode and I can't stand it when she gets bossy like this. I wasn't giving him "fuck-me eyes," at least not consciously.

"My 'nice boyfriend' might have me out of a job soon," I say to remind Jane. She seems to be conveniently forgetting Peter's transgressions.

"You can't know that's true unless you actually talk to him!" Her black eyes are flashing and boring directly into mine.

"Fine!" I yell at her, straining to be heard over the party.

"Then what are you doing?"

"I don't know!" I cry, and I mean it. I was toying with the idea of going up to Caleb's room before Jane accosted me, but I hadn't made up my mind yet.

"Well, you'd better figure it out before you really fuck up your *real* life. This isn't some virtual drama that you can leave on your laptop, Alex. I thought you had evolved past this. I know it was really hard for you when your dad died, but I can't watch you torpedo your sanity with Caleb again."

"Jesus, Jane."

"Alex, I'm looking out for you." She reaches out to touch my shoulder and I shrug her off.

"You're supposed to be supporting me! Why are you on Peter's side and not mine?"

"This isn't about 'sides.' Part of supporting you is telling you when I think you're making a huge mistake." Now she's giving me social worker talk, and it makes me want to die.

"Fine." I sniff.

"Alex, I mean it." Jane's incredibly stubborn and I know she's not going to shut up unless I acknowledge that she has a point. She *does* have a point. But that doesn't mean she gets to decide how I live my life.

"Okay! You're right! Just don't talk to me like I'm one of your wayward patients."

"Well, then stop acting like a destructive teenager. I can't help you if you don't help yourself," Jane says, crossing her arms.

"Can I finish my conversation now?" I ask her somewhat petulantly.

"If that's what you want to do, I can't stop you," Jane says, looking truly chagrined.

I know that Jane's advice is sensible and that she's saying these things because she cares about me. But she doesn't understand that I'm not good and strong like she is, and her fighting me on this like she's my mother only makes me want to go upstairs with Caleb even more than I did before we started yelling. Maybe I *want* to torpedo my sanity—or at least test it. Maybe I'm not meant to have the staid life that I'm heading for with Peter. Maybe I'm better suited for something more debased and messy. I'm only twenty-five—is this really my forever? Being the wife of a finance guy, going to bed early, cooking chicken?

Besides, how dare Jane imply that I would just hop back into bed with Caleb before clearing things up with Peter? I definitely wouldn't do that. I probably wouldn't do that.

I walk back to Caleb, leaving Jane in the alcove, shaking her head.

"I'll come up and see your new project," I tell him.

"Good," he says. "Come with me."

Chapter Nine

Caleb's room is in the attic. It has low, slanted ceilings. He's so tall he can only stand upright in the center. The space feels familiar even though I've never been here: He has the same *Blue Velvet* poster, with Isabella Rossellini's long white neck and Kyle MacLachlan's cherubic face stretching across a background of purplish navy. He's even got the same white sheets and comforter, though I notice he has a new clear plastic desk in one corner of the room with an enormous Apple desktop computer perched on top of it.

He goes right over to the computer, turns on a lamp, and sits down in an Aeron chair. Even though Caleb has been marginally employed since college, selling the occasional photograph or sculpture, he can afford expensive furniture because of monthly checks from his father, the East Texas oil magnate. Caleb doesn't really like to talk about his background—I suspect he feels like it destroys his street cred. So when people ask about his childhood he just tells them that he grew up in Port Arthur, "like

Janis Joplin," which he hopes will make them think he had a gritty, unhappy past. He leaves out the McMansion he grew up in and doesn't talk about his kind and generous parents, Bob and Leigh Ann.

When we were together, Caleb took me down south to meet them just once, for Christmas three years ago. I didn't realize I was walking into a trap until I got there. Caleb always said that what his mother really wanted was for him to marry some boring blond cotillion girl who went to their country club. It turned out that, in an attempt to scandalize her, he had sent his mother links to a column I had written in college about anal sex and he had made a big deal over the family securing a menorah in addition to their customary tree and stockings, because he didn't want me to feel "alienated by their Jesus love." He ignored my protestations that my family hadn't celebrated Hanukkah since I was twelve.

His attempts to pit us against each other backfired. Leigh Ann, a chain-smoking good old girl with hair bleached just a shade lighter than respectable, loved my column. "It reminds me of Jacqueline Susann, honey," she told me, laughing. And she was perfectly happy to accommodate my fake cultural heritage with a lovely silver menorah. In fact, Leigh Ann and I got along so well that she still sends me e-mails from time to time, updating me about her online jewelry business (Leigh Ann's Baubles) and keeping me posted on Bob's golf scores. I'm wondering if Caleb knows that his mom still sends me e-mails every quarter when he pulls a stool close to him and beckons me over.

The only light in the room is coming from that lamp and his computer screen. The background on his screen's desktop is a photo of Serge Gainsbourg and Jane Birkin gallivanting down a Paris street. Jane's wearing hot pants, and Caleb clicks on a QuickTime file next to her slender left leg. "I remember when we were fighting toward the end," he says. "You called me a snake once."

I try to remember the specific incident, but I can't. "I did?"

"Yes. And I thought a lot about that." This surprises me. I always assumed that Caleb tuned me out when we were arguing.

"So I thought—what do snakes do? They shed their skin. And when we broke up I figured I had to shed my old self. So I decided to measure the surface area of my skin, and then I made a giant ball of masking tape that was the same size." He gestures over to a three-foot-tall white ball that's sitting in the corner of his dim room. Even without the overhead light on I can see that there are bits of dust and flecks of grime sticking to its surface.

"So then I had this giant ball of masking tape, and I thought to myself, what am I going to do with this giant ball of masking tape? And then it hit me." He clicks the play button on the screen. An image appears of Caleb dressed all in white. I recognize the space—it's his studio in Ditmas Park. I watch the screen as he rolls the enormous ball of tape back and forth across the long room. I wait for something else to happen. Is something else going to happen? Nope. Just more of Caleb pushing the ball back and forth, back and forth.

Caleb looks over at me expectantly, waiting for me to comment. What I want to tell him is that this is exactly what people hate about modern art. Instead, I muster the strength to say, "The sound of the tape against the floor is really . . . visceral."

"Thanks. That's exactly what I was going for." He leans

toward me and kisses me tenderly on the forehead. "I missed you, Alex. Nobody gets me like you. When I was doing that series with the taxidermied pigeons, everyone else dismissed it. But you were behind me all the way."

I don't respond—I'm still reeling from the white lie I just told and I want to avoid another one—but Caleb doesn't seem to notice. He stands up and announces, "I want to show you another piece I've been working on. It's down in the basement. Stay there. I'll be right back."

"Okay," I say, not really sure why I'm agreeing but thinking it's better than being downstairs at the party. As he walks away I lean forward to look once again at his computer screen. I was so angry at Caleb when we broke up that I forgot his good parts, and for a minute I wonder if I dismissed him too quickly when we broke up. Maybe he's no longer the enfant terrible I remember. Lots of decent people don't know how to handle sudden death—many of my good friends avoided me right after my dad died because they didn't know what to say. It was just immaturity, not pure evil.

And Caleb was capable of some really tender moments when he wasn't being an asshole: bringing me coffee in bed on weekend mornings from my favorite little shop near his apartment, buying me the perfect French journals from obscure stores in the Village, keeping me company late into the night when I couldn't sleep.

"Ah, your little smiley face," Caleb says wistfully from behind me, and I jump and turn around. "I missed that, too." He smiles at me and walks out of the room, his upright carriage emphasizing the broadness of his shoulders.

It's like a bucket of frigid water has been thrown onto my nostalgic reverie. Maybe it's not Adam who sent BTCH the dirt on me. It's Caleb. Caleb, who is in Brooklyn and not in a remote yurt. Caleb, who doesn't believe in privacy. Caleb, who thinks of my body as an extension of his little art projects. Caleb, that bastard.

But what could he have sent? I definitely didn't let him take any nude videos, photographs, or whatever when we were together. Unless he took them without my consent? When I was sleeping? Or maybe he did something more sinister: Maybe he altered an existing picture of me in Photoshop to make it look like I was giving someone a blow job, or something else equally lewd. Maybe he named it *Alex Is Submissive* and called it art.

I run to the door and look down the hallway. There's no sign of Caleb. I go back to his computer and go straight to Gmail. Luckily he's still signed in, and I can see all of his recent sent messages. I scroll down through pages and pages of sent messages. I see e-mails to Bob and Leigh Ann confirming a Labor Day trip back home. I see e-mails to a bunch of different girls, including one to Stacia, with a subject line that reads, "Last night at your apartment." I always knew he was fucking her! I see e-mails to several different galleries with a file of Caleb's video, *snake skin*, attached. What I don't see are any e-mails to Breaking the Chick Habit's Gmail account, or to any other names that look like they could belong to the person who runs BTCH.

I glance behind me to see if Caleb is coming, and then I take to his hard drive. I look through as many photos as I possibly can in quick succession: dead pigeon, dead pigeon, dead pigeon, street sign, dead squab, dead pigeon dressed in a miniature postal worker's uniform, dead pigeon dressed as a doctor, view from the Williamsburg Bridge. I'm not seeing anything here that is even remotely sexual or ominous. Now I'm really starting to sweat. How am I not finding anything?

I'm about to give up when I see a folder marked, ominously, "Alex." Though he claims to have quit the Internet, Caleb is pretty tech-savvy when it comes to sending large photos into the ether. I bet he would have chosen a more secure connection than just e-mail to share this creepy business with that vile hate blogger.

I glance over to his bed. He always liked to draw when he was under the covers, so the sheets were always grainy with graphite shavings. I remember feeling them against my bare skin when I was trying to sleep. I picture photographs of me sprawled out on that bed, asleep on my side, my unconscious self so open and vulnerable.

But I can't find out immediately whether my imaginings are accurate, because the folder is password protected. I try entering every combination that might have meaning for him: his name and birth date (Caleb423), his first pet (Fluffers, a finicky Siamese), his favorite artist (Twombly). Finally the nickname of his first car (El Guapo) gets me in.

Inside the folder is a single file. I click on it, feeling the whiskey rise in my throat, and open . . . a photo of me, smiling at the camera, fully clothed. I recognize the shot—it was taken during graduation week, during our first flush of love. My pixie cut had just started to grow out and for whatever reason I thought it was a good idea to bleach small chunks of it platinum. I'm not wearing any makeup but my cheeks are freckled by the sun and rosy from drinking.

At first I'm furious with Caleb: How dare he idealize the notion of me when he treated the real me so terribly? But then I realize: That's how Caleb *was,* the whole time we were together. Of course he would rather look at a static photo from a happy time than deal with my actual self. Peter might not be the man I thought he was, but at least he has always appreciated me for what I am. He never tries to distance himself from my emotions or my work—he confronts them head-on.

Jane's right: I am better than this. I don't know for sure that Caleb isn't somehow connected to BTCH, but the fact that I'd even violate his privacy shows how messed up my head is right now.

I close out of the image and the folder just as I hear him coming up the steps. I've just moved away from it when Caleb comes back into the room. He's holding a preserved dead sparrow wearing a knitted cap.

"Thanks for showing me the video, but I have to run," I say before he can begin to explain the dead bird.

"What? Why?"

"I just do." I brush past him and hustle back down the stairs, stopping on the landing so I can scan the crowd. I have no idea how long I've been gone, but from the looks of it probably about forty-five minutes or an hour. The kitchen is not quite as packed as when I went upstairs with Caleb, but the party has not yet reached its tipping point, when groups of friends and couples start leaving en masse. I see Cheyenne and her bandmates, a clot of metal in a sea of blacks and plaids. They're drinking from blue and red keg cups, and I see Chey throw her head back in laughter, a look of pure pleasure taking over her entire open face.

Standing there on the landing I am struck by the contrast between myself and my friends: I'm driving myself bonkers searching for something that doesn't even exist in the physical world while they are actually living. How did I get so disconnected? Chick Habit, and all its attendant stresses and woes, is still just a website.

Then something else hits me: If Caleb isn't connected to the hate blogger, I'm back to square one. I feel despair creep over me. It's so much easier to parse something nefarious when you can understand the person and his or her motives. What if this is simply random Internet terrorism? Something that could happen again and again, for no reason at all?

I realize I need to find Jane immediately and patch things up. I can't afford to cock up any more of my real-life relationships. I scan the crowd but I can't see her anywhere, though I do see Julia and that skinny girl, what's her name, still standing near the booze table, deep in conversation.

I push my way over to them. "Sorry to interrupt, but have you seen Jane?"

"I think she's out on the stoop," Julia says. What's-her-name just stares at me. "Is she okay? She looked pretty upset when she was on her way out there."

"I should check on her," I tell Julia, nearly sprinting past her.

I run through the darkened main room, which is almost entirely empty, and throw open the heavy door. Sure enough, Jane's outside on the stoop, talking to an acquaintance from college, Anna. I don't know Anna that well, but she and Jane have been close since they played on an intramural soccer league together in college. Jane's smoking a Camel Light. She only lights up when she's had a few, so I know she's pretty drunk. I'm hoping this means she is in a forgiving mood.

"Thank God you're still here!" I say, testing the waters.

Jane regards me coolly. "Yep, still here."

Ouch. So maybe not so forgiving. I turn to Anna. "Hey, Anna, good to see you."

"Nice to see you, too," Anna says cautiously. From the look on her face I suspect that I've just walked into a major bitch session about yours truly.

Since their conversation clearly can't continue, Anna stubs out her cigarette and says to Jane, "Catch you later, J." She pushes open the heavy door and disappears back into the party.

Neither Jane nor I says anything for a few minutes. I desperately want to beg for her forgiveness immediately, but I'm too nervous. She might still be pissed, and I don't want to get another lecture, not now. Finally, Jane blows smoke out of the side of her mouth and says, "So, did you fuck up your life or what?" I exhale with relief. At least Jane's still speaking to me!

"I didn't. You were so right. I need to get a grip."

"Damn straight I was right."

"I'm so sorry, Jane." She's still got her face in a tight little grimace.

"Please tell me that you didn't touch him, even a little."

"I didn't!" I hesitate and then add, "I did, however, read his e-mail."

"Whaaaaaat?!?" She drops the cigarette from her fingers and she raises her eyebrows nearly off her face.

I explain to Jane about the smiley-face tattoo and the locked folder and the ordinary, not-scandalous photo of me, ending with, "So I realized that I was losing my mind, truly, and high-tailed it outta there."

"I'm glad," Jane says, her tone still firm. "But I really do hope this is a wake-up call."

"It really is. I'm going to go back home right now and have an honest, serious talk with Peter."

"I'm not just talking about Peter." Her concern face is back on.

"What do you mean?"

"You're obsessed with this job in a really unhealthy way. You don't eat properly, you don't go outside. You wear that tragic muumuu all the time. You are neglecting people you love. I know that Chick Habit has been good for your career, and I've tried to be supportive because I love reading the site, but I think after all this hate-blog, Rebecca West nonsense dies down you should seriously reevaluate what it is you're doing."

"Wow, Jane, tell me how you really feel." My head is spinning. How long has Jane felt this way?

"I'm just telling you what I'm seeing. It never seemed this bad before and I thought you would adjust eventually. But after this week, I don't think it's right for you." She says this gently. Her tone is completely different than it was during our first confrontation.

"Well, Jane, it's not like I have a whole lot of other options in this business right now. And before this week everything was going pretty okay." I say this bitterly, not because I'm mad at Jane for being honest or because I think she's wrong, but because

I really have no idea what to do—about the job, about Peter, about any of it.

"I'm not telling you to call up Moira tomorrow and quit your job. I just think you should think about your situation."

All of a sudden I am very, very tired. I don't have the energy to argue with Jane, and I certainly don't have the energy to contemplate leaving Chick Habit and finding another job. We stand there in silence for a bit, not looking at each other. I can hear Jane sighing a foot away from me.

"Can we just go home now?" I ask.

Jane says, "Yes, we can just go home now. Do you have the number of the car service?"

"I do." I take my phone out of my canvas bag and turn it on. Immediately I see that I have four messages waiting for me, but I ignore those for the time being and call the car. "Five minutes," the dispatcher tells me, and just three minutes later a beat-up Town Car arrives.

Jane must be exhausted, too, because she falls asleep immediately upon sitting down in the big backseat of the car. I tell the driver that there will be two stops, Jane's place and then mine. Against the background of muted techno music I listen to my voice mail, bracing myself for Peter's sad disapproval.

The first voice coming out of my iPhone is not Peter's deep one but Moira's jaunty Irish brogue. "Love, where are you? I have news about tomorrow! It's about nine P.M. Call me or IM me when you get this."

The second message is from my mother. "Hi, Alex. I just wanted to hear your little voice. If you can give me a call tomorrow, I'd love to catch up." I feel guilty for not calling her, but I don't know how I'd explain the madness of the past few days.

The third message is also from Moira. "Alex, seriously, call me. It's eleven. You know how to reach me."

The fourth message is Moira again, the brightness in her voice replaced by total annoyance. "Alex, if you would deign to return my phone call, I would tell you that you need to be camera-ready at six thirty tomorrow morning. That's when the *Today* show is sending a car to pick you up. Be prepared to talk Rebecca West by seven fifteen. This is huge for Chick Habit. You'd better be ready."

Despite my exhaustion I have an immediate surge of conflicting reactions. The first is: Squeee! I'm going to be on the *Today* show! This is a lifelong dream of mine. As much as I roll my eyes at the dog-grooming tips and missing-white-woman news stories, I do have a sincere love for Natalie, Savannah, and the rest of the crew.

My second thought is: The hate blogger is going to lose her mind when she sees me on TV. Is this going to hasten the release of whatever it is she has on me?

Which brings me to my third and most distressing thought: When the Rebecca West story was just on our humble website, I could pretend it wasn't that big a deal. If it's on national television, it might actually ruin her life for real.

All of these thoughts are roiling in my brain as the car pulls up to Jane's apartment. She wakes up just as the car stops.

"Hey," I say, deciding not to bother her with the latest turn. Jane's made it pretty clear that she's had enough of my drama for the day.

"Hi," Jane says, rubbing her eyes and smearing her mascara. "I know I was a total pain in the ass today, and I'm sorry."

"S'okay. I love you, you know? I just want what's best for you."

I nod. "Good night." We hug and she gets out of the car.

It is only after Jane leaves that it sinks in that Peter hasn't called me tonight. Or if he has, he realized my phone was off and he didn't leave a message. I can't say I blame him, since I've been such a deadbeat about calling him back this week. But I'm scared about going home, because I don't know how he's going to react when I stumble home far past midnight, and not even for the first time this week. I also don't know how to broach the subject of the Omnitown report. I know I might not like what I hear, but I need to find out what's going on so we can move forward.

The car pulls up to the curb outside my apartment. The driver tells me it's going to be $22, which is when I realize how far away from home I really was. I hand him a ten and a twenty and tell him to keep the change. As anxious as I am about facing Peter, I'm here at the door and I have no place else to go. I open our squat door as quietly as I can, in case he's still asleep, but I see him sitting up on the couch reading in a T-shirt and boxer briefs as soon as I step into the light. There's a pillow and a blanket next to him. He puts down what appears to be the Omnitown report and looks at me.

"You're finally home." There's a mixture of relief and frustration in his voice, but his face is impassive. I can't read it, which is rare; I can usually tell what Peter's feeling from his expression. I decide to launch into extreme apology mode and hope that his blankness is just exhaustion.

"I am. We really need to talk, I just—"

"Shut up, Alex, seriously. Just shut up." I freeze. Peter's hardly ever spoken to me like this before. He doesn't seem tired at all now.

"But I just want to explain—"

"I don't want to hear your excuses right now. I'm so angry and confused that I don't know what to say. We need to sit down and have a real talk about the way you've been acting these past few days but it's three in the morning and as I've told you a million times already, this is a huge week for me at work." His voice gets louder and louder throughout this speech until he's shouting at me, nostrils flaring. This is the angriest I've ever seen him. I try to remember the last time he yelled at me like this, but I can't. "Have you had a fucking lobotomy or something? What is *wrong* with you?"

I am so shocked at being yelled at that instead of confronting him about Tyson Collins I start babbling. "I know, I just . . . Work's been crazy and there's all this . . . stuff going on. I just wanted . . ." I'm starting to cry, and I see Peter's face harden.

"You just nothing. You haven't thought about me for a second in days and right now my priority is sleep, not listening to whatever it is you have to say."

"Okay," I say, resigning myself to another day of not telling Peter about the Becky West fiasco, which is about to reach the next level, and another day of pretending I didn't read what I read at the kitchen table this morning.

"Good," he says. He plumps the pillow angrily, lies down on the couch, and turns over so his back is toward me.

I go to the bathroom to clean off my makeup and put cold water on my hot, tearful face. Maybe Jane was right. Maybe losing my job would be good for me. Maybe I shouldn't go on the *Today* show.

Then I look up at my newly clean face and wonder, Will they provide a makeup artist on set?

THURSDAY

Chapter Ten

My iPhone's ring wakes me up. I don't immediately see the phone, but the ringing is so close to my head, I realize that the cell must be somewhere in bed with me. My eyes are so dry from last night's sedative-and-booze combo and a possibly perilous lack of sleep that I can only open them partway. I grope around for the phone and manage to pick it up and shove it against my ear.

"Hello?" I croak out.

"Where the fuck have you been, love?" Moira says. She's the only person who can make the word "love" sound menacing.

"M-my phone accidentally got turned off in my purse," I stammer, pleased that I can come up with a plausible excuse before I've ingested coffee.

"Did you get my messages?"

"Yes."

"And will you be ready in thirty minutes when the car from *Today* arrives at your hovel?"

I pause for a second and collect my head. My dithering of the previous night seems to have dissolved in the early morning sun. It's suddenly completely clear to me that the only choice is to push forward. I've already sacrificed so much to this job that to give up now—and possibly lose it—seems ludicrous. Even though this isn't the way I wanted to end up on the *Today* show (ideally, I'd be appearing because of a serious ten-thousand-word article I had written that made people change the way they thought about women in politics), I shouldn't pass up this chance. I can deal with Peter later.

"Yes," I say, my voice steady with my new resolve.

"Good." Moira's voice relaxes immediately. "Molly is doing your first post of the day but after you've been on the telly you need to go right back home and fill your quota."

"Of course," I say, wondering how the hell I am going to get through another hungover day. This job is hard enough when I've had my eight hours and the strongest thing in my system from the night before is Sleepytime tea.

"Right, then. Take a shower and put on something presentable. Remember: Colorful V-necks are best. Avoid patterns. They'll do your makeup so go in with a bare face. Sit up straight, and speak clearly."

I remember now that Moira is a veteran of the morning talk show circuit from her days at the fusty lady mag. She was a celebrity correspondent and would comment on pressing famous-person issues like Reese Witherspoon's new haircut and how quickly Jessica Alba lost her baby weight.

"Got it," I tell Moira, grateful for her practical advice. "See you back online in a few hours."

I hoist myself out of bed and notice immediately that Peter is not on the couch. In his place is a neatly folded blanket with a perfectly plumped pillow atop it. I'm more surprised that he folded the blanket than anything else; that he's gone is not a shock. He occasionally leaves for work before six and he wants to avoid seeing me. I'm still angry and hurt when I think that he might be keeping pivotal job information from me, but I'm also feeling guilty about pushing him away.

But now is not the time to indulge myself in feelings about my relationship. I need to be in Terminator mode.

The shower refuses to heat up; the water doesn't even reach its normal tepid heights. No matter. I hop in, lather up my shampoo without even minding the downright cold temperature, and clean my face with the fancy face-scrub I use for special occasions. I hop back out approximately three minutes later and rummage around in my closet until I locate the one dress that fits Moira's qualifications: a cerulean wrap dress from Forever 21 that is miraculously clean. I throw on the dress with a pair of pointy-toed sling-backs that I only ever wear for job interviews.

I hear the sound of a car pulling up to the curb and I glance at the clock. It's 6:28. I go outside, my hair still dripping, to find a gleaming black Town Car sitting next to a bunch of trash out for garbage collection. I pick my way around an old air conditioner and get in.

"Hi."

"Hey," the driver says back to me. He's wearing a pressed black suit and bears a striking resemblance to Steve Buscemi. Since I've made it to the car on time, I relax into the backseat, which is when my head starts pounding with caffeine withdrawal.

"Can you pull up here?" I ask him when I see a bodega.

"Sure."

"I'm just going to get some coffee, do you want some?"

"That would be really nice, thanks," he says.

"I'm Alex," I tell him, extending my hand.

"Tim," he says, shaking it firmly.

I walk in and am momentarily soothed by the quiet hum of the morning show. They announce the weather (it's going to be a hot one today!) and then segue into playing some bouncy Taylor Swift song. I pour two large coffees, one for myself and one for the driver, and liberally dump milk and sugar into both.

I get back into the car and hand Tim his coffee. As the caffeine starts to hit my system I am struck by an inescapable sadness. I'm living my dream—how many mornings while watching the *Today* show have I fantasized about gabbing with Kathie Lee?—and yet no one knows: Peter's barely speaking to me; I haven't talked to my mom since Monday; and Jane has no idea I'm about to be on TV.

I look down at my phone to push off the gloom and see that our daily traffic report from yesterday has come in. The Rebecca West post has two million page views, making it the most popular post in Chick Habit history by a multiple of three. I tell myself that this video is officially real news and that the *Today* show would run a segment on it whether or not I agreed to participate. I tell myself that if I didn't publish the video, Molly sure would have, so what's the harm? I'm just doing my job—and doing it well.

Traffic is moving briskly this early in the morning, and at the base of Manhattan Tim tries to make some light conversation. "So what are you going on the show for?" he asks, craning his neck back to look at me at a stop light on the West Side Highway.

I consider making up something more respectable, for instance: "I run a booming macaron bakery called Bakerista and am going on to do a cooking demonstration with Al Roker." But instead, I go with some version of the truth. "I write for a website and yesterday I posted a piece with a video of a pseudo-famous person doing drugs and taking her shirt off."

Tim's eager, wizened face scrunches up. "Oh," he says, then turns back around. He's pretty quiet for the rest of the trip to midtown, but as we pull up to the studio, with its enormous wraparound window replete with tourists standing behind the barricades outside, he wishes me good luck with a genuine smile.

"I'm sorry I wasn't better company this morning," I say.

"You'll be great!" he says, and for a second I believe him.

It's 6:50 A.M. when I check in with a security guard and am promptly ushered into a dingy, windowless room where a motherly woman named Barb immediately comes at me with a tincture of foundation in her meaty hand. She tells me, almost under her breath, "Christ, hon, it's going to take our industrial-strength concealer to fix that mess under your eyes."

I'm strangely grateful for her honesty and smile up at her as she dabs something thick on my sleepless circles. "Thanks. I didn't get much sleep last night."

"It shows. But don't you worry, we'll fix you right up."

I close my eyes, relaxing into the feeling of Barb's fingers on my face. A few minutes later a hairstylist who doesn't introduce herself gets to work on my still-damp, stringy hair.

With a genuine hair-and-makeup team working to cover my bad decisions of the last few nights, I start to get genuinely excited about this appearance. Tyson Collins—or executive X from Omnitown—might see the spot and realize how indispensable I am. Rebecca West's feelings aren't *really* my problem, are they? It's not my fault that her family is so fame-whorey.

I'm almost fully relaxed when the whine of the hair dryer goes silent and Barb snaps me out of my calm with a cheery, "Okay, hon, you're all set!" I open my eyes and barely recognize the reflection in the mirror. I certainly look less tired, but I don't quite look like myself, either: It's like I'm wearing the Kabuki mask of a third-tier starlet. At least those under-eye bags have disappeared.

I'm shuttled off to wait in the greenroom, a similarly shabby little place with threadbare furniture and an anemic-looking fruit basket. I'm momentarily let down: I thought the digs would be swankier than this, and the snacks more delicious. But I don't have time to consider this because I'm immediately met by a harried producer, Tammy, who is wearing a headset and a determined look in her green eyes. "Okay, so you're the one who posted the Becky West coke tape, right?"

"Yes, that's right." I try to sound as confident as possible. I've watched enough morning TV to know that showing self-doubt is televisual death.

"Ann's going to be interviewing you. Usually I have more time to prep our guests but our producer couldn't reach you last night." Tammy's voice is accusing and I start to get anxious.

"Sorry. I had turned my phone off."

"Too late now. I've written down some topics on these." Tammy hands me a stack of multicolored index cards. "I can't guarantee where Ann's going to go with this one, but you'll at least have some idea about what we're going to discuss."

"Thanks," I say, trying to sound calm. But the makeup chair relaxation has worn off. A flubbed appearance on national television could make me my own video meme—if I say something embarrassing or indefensible it could whip around the Internet all day. Maybe not with the velocity of an angelic blonde doing blow and taking off her top, but still.

"We weren't able to locate Becky West," Tammy adds. "We asked her to come on the show, but she didn't respond to any of our inquiries."

"Huh," I say. That seems odd. Why wouldn't she want to set the story straight? Wouldn't Darleen at least want to reprise her role as aggrieved party on the *Today* show couch?

Before I can ask Tammy any of these questions, she's hustled off down a dim corridor. I shuffle through the cards, and this interview seems soft enough: Savannah wants to talk about the habits of college girls today, privacy online, and Darleen West's divisiveness, in particular the Chick Habit campaign against her. I am just beginning to fully process these lines of conversation when Tammy bursts back into the greenroom. "You ready?"

"As ready as I'll ever be!" I say brightly. As an avid student of the *Today* show I know that perkiness can cover a multitude of sins.

I follow Tammy's hunched shoulders down a labyrinthine hallway and out onto the *Today* show set. Unlike the lumpy back rooms, the actual set is crisp and bright, and the sun is streaming in on this perfect July day. As I walk past the big window onto Rockefeller Plaza, I look out at the beaming faces in the crowd. One squat woman is holding up a sign that says HAPPY 40TH ANNIVERSARY, MORTY! and I am briefly but sincerely touched. I wonder if this studio is so steeped in earnestness that it is rubbing off on me, like some sort of anti-snark solution.

Tammy brings me to a low, comfortably plush beige couch. There's a matching beige chair next to me, and I know that is where Savannah will sit. But when Tammy returns it's not with attractive Savannah but with a woman I don't recognize. She's wearing a boxy bright red suit and sensible, two-inch black heels. Her dyed auburn hair is higher than her heels and appears to have about a can of hairspray locked into it.

"Howdy," the stranger says. "I'm Internet safety expert Joellen Maxwell."

I've never heard someone introduce herself by citing her expertise before. I spit out, "Hi. I'm Chick Habit associate editor Alex Lyons."

"Oh, I know who you are, sugar. They briefed me on you last night."

Damn it. I really should have been answering my phone. "I didn't know someone else was going to be on with me," I say, trying to hide my surprise. "It will be nice to have a discussion partner!"

"It sure will!" Joellen affirms this as she settles to the right of me on the couch, neatly crossing her hose-covered legs.

Before I can ask my pert partner some leading questions to

figure out how exactly she'll stand in what I assume is opposition to me, Savannah Guthrie appears on set and walks determinedly toward the cushy chair next to me.

Whenever people meet celebrities in real life, their first comment is usually, "They're so much smaller in person!" This holds true for Savannah, who is impossibly petite and put-together. She's wearing a magenta sleeveless shell and a slim-fitting light gray pencil skirt. Her glossy shoulder-length hair shines in the studio lights as she gracefully sits down and angles herself toward us. I'm just able to register that someone is saying, "And we're live in five, four, three, two . . . ," and then Savannah is speaking.

"It's seven thirty, and we're starting this half hour with the story of a celebrity child exposed. Rebecca West is the successful daughter of 'Genius Mom' Darleen West. A video of Becky partaking in an illicit substance has become an Internet sensation since it was posted yesterday at one. For more on this story, we go to NBC's Jeff Rossen in the Wests' hometown of Omaha, Nebraska."

A producer says, "And we're out." Instead of talking to either me or Joellen, Savannah reads her notes intently. Behind Savannah's head I can see a TV rolling footage of Rossen—*Today*'s investigative reporter—framing the Becky West story for the audience: "Just two days ago, America thought of Becky West as a model daughter. She made the dean's list at MIT three semesters in a row and has a promising future as a robotics engineer. Becky is one of four quadruplet daughters of parenting expert and Nebraska state senate candidate Darleen West, whose highly controversial bestseller, *How to Raise a Genius, Times Four,* encourages parents to be tougher on their children. Becky has only ever had praise for her mother's methods."

I hear the show cut to the clip of Becky on the *Today* show a few years back, telling Ann Curry, "I don't regret a thing," and then Jeff Rossen is back.

"But a shocking video published yesterday by the gossip website Chick Habit shows that even the most accomplished young women can have serious problems." I hear the sound of Becky West snorting those lines reverberate throughout the studio and am mildly annoyed at Rossen's characterization of Chick Habit as a mere "gossip website." Aren't we a bit more than that?

"The publication of this video has started a national debate about the blurred line between public and private behavior. The West family would not respond to our interview requests, so we asked people in Omaha, where the Wests are local celebrities and Darleen is running for state senate, what they think of Becky's alleged drug use."

I take my eyes off the TV for a second and notice Savannah's still looking studiously at her notes, rubbing her left temple occasionally as if she is massaging the information into her brain. Joellen is sitting perfectly still, her smile undimmed even off-camera. I turn back to the screen, where Rossen is now holding the camera in front of a teenage girl inside what appears to be an upscale Omaha mall. "Whatever Becky West wants to do in her, like, free time, that's her business," the girl says with an appropriately adolescent sneer. "It's not, like, anyone else's place to judge."

The camera cuts to a matron in her fifties with a bad perm

and an expensive-looking tennis bracelet. "It just makes me so nervous for my kids," she says. "They could make one dumb mistake and it could follow them for the rest of their lives. This girl needs private help, not publicity."

Finally, a man in his midtwenties with an air of skeeziness about him, whose skinny, unshaven neck is sticking out from an oversized T-shirt, says, "That Becky girl should know better than to let someone tape her. You gotta be a moron in this day and age to think that anything that goes on tape is going to be private forever."

"Is this young man correct? Does a person's expectation of privacy disappear the second someone hits record? For NBC, I'm Jeff Rossen."

Like one of Becky's robots, Savannah immediately snaps her head up to the camera with a sanguine expression. "Joellen Mitchell is an Internet safety expert, and Alex Lyons is an associate editor at Chick Habit. Welcome to you both. Alex, I wonder if you could tell us a little bit about your decision to post this video of Becky West. Were you worried about violating her privacy?"

I wonder if the beads of sweat collecting in my armpits are bleeding through my $19 dress. I know that silence is deadly on these shows so I just open my mouth and let the words fall out.

"Darleen West has positioned her daughters as, ummmm, aspirational figures, and in doing so has turned them into public figures. The video of Becky had clear news value *because* Darleen has used her daughters in the pursuit of her own controversial platform. I don't think that we violated Becky's privacy by publishing this. This is information the public has a right to know about." I don't think I sounded like a total moron, so I finish my sentence with a cryptic half smile. Savannah's expression doesn't change, so I can't tell if she thinks I'm full of it.

"Joellen, what do you think about Chick Habit's decision to run this video?"

"Well, darlin', I think it's just a pathetic state of affairs. We should be building America's children up online, not tearin' 'em down. Certainly a gal like Becky West can't expect the same level of privacy as a regular person, but it is the responsibility of our journalists and bloggers to be above this kinda thing." She's looking right at Savannah when she says this, and she's tilted slightly away from me as if I'm not there. Joellen's tone is think-of-the-children drippy.

"Alex, have you heard the news that Becky West has been receiving death threats?" Savannah asks me firmly but not aggressively.

Jesus. "No, I hadn't heard that." I've gotten death threats before, too—anyone who has worked on the Internet for more than a week has—but it sounds so much more serious when Savannah says it. I can feel my cheeks reddening with shame.

"Do you still stand behind your decision to run this?" Savannah sounds neutral like she always does, and I can't tell what answer she wants to hear.

"I do," I say, though my voice is wavering and I just know that my pit stains are showing. "This video would have made its way online whether or not I published it. Of course I think it's awful that she has been receiving death threats, and in no way do I condone that behavior. But the fact of the matter is that Becky is a celebrity now, and she needs to consider that before she acts."

I can't tell whether or not I actually believe what I just said, but I'm relieved that at least I came up with something coherent. I glance over at Joellen, who looks appalled.

"I'm sorry, I just think that is so darn terrible," Joellen says, her voice becoming cloying and saccharine sweet. "Becky is a good kid who made a mistake, and you're just a big ol' cyber-bully."

"Becky is a grown woman who should be able to deal with the consequences of her actions. Don't infantilize her!" I say, my voice rising. I fight to calm down because I know it's a mistake to lose my temper—even though she's the one calling me names, Joellen will come out looking better than me if she keeps her cool and I lose mine. I'm looking at her for a response when Savannah interrupts.

"I'm sorry, we've got ten seconds to go. The lesson here?"

Even though I see Joellen opening her lipsticked mouth I make sure I get the last word in. "No matter how old you are, you need to be aware that anything you record could end up all over the Internet." Joellen lets the air run out of her and I detect a slight pout. Savannah is all business, moving fluidly to the next segment.

"Thanks to Alex Lyons and Joellen Maxwell. Next up, we've got Basil, the miniature dachshund who saved his owner's life by dialing 911 with his paw!"

I hear the clip of Basil barking and panting start to run. Then I realize Basil is only barking—I'm the one breathing so heavily. Savannah finally makes eye contact with me and says a sincere, "Thank you for coming."

I mumble, "Thanks for having me," and I flee before I have to make nice to Joellen, who is still sitting smugly to my right. I scurry past Tammy, who's standing near where she brought me onto the set. Then I head back the same way I came, through the maze of hallways to the dumpy greenroom, where my canvas purse is awaiting me. I plunge my hand in and grab my iPhone immediately, hoping no one I know—save Moira—decided to flip on *Today* this morning. Most important, I'm hoping BTCH hasn't gotten wind of this yet. Deep down I know there's no way the hate blogger won't find out about my appearance on a national television show, but I can't deal with any further threats right now.

There's a text awaiting me from Moira.

Moira Fitzgerald (7:41 AM): All press is good press!

I'm not sure if Moira means that in a positive way. Maybe it wasn't so bad after all? I look down at my armpits, first the left, then the right. The dark circle on the left side is perceptible in person, though the right one is barely apparent (I've always wondered: What is the deal with disproportional pit stains?). Hopefully under the bright TV lights both stains disappeared.

There's a junior producer loitering in the greenroom who looks about twelve. She takes me to the elevator and says, "Good job," with as little enthusiasm as possible right before the doors close.

Tim is waiting for me where he left me off this morning. "How'd it go?"

"Okay, I guess," I say as I climb back into the slick backseat.

Once I'm settled back into the car I log into my Chick Habit e-mail account to see if BTCH has contacted me again. I bet this Becky West death threat info has invigorated her. If nothing else it will give her some weird moral high ground: She might be harassing me, but I caused someone to fear for her life. And she wouldn't be wrong. Even though death threats are almost always just a lot of hot air, if Becky's life is actually in danger, I don't know that I could ever let myself off the hook.

I don't see any e-mails from the BTCH address, and there's nothing in my inbox from Rebecca or Darleen or even any of their lawyers; what I do see is 532 unread e-mails, all from names I don't recognize. I click on one in the 200 region, from a woman named Cheryl Carolla.

To: alex@chickhabit.net
From: Cheryl Carolla <ccarolla@aol.com>
Subject: You are a cyberbully!

Young lady, you should be ashamed of yourself. Darleen West is a god-fearing Christian woman and you have just defiled her on national television. Her daughter is a good girl at heart, and you had no place airing out their private family business on your smutty little website. That Joelene woman was right, you are a cyberbully!

Well, that was a pretty mild, literate piece of hate mail. I click through to the next e-mail.

To: alex@chickhabit.net
From: Morris Saverin <morris223@hotmail.com>
Subject: Die Cunt

U shold go fuck off and die u ugly cunt. Get ur teeth fixed first + take care of ur pit stainz too.

Ugh. This one stings. I only get this sort of response when our content appears in front of a wider audience than our Chick Habit regulars. The usual stable of readers might be tough to please, but they hardly ever attack our looks (it's not very sisterly) or use derogatory words for vagina as an insult. And you *could* see my pit stains! Why didn't Moira say anything?

I keep scrolling through the mail, my hope that I did a decent job on *Today* shrinking with each missive. The ratio of hate mail to support mail is about nine to one (typical subject line: "You're An Asshole"). I pick one of the nice e-mails to see if reading it makes me feel any better:

To: alex@chickhabit.net
From: Lisa Rodgers <lrodg1234@starpower.biz>
Subject: Way to go!

I'm so glad someone is out there showing what Darleen West is really like. I've known Darleen since high school, and let me tell you, she's been pulling this shit since we were 16. Ever since we were on the cheerleading squad together and she forced me to be at the bottom of the pyramid, I've known she's a phony. Good on you for showing the world that Darleen West is a hypocrite!

—Lisa

Nope, that just makes me feel worse. I'm only enabling sour old grudge holders. Deep down, even though I still feel conflicted about this whole debacle, I hoped that I might change the way some people think about the nature of privacy and celebrity, but I guess that's a lot to ask from a five-minute TV segment.

At least I'm pretty sure that my mom hasn't seen my performance this morning—not yet, anyway. In the grand tradition of academic parents, she doesn't own a TV, and she's such a Luddite that she only knows how to check her e-mail from our home computer, so if some well-meaning soul sent her the link to my appearance, she wouldn't see it until tonight, which gives me some time to explain it to her. Hopefully with the right spin, I won't be such a disappointment.

I remember the first post that BTCH did, the one with the photograph of me from the local Connecticut weekly and the quote about how much I loved Hillary. BTCH had wondered what had happened to that sweet little girl. That's what my mom would be thinking if she had seen my morning show appearance.

But I can't think about my mom too much longer, because just as Tim pulls up to my apartment, I get a text from Jane.

Jane Rivera (8:22 AM): Got the intel from Leon. Call me when u get this.

* * *

Jane picks up on the second ring. "I'm about to see a client so I need to make this quick."

"Okay, go!"

"Leon says that the hate blogger is based in Fort Greene. He's been able to pinpoint the address to a big collection of condos called the Phthalo on Carlton Avenue, but it's unclear which of the seventy units the IP address is coming from."

"Damn, Leon is amazing. I really appreciate your doing this for me, especially since I've been such a massive boil on your butt this week."

"No problema. I'm over it already—just handle your shit, girl."

"I will."

"And by the way, I thought your hair was amazing on the *Today* show."

"You saw it?"

"It was on in the kitchen at work when I was making coffee," Jane says, a laugh in her voice.

"Besides my hair, was the rest of it a total disaster?" The line goes dead for a second and my heart stops. "Jane?"

"You really got into it with that Southern belle, didn'tcha."

"I did." I can't tell if Jane thinks this is admirable or embarrassing. Her tone leans toward the latter.

"It made for very good TV." Now I know she's just trying to find the one positive thing to say so that she doesn't have to lie to me about how great I was. I appreciate the kid gloves—not usually Jane's style but she knows how rough it's been for me this week. And hey, at least I seemed to entertain her.

"Thanks?"

"I gotta run, but check in with me later." From the warmth in Jane's voice here, I can tell she's over our tiff from last night, and I'm so relieved. I need at least one person fully in my corner.

"Love you."

"I love you, too."

I hang up, thoughtful. I've never heard of the Phthalo before. It sounds pretentious and expensive—I can imagine the faux marble in the lobby without even seeing the joint. But hold on a minute: Didn't Tina say the hate blogger lived in Greenpoint?

Chapter Eleven

By the time I get settled at my laptop it's a little before nine. The air conditioner hasn't been running since I left the house, so there's an unbearably stale, fetid quality to the air, some combination of bathroom mold and Peter's soiled workout clothes. I shed my cheap sweat-stained TV dress—surely made of some synthetic fiber of the devil; in fact, in college I once wrote about the horrid sweatshop labor that those fast-fashion emporiums use. Maybe my pit stains were just penance for wearing something from Forever 21.

I pull out the breezy cotton comfort of my eyelet muumuu from the depths of my bag and put it on. Though it's been crumpled down there, when I yank it out, it has magically shed that old-sheep smell that was following it around. What to do first—ask Tina about the discrepancy, or Google "Alex Lyons + the *Today* show"? Am I an aggressor or a masochist? I guess I'm still slouching toward the latter because I decide to Google myself first.

The first thing that comes up is the *Today* show's own page. But right below that, I see a link to the website of a TV show called *Chat Skewer*, which sends up all the daily talk shows. The headline I see through Google is ambiguous ("I Have a Secret for Chick Habit Writer Alex Lyons"), but when I click through to the post itself, it's a freeze frame of my adolescent nightmares.

Chat Skewer features a screen shot of my appearance this morning. My face is screwed up in a furious scowl, and a huge Photoshopped yellow circle with a big flashing arrow points to my armpit. The punch line, of course, is that the blogger's "secret" for me is Secret deodorant. Hardy har. But below the screen shot and the easy joke is a blistering indictment of, well, me:

> Perspiring Chick Habit writer Alex Lyons talked with Savannah Guthrie this morning about Rebecca West, the coked-up daughter of "Genius Mom" Nazi Darleen West. Lyons got into an impressive brawl with big-haired "Internet safety expert" Joellen Maxwell. Both these broads are pretty annoying, but Lyons said something that we here at *Chat Skewer* take as a personal challenge: "No matter how old you are, you need to be aware that anything you record could end up all over the Internet." So, monsters, your task is to find embarrassing recordings of Alex Lyons. Here, I'll start:

There are two videos below that scathing paragraph. One is the *Today* show appearance in full; the other is another blasted video from my freshman-year a cappella performance, poncho and clown hair and all. This video isn't the one that BTCH put up; no, this time I'm belting my wee heart out to Wilson Phillips's "Hold On." During the chorus I am doing a particularly heartfelt fist-pumping motion as I hold the notes in "hoooooold ooooon."

Chat Skewer goes on:

> Normally, we stay out of these sorts of Internet fisticuffs, but when we heard that Rebecca West was getting death threats we felt like it was our mission to give Ms. Lyons a taste of her own medicine. Here's her e-mail—alex@chickhabit.net—if you'd like to share your thoughts with her.

Oh my god. The idea of an endless stream of insulting e-mails coming my way makes me nauseous yet again, and for a second it's so bad I contemplate running to the bathroom. Now it's not just BTCH on the warpath to humiliate and harass me—*Chat Skewer* has opened up my public embarrassment to the crowd.

I remind myself it's really too soon to gauge how destructive this call for recordings is going to be, and the desire to hurl disappears. For one thing, *Chat Skewer*'s traffic is mediocre, so only a hundred or so people might actually read that post in the first place. Furthermore, I'm sure none of these "monsters" has any idea who I am, so their incentive for scouring the Internet to find evidence of my personal idiocy is fairly low. The wild card is the same wild card I have with BTCH—I don't actually know what's lurking out there in the untrammeled digital woods. It could be anything, and anyone with a serious vendetta could do real damage to my reputation.

While I'm pondering this I hear from Moira:

MoiraPoira (9:03:42): I'm glad you're back, because I need you to get cracking on your quota for the day. Molly's already been posting away for several hours.

Alex182 (9:04:17): I'm on it.

MoiraPoira (9:04:56): Great. I've got an easy one for your first post today. Put up the clip of yourself from the *Today* show.

Alex182 (9:05:24): You can't be serious.

MoiraPoira (9:06:11): Of course I'm serious! It's fantastic press for the site!

Alex182 (9:06:24): Don't you think it's a little self-aggrandizing?

MoiraPoira (9:07:02): You say that like it's a bad thing, love.

Alex182 (9:07:44): I just don't think the appearance went that well.

MoiraPoira (9:08:21): Why would you think that? It was brilliant! I cheered in my living room when you gave it to that fearmongering slag. Her "think of the children" crap made me sick.

Alex182 (9:08:45): I'm worried I sounded a little unhinged.

MoiraPoira (9:09:24): I've said it before and I will likely say it again: Grow. A. Pair. Alex. You made an impression. People will remember Chick Habit, and probably remember you, after seeing that appearance. I wasn't going to tell you about this, because I didn't want it going to your head, but I got another call from Tyson Collins after your *Today* show appearance.

Alex182 (9:09:40): And?

MoiraPoira (9:10:11): And he raved about it. He said, and I quote, "That li'l girl's got some spitfire in 'er." You've got to get over wanting everyone to like you if you want to succeed in this business.

Alex182 (9:10:20): OK.

MoiraPoira (9:10:37): Good. Hop to it because I need it for the 9:30 slot.

Even though I'm gratified by Moira's praise, I try to do moderate damage control with the post, making the wording as banal as possible. I know most of our readers can't watch video at work, even during their lunch breaks, so as long as I keep the write-up vague, maybe they won't know how intense the actual appearance was. I don't even mention Rebecca West by name, though I do tag the post with her name and her mother's and a lot of variations of the phrase "Rebecca West coke video." I write just under two hundred words, mostly about how shiny Savannah Guthrie's hair is in real life, and call the post "Chick Habit Makes It to the *Today* Show." I file to Moira at 9:29, knowing that she won't have time to send it back to me to make it more controversial or specific.

MoiraPoira (9:31:11): You are such a wuss.

Alex182 (9:31:45): Sorry.

MoiraPoira (9:32:18): Too late now. On to the next. I don't have anything for you this second so you're going to have to find your own topic. I need the next post from you at 10:15, so get on it.

Alex182 (9:32:58): Word.

I have just enough time to confront Tina before I scour the web for something new to write about. It seems like a small mistake—confusing Greenpoint for Fort Greene—but she's always been so bizarrely secretive that it makes me suspicious. (Once I asked her if she had any siblings and she replied coolly, "I don't see how that's relevant.") I used to think that she was so private as a reaction to working online—she was so public there that she needed to keep something for herself. But now her guardedness, combined with her warning about stepping off her beats, seems a whole lot more sinister.

Maybe it's my hangover talking, or the lack of sleep is making me nutsy, but I'm really starting to think that she could have something to do with BTCH. She knows how upset I get when there's controversy—maybe she thought a really disturbing hate blog would drive me to quit. It's possible she thinks that if I weren't around she could hog more scoops and get more bonus cash.

Alex182 (9:33:18): Hey

TheSevAbides (9:33:24): Hello

Alex182 (9:34:10): I had a question for you about our hate blogger.

TheSevAbides (9:34:45): Oh right—I had almost forgotten about all that junk.

Alex182 (9:35:19): That's weird. You seemed pretty upset about it just two days ago.

TheSevAbides (9:36:01): Well, it's been a busy week and I've had other things on my mind. In fact, I'm pretty busy now, so what's your question?

Alex182 (9:36:42): Well I had someone do some extra sleuthing for us, and he tracked down Breaking the Chick Habit's IP address to somewhere in Fort Greene.

TheSevAbides (9:37:15): Right, which is what I found, too.

Alex182 (9:37:48): No, you said the hate blogger was in Greenpoint.

TheSevAbides (9:38:29): No, I said Fort Greene.

I decide to pull the most passive-aggressive move in the Internet playbook: I look up our original conversation, copy Tina's old IM, and send it to her.

Alex182 (9:39:11): TheSevAbides (8:25:13): But I was able to see that her IP address is from Greenpoint, so at least we know she's local.

Alex182 (9:39:22): Does that ring any bells?

Tina's IM goes idle for several minutes. Just when I'm ready to give up and start scrolling for a topic to post about she writes back.

TheSevAbides (9:43:02): The two names sound a lot alike. So I made an honest mistake. What does this have to do with anything?

Alex182 (9:43:49): Never mind. You're right, it was probably just an "honest mistake."

Without responding, Tina signs off of chat.

That wasn't how I wanted that conversation to happen—but what did I expect? That Tina would just admit she had cooked up a dastardly scheme to drive me crazy and would beg for my forgiveness?

I'm racking my brain for something, anything, that would explain Tina's location-based mix-up. Then in the overflowing junk room of my mind a thought surfaces: Didn't Molly tell me she lived in Fort Greene when I saw her at the Cactus Inn?

Molly has even more of a motive than Tina—she's been baldly hankering for our jobs since her first day at Chick Habit. If she were BTCH it would explain why she knew about the hate blog so early on. And furthermore, no one in this business is actually as nice as Molly is obviously pretending to be.

Then the paranoid voice in my head homes in on an explanation: Tina and Molly are somehow in this together.

Maybe it's just the lack of sleep and the stress talking, but that would explain Tina's mistake—though it doesn't explain why she and Molly have formed some kind of deranged alliance.

Maybe I'm all wrong about Tina, and Molly's the one behind this cruel plot.

I decide to pump Rel for information. Rel's temper is so flare-based it's possible that she's forgiven me for posting the Becky video by now.

Alex182 (9:50:11): Hi

Wienerdog (9:50:23): Yo.

Alex182 (9:51:02): I'm sorry about the other day.

Wienerdog (9:51:34): No big.

Alex182 (9:52:10): Thanks for understanding.

Alex182 (9:52:15): Hey, do you think Tina's been acting weird lately?

Wienerdog (9:52:49): No weirder than usual. Tina has always been one odd bitch.

Alex182 (9:53:01): True. But I feel like she's been extra shady lately.

Wienerdog (9:54:33): I haven't noticed anything, but I haven't talked to her since we went to Coney Island.

Alex182 (9:55:10): Word.

Alex182 (9:56:04): What about Molly?

Wienerdog (9:56:36): What about Moira's special little princess?

Alex182 (9:57:06): Have you noticed anything strange about her?

Wienerdog (9:57:44): Is this a bad episode of Law and Order SVU? Why are you asking me all this shit?

Alex182 (9:58:13): It's a long story. I'll explain later.

Wienerdog (9:58:42): Whatever.

Rats. I can't just accuse Molly of being the hate blogger without having a more damning piece of evidence than just the Fort Greene location—tens of thousands of people live in that neighborhood. How can I trust my logical powers at this point anyway? I've probably had ten hours of sleep in the last four days.

I decide to take a break from sleuthing by checking my e-mail. Perhaps BTCH has responded to my *Today* show appearance.

Et voilà: Here she is.

From: Breaking the Chick Habit
To: alex@chickhabit.net
Subject: Today Show, Tomorrow's Show

Hello, My Dear,

Apparently you're really sweating about the information I'm planning to reveal about you tomorrow. I could tell from your leaky armpits on the Today show this morning. I truly relished your little performance, particularly the gif of you that's making its way around the web. What, you haven't seen it yet? Here's an eyeful:

My canny hate blogger has made a gif of my mouth opening in an exaggerated fashion, after which she's reddened my eyes and inserted foam around my mouth so that it looks like I'm rabid. As gifs go, I'm not that impressed.

Even after your bilious little performance, I'm still willing to strike the deal I made you yesterday: Take down the Rebecca West post and offer up a true apology. If you don't get this done by 11 AM tomorrow, you will rue the day you ever heard the name Becky West. I'll put on a little show that you'll remember for a lifetime.

Kisses,
BTCH

Maybe I've toughened up in the past twenty-four hours, but I'm not as shaken by this missive as I was by the first one. And then I read the postscript:

> P.S. I was so sorry to hear that your father, Jim Lyons, died so suddenly two years ago. It's very rare for a man of his age and fitness level to have a heart attack like that. Perhaps your dear old dad had a taste for narcotics just like Becky West . . .

Now I am legitimately terrified. This has suddenly escalated from painful sophomoric prank to aspersions cast on the character of my *dead father.* For a second, I even wonder if BTCH knows something I don't: Maybe my stern, moral daddy had some secret, sullied life that my mom and I never even imagined. I can't believe that's true . . . unless . . .

Suddenly, the notion that naked photos of me might be leaked online is the least of my troubles; a homemade-sex-tape reveal seems almost quaint (though I still hope there's no soundtrack). What if Dad *had* been hiding some secret?

I don't know what I'm supposed to do next. Do I call my mom and ask her about Dad? That's going to really upset her, and possibly just for a psychotic bluff. Do I acquiesce to the hate blogger? I can't. Even if I wanted to, my post belongs to Chick Habit and I don't have the power to take it down.

How could Molly know all this stuff about my family? Unless Tina's Internet ninja skills are propping up the whole enterprise . . . Are my coworkers really so competitive that they'd go to these lengths to ruin me? Am I just completely unraveling?

I decide to do the only thing that makes sense anymore. I owe Moira a post in about twenty minutes and I don't want to mess up the one thing that's actually going gangbusters for me. Chick Habit won't stop for my drama.

The first thing I find that's worth a few hundred words is a new study that shows that when you liposuction out fat, it doesn't disappear forever—it merely redistributes. For instance, if you suck out that troublesome fat in your lower belly, it will find its way back into your arms or your upper abdomen.

I read an article a while back in one of the lower-rent tabloids (*In Touch*, *OK!*, or *Life & Style*—definitely not *Us Weekly* or *People*) about Kirstie Alley's failed liposuction attempt. The tabloid in question had said that Kirstie Alley's fat was too stubborn to disappear entirely. They used a singularly unpleasant photo to illustrate Alley's immovable weight.

A minute or two of searching leads me to the story in question—I lift the photo, save it to my desktop, and use it to illustrate a post that I end up calling: "Sorry, Ladies, Liposuction Sucks." I also make a joke about Kirstie Alley's neck rolls. I know the commenters are going to go totally apeshit about this bit of unnecessary meanness. Any comment on a woman's figure, even one that could be construed as positive, gets defined as "body snarking" by at least one sensitive soul. "I thought this place was above nitpicking on women's bodies," is a typical response to pointing out, say, Bristol Palin's obvious plastic surgery.

Usually I won't go there with my celebrity posts—after all, I'm no supermodel myself—but something about the hate blogger's attempt to control me has pushed me over the edge. How dare she tell me what I can and can't write about? Who died and made her queen of the motherfucking Internet? I will not be shamed into being "nice." I just won't. Especially not when she's upped the stakes by threatening my family.

I file my lipo post to Moira at 10:10.

MoiraPoira (10:11:13): Oooh you're really getting nasty now. You're really starting to sound like a hardcore Fleet Street hack. I love it.

Alex182 (10:12:01): I'm glad.

MoiraPoira (10:12:43): Since you've done two posts so quickly you can go take a break now. Have you eaten anything at all today?

Alex182 (10:13:32): Just coffee this morning.

MoiraPoira (10:14:02): Well off with you—go get some food in your tummy. You can even sit down and eat it away from the computer. That is my gift to you.

The second I stand up I realize how woozy I am. Probably from the three hours of sleep and the no food and the hangover. I find my sandals, grab my canvas bag, and head out into the daylight to get some sustenance. I'm not going to eat slumped over my computer, and, in fact, I'm not even going to have a salad today. I don't even like salad. I just eat it because grilled chicken with greens is what girls eat for lunch. So it was decreed by the

Girl Council sometime in the late eighties, and unlike the big floppy bow ties and the Easy Spirit pumps, that salad remains a dowdy staple of the working-woman crowd.

I march outside determined to get some real sustenance, maybe even pizza (secondary query: Can I find someplace to sell me pizza at ten in the morning?). If I find it, I'm going to have not one but two slices. I'm about to cross the street when I hear the cheerful *briiiiing* of my phone informing me that I have a text message. I pick it up with a sigh; it's probably just Moira reneging on her promise to let me eat lunch untethered from a machine.

But when I look at the phone I realize that it's not Moira at all.

> Peter Rice (10:15 AM): My mom called. She saw you on the Today show. What the fuck is going on?

Oh shit. After all the intensity of this morning I had conveniently forgotten about my problems with Peter. Of course his mom would watch the *Today* show. I can just imagine her chagrin at watching me sass a "certified" Internet safety expert in front of millions of people. What will she tell the bridge club?

That unfairly snide thought is replaced immediately by a real fear: What if I actually do lose Peter in all of this? I'm pretty sure nothing is worth that.

> Alex Lyons (10:15 AM): It's a really long story. I promise I will be home and awake tonight and we can talk it out.

Peter Rice (10:15 AM): No. This is not waiting another minute. I am coming home now. I'll make some excuse about a family emergency. I can't take this shit.

Suddenly I'm not so hungry anymore. I decide go to back inside and get some more work done, just in case Peter and I have a blow-up fight. I duck back into the midget door and flop back to the couch, scrolling through my RSS feed halfheartedly.

It's odd to get a furious communication via text. Even though Peter and I have fought more this week than in the entirety of our yearlong relationship, I can barely imagine what his voice would sound like if he had said those words aloud to me. When he gets pissed—like he did last night—the Long Island accent that's been tamped down through years of fancy Catholic school comes out around the edges. He starts dropping his *R*s and elongating his vowels when he's truly enraged. I've only seen him that angry a couple of times, most recently with a representative from AT&T customer service.

I'm not sure how long it will take Peter to get home—he's much thriftier than I am, so even in a so-called family emergency I'll bet he's taking the subway, which is on a non-rush-hour schedule. To bide the time and mask my anxiety, I find an article to post on, about Duchess Sarah Ferguson's latest comeback attempt.

I've always had a soft spot for Duchess Fergie. She seems sweet, if terminally dim. And I appreciate that she's never prim and proper and perfect, like the unerring Kate Middleton.

Fergie's comeback 4.0 involves a new children's book she's written, which is meant to teach the pre-K set how to apologize.

It's called *Little Red Makes a Mistake*. I find a clip of her promoting the book on the OWN network and write a few hundred words about Fergie's past struggles. I find a screen shot of Fergie looking truly abashed and call the post "Fergie Begs for Forgiveness: How Could You Stay Mad at That Face?"

I file to Moira around twelve. Just as I hit send on the IM notifying her that the post is ready, Peter bursts through the door, sweat dripping through his once-starched white shirt. His tie has been loosened to the point that it's almost falling off his neck.

"What happened to you?" I ask, gasping. Peter not only never loses his temper, he also never looks this undone.

"The F stopped running at York Street and I had to walk the rest of the way in this fucking ninety-degree heat."

"Jesus, Peter, why didn't you take a cab?"

"Jesus, Alex, what's *wrong* with you? I'm not here to talk about how I got home. I'm here to find out why the fuck you were on TV this morning and why you've been acting like a total lunatic all week." He's so angry that he's breathing hard, and his shoulders are moving up and down in a jerky, uneven way, as if controlled by a drunken puppeteer.

"It's a long story," I say, shifting uneasily on the couch and trying to look away. "But you should already know part of it."

"It had better be a long story. Why don't you start from the beginning," Peter says, taking his tie off completely and sitting down right next to me so I can't avoid his face.

"Have you heard of the Genius Mom?" Even though Peter's furious with me, it's a relief to finally have the chance to tell him the whole sordid tale. He's looking less angry now, more expectant.

"That lady with the quadruplets? Who had that crazy op-ed in the *New York Times* that all the moms in my office got pissed off about?"

"That's the one. Well, on Tuesday someone sent me a video of one of her daughters snorting a ton of coke. And I published it. So that's why I was on the *Today* show. To talk about it."

"Why didn't you tell me?"

"Because I was furious at you," I say, looking him right in the eyes.

"What are you even talking about?" He looks thoroughly confused now and a little agitated—his mouth's hanging slightly open, and I can tell he's anxious to hear the explanation.

"You left your Omnitown report on the kitchen table. I read it." I try to say this as calmly as possible. I want to seem cool and collected—the superior ice queen that I've never been able to be.

I watch his face as he processes this information. It falls almost immediately. "Where do you get off reading that report? It's confidential information. I could be fired if my bosses ever discovered that you saw a single page." He's so soaked with rage at this point that I can almost see it dripping from him. So much for keeping the frosty upper hand. I fire back at him.

"What, so your job is so much more important than mine that you don't care that I could be laid off tomorrow? How could you not warn me! I published that video in part because I needed the page views so that I wouldn't get canned!"

"I don't think my job is more important than yours, but yours certainly isn't more important than mine," Peter says bitterly. "You're not the one with college loans that you'll be paying off for the next decade."

"What's that supposed to mean?" I ask him defensively.

"You could always find something else to do for work. And maybe you should. Publishing this Genius Mom shit is beneath you." Peter leans back into the couch. I can tell he thinks he landed a harsh blow.

"And how would I support myself in the meantime? You know my mom can't help me out anymore." I want to scream that his principles can't pay our rent, but before I can say that he replies.

"I would be happy to support you while you get back on your feet," Peter says with a sniff.

"Oh, so with your big fancy job you can support your good little homemaking lady. I just knew you'd be on your moral high horse about this," I say as I stand up, ready to launch into my own self-righteous tirade. "Where do you get off judging me about where I decide to work? You work in finance, for God's sakes, not exactly the most morally impressive career. Who are you to tell me what's wrong or what's right when it comes to my job? My publishing that video might be bad for one family, but what you do almost bankrupted the country!"

Peter's eyes become bloodshot and the usually delicate vein running along the left side of his forehead begins to pulsate. "Don't you *dare* try to turn this around on me. What do you even *care* about the banking industry? You fell asleep halfway through *Inside Job*! Telling you anything about my report would have been illegal. I haven't done anything wrong here."

I snort with what I hope is an appropriate level of derision. "Nothing wrong? You care about holding on to that stupid Polydrafter job more than you care about our relationship."

"Oh, because your job hasn't caused you to lose any kind of perspective at all," Peter sneers. "You seem to have forgotten the real me in your obsession with this website and your fake virtual drama. It doesn't take a psychologist to see that you're avoiding dealing with your dad's death by immersing yourself in this frivolous bullshit."

"How dare you bring my dad into this!" This is the most hurtful thing Peter's ever said to me, in part because I know there's a kernel of fact in his assessment. My shoulders droop and I feel like my chest is caving in.

"Because it's true, Alex, and you know it. You've turned me into some two-dimensional heavy who doesn't support or understand you. You're not letting me in at all. You're sneaking around, reading papers that don't belong to you. All that's real to you these days is what goes on the Internet and what happens in your crazy-ass skull."

I open my mouth to try to argue with Peter, but I know that he's right. I've been treating my entire life lately like some elaborate game of cat and mouse, searching for some jerk who says mean things about me, obsessing over some girl I've never met. My real life—the life with Peter and my mom and Jane—is happening without me, and I've been too self-absorbed to notice it.

My self-righteousness deflates and I hang my head. "I'm so sorry."

Peter sighs. "It's too late now, Alex. This week has been bad, but if I'm honest this job has changed you. You've become more insular and weird and selfish over the past couple months. I thought you were figuring it out, but now it seems like this version of you is here to stay."

"It's not! I swear, I'll go back to the girl I used to be." I'm crying now, huge ugly sobs replete with a snot avalanche. Usually when I cry Peter will rush to comfort me, but not today. He sits on the couch and stares off into the bedroom before abruptly getting up and moving toward his closet.

"I need some space," he says, shoving his work clothes into a gym bag. "I'm going to spend the night at Doug's." Doug is his buddy from work who once called me a ballbuster and didn't mean it as a compliment. "I don't know when I'll be back."

I know I'm not in a position to argue with Peter. He's right—I've taken him completely for granted. But I still manage to say quietly, "Please don't go."

"I have to. I need to think about everything, and you need to figure out what you want."

"What do you mean, 'what I want'?" I say, still sniffling. "I know what I want. I want to be with you!"

"I don't mean about us. This person I've been living with since you started working at Chick Habit isn't you. You need to figure out how to be yourself again."

Peter finishes packing up his things. I watch his back muscles tense as he changes into a fresh shirt. I don't have the heart to tell him what my new fear is: that this is me now, and that there's no going back.

Peter doesn't say anything else before he leaves. Though I don't think he means to, he slams the door behind him.

After Peter's left, the silence in our empty apartment is oppressive. I know what I *should* be doing right now, which is going back to Chick Habit and marching roughshod through my day like a zombie stomping down a village square. But I can't bring myself to go back to the computer. I'm too sad and shocked. I would call Jane, but she's had enough of this for one week and would be furious at me for screwing things up with Peter anyway.

I look down at my iPhone, which is sitting next to me like a tiny electronic companion. It's blinking furiously with new e-mail messages. I click on a few at random, all from strange names that I've never seen before.

> Sent at 11:45: "You should kill yourself."
> Sent at 11:46: "You're a terrible person."
> Sent at 11:47: "You should be thrown in jail."
> Sent at 11:48: "Girl, I'm just being honest with you. You need a nose job. I know a great plastic surgeon."

I decide I need to talk to the one person who is genetically hardwired to provide me with solace. I start dialing the 860 of my mom's cell phone number, hoping that she's taking an early lunch and can talk to me. The phone rings five times, and I'm about to end the call when I hear her worried voice on the other end.

"Alex?"

"Mommy?" I sniffle. I can hear the quaver in my voice.

"Alex, what's wrong? Have you been crying? Why haven't I heard from you?"

"P-P-Peter and I just had a huge fight and I posted this mean video and I might lose my job and—and—and—" I dissolve into tears.

"Slow down, puffin. I don't understand what you're talking about, but it can't possibly be all that bad."

I explain the whole thing to her, in an abbreviated, snot-filled, heaving kind of way. I don't think she fully understands the stuff about the hate blogger—she can barely use e-mail and only goes online to research stuff for her classes. She definitely doesn't get the impact of the *Today* show, since she hasn't owned a television since after the Watergate hearings. As a pop culture lover since birth, I think I chose my friends as a kid solely based on how much cable I could mooch off of them. My mom has heard of Darleen West, though, because some of her students' parents were annoying West acolytes.

"Let's separate the Peter thing from Chick Habit issues," my mom says after I vomit out the story to her, as if they were still two separate problems and not a knotty, intertwined disaster. "It sounds like you were just doing your job for Chick Habit, but I can understand why it makes you feel so terrible. But what's done is done. You can't take it back."

I sniffle an assent.

"Why don't you start looking for another job if Chick Habit is making you so miserable? Something that's maybe a little deeper?"

"Do you know what the market's like out there right now in media? It's not like new jobs are just growing on trees, especially now that I've possibly humiliated myself on national television *and* put an innocent kid's life in danger."

"But you're getting death threats, too. How seriously can you take these messages from nutty strangers?"

This reminds me of what BTCH said about Dad, and even though I didn't want to bother Mom with it, I'm feeling so fragile I can't help myself. "Did Daddy have some secret life we didn't know about?"

"What do you mean, a 'secret life'?" She sounds puzzled and a little sarcastic.

"Ummm, I mean, like, did you ever find out after he died . . . that he like . . ."

"That he like what?" she says.

"Like, did stuff . . . away from us, that was bad?"

"Use your words, Alex," my mom says, which is something she used to tell me when I was little.

"This crazy person on the Internet said that Dad was a secret drug addict!" I nearly shout.

Mom starts laughing so hard she can barely breathe. "Your father? Drugs? Alex, your dad wasn't perfect, but he wasn't out cruising Hartford for illegal substances in his spare time."

"How do you know for sure?" I ask this timidly, seeking reassurance.

"Al, when you've been married for thirty years, you'll understand. Besides, your dad and I worked together and lived together—I saw him almost every waking hour of every day. Unless he cloned himself, I'm pretty sure this terrible person is just baiting you."

"Aren't you worried that she's trying to impugn Daddy?"

"Not really." Mom laughs. "It's the most exciting thing that's happened to me in ages."

"How can you say that?" I can't believe she's not taking this more seriously. She must think my life is one big creative lark, like I'm some acerbic girl Friday from one of the thirties romantic comedies she holds so dear. But I'm not Rosalind Russell tripping down the city streets in spectator heels.

"Because I have some perspective, puffin. I know who your father was, and some stranger can't take that away from me. And hey, your dad's dead—it's not like he's going to be hurt by this if this nutter decides to go public with this information."

"I guess." I'm starting to feel disoriented, like I've lost sight of the bigger picture.

"This situation is not so horrible. You could look for something in another field, if Chick Habit is really that bad. You could even temp for a while. You're such a smart girl, Al, and you're so young, and life's so short. You can do whatever makes you happy."

I bite my lip and go silent. Somehow her sensible words break through where Jane's and Peter's could not. The foundation of my swirling week has now crumbled, and saving my job suddenly seems like a really shabby excuse for my behavior. Happiness—mine or anyone else's—hasn't been at the root of the whole Becky West/hate blogger fiasco. It's been all about that fleeting costume jewelry: notoriety, posturing, and success.

"I don't know what will make me happy." I start crying, because it's true. I still love Peter and hope to salvage our relationship, and even though he makes life better, he's not responsible for my happiness. Chick Habit, as stressful as it is, was a delight at first, before the traffic pressure started raining down. Now it's just a source of anxiety and dismay.

"I don't even know if I want to be a writer anymore," I add through the tears. I'm afraid that having a job like this is the only route to being a working writer these days, and I don't know that I can take it for the long haul.

I always try not to break down in front of my mom. I want to be strong for her, to give her one less thing to worry about. She was so proud of me when I got the job at Chick Habit, and I hate that I might be disappointing her or puncturing her image of me as confident and flourishing. But somehow, with our voices traveling in the ether, I say things I wouldn't be bold enough to say to her face—maybe shouldn't say at all. She's hasn't responded for at least a minute, and I'm worried that she's crushed because I'm so upset.

"Mom? Are you still there?"

"I'm still here, honey, I'm just thinking," she says in a smooth, deliberate way. "I never wanted you to feel forced into a life that you don't want. The last thing I wanted was for you to end up like me, with your true passion deteriorating in a drawer somewhere, and now I'm afraid I've pushed you into this mess."

"But how do I know if this is the right way to my true passion?" I thought the Chick Habit job could lead to something better but now it feels like a dead end.

"I can't answer that for you," she tells me. Damn it. "You need to sit with yourself—without the thousand distractions it sounds like you have—and figure out what it is that you want. I'm so, so sorry if my example has made it harder for you to know what that is."

Now I go silent. I thought my mom would have an easy, soothing answer for me. But now I realize that was a foolish expectation. I have to take responsibility for my own choices. This isn't, exactly, about publishing the Becky West video or its consequences. It's about slowly stumbling down my own path, which unfortunately doesn't happen in a twenty-four-hour news cycle.

At least the hugeness of this thought has caused me to stop crying.

"Alex?"

"Yee-aah?" I say haltingly, trying to pull back the last of my tears.

"Are you going to be okay, baby? What about Peter?" My mom really does love Peter and considers him part of the family at this point, and I can hear the worry in her voice when she says his name, like it's slipping through her fingers.

"I'm just as confused about Peter as I am about my work. I want him back but I don't understand why he didn't tell me that I might lose my job." The whine is starting to creep back behind my sentences.

"Do you want my advice?" she asks gently.

"Yes." I try to say this crisply, to iron out that whine.

"I think you were a real dummy to read his report." "Dummy" is the word my mom reserves for waiters who screw up her order and politicians who cheat on their wives.

"Mom!"

"It wasn't your business. You think I'm a pretty good judge of character, right?"

"Yes." It's true—after decades of teaching, my mom can read the faces of her students on the first day and tell whether each one is going to be a disaster or a delight. I used to find this trait infuriating. When she would tell me that the parents of a new acquaintance had "cruel expressions," and that I should watch out for their child, I would tell her she had no idea what she was talking about. But invariably that kid would end up snubbing me in some dramatic way/getting heavily into drugs/becoming an arsonist.

"Peter has a good face and a good heart. I know you think he betrayed you, but you have to understand how that report put him in an impossible position. And remember that the company hasn't been sold *yet*." I smile ruefully—her listening comprehension is better than my reading comprehension. "Maybe he would have told you when it was really happening. You never know. Right now it's just classified information about a potential sale. It wouldn't have been worth upsetting you if it turns out that the sale doesn't go through, right?"

"Yes." I sigh, conceding to her reasonable explanation.

"Okay," she says. "Listen, my lunch hour is almost over and I have to get back to the kids. But I can be late if you need me. Are you going to be all right?"

"I guess so." I say this because I don't want her to spend all day fretting about me. I don't know if it's true yet—I couldn't bring myself to tell her about BTCH's sexposé threat, the details of which I will only disseminate if I have no other choice.

"I believe that you are going to be okay, because I believe in you."

Chatting with Mom made me feel temporarily better, but ten minutes later, the enormity of my problems comes back to me. I started off this week as someone with a decent job, a stable relationship, and a sweet domestic existence. Soon I could be a single, unemployed lost soul whose ass is plastered all over YouTube, living in an apartment she can't afford, trying to figure out what the hell she's going to do with the next thirty years of her life.

I can't face returning to work right now. I know Moira is going to be livid, but I just can't bring myself to care. She can fire me if she wants to fire me—and I bet the success of the Rebecca West post will give me a little leeway anyway. I've already reached my page-view quota for the month, and it's only the second week of July.

I turn off my phone so she can't reach me and rummage through my bag until I find the Xanax that Jane gave me yesterday. I crawl into our bed—though maybe now it's just *my* bed—and the sheets are crisp and cool because they're sitting right below our one good air conditioner. I pull the covers up over my head and cry until my sobbing slows to periodic jagged sniffs. Finally my breathing becomes regular and I fall fast asleep.

FRIDAY

Chapter Twelve

I wake up because the sun is shining directly in my eyes. As I rub them and stretch my arms, I realize that I haven't woken up naturally—that is, without an alarm or a burst of unconscious anxiety—in six months. I have fifteen full seconds of peace as I unfurl myself across the bed before I remember everything that happened yesterday. Still, everything seems a little more manageable in the clear sun.

I pad over to the couch, still muumuu-clad from yesterday. I turn on my phone and see that it's seven forty-five, long after I should have been online. I have fourteen missed messages. I hope one is from Peter, but I'm not expecting much. The last time we got into a Chick Habit–related fight—it was about the fact that I wouldn't get off the computer at nine P.M., even though I was finished with my work for the day—he stopped speaking to me for a full twenty-four hours. And this is of a different magnitude altogether.

Still, I have a shred of wishful thinking left when I look through the missed messages on my iPhone. Thirteen are texts from Moira:

Moira Fitzgerald: WHERE THE FUCK ARE YOU

Moira Fitzgerald: WHERE THE FUCK ARE YOU

You get the drift. The fourteenth is a message from a New York City–area number I've never seen before. Maybe it's from Doug's landline? My mom's advice has put things in perspective for me, at least a little: There *is* a world outside Chick Habit and I need to start engaging with it. I decide to pick up the message before going back to my computer and possibly getting fired. Which in some ways would be a relief.

A gravelly male voice fills my ear. "This is Robert Shapton, *New York Post*. Sources are telling us that Rebecca West has been missing from her off-campus sublet in Cambridge for at least forty-eight hours. We'd like a comment from you. It's about seven A.M. on Friday now, and I've just gotten into the office. If you'd like to respond before six tonight, my number is 212-555-3049."

My heart sinks. I believed my mom when she said that the death threats were a lot of hot air from a sea of randoms—that's always what *my* death threats seemed like, anyway. But now it seems like Rebecca might actually be at risk. That would explain why she hasn't responded to me or anyone else since the story broke two days ago.

The most benign interpretation for her disappearance is that she's gone into hiding out of extreme embarrassment, the most sinister that she's been kidnapped or hurt in some other awful way. The worst-case scenario is that she has some heretofore unknown mental instability, and my publishing that video pushed her over the edge into self-harm.

An image appears in my head of Becky in the days before I published the video. She's bopping around Cambridge—maybe with a friend or two at her side. Like any normal college student she's heading to classes with a bag over her shoulder, smiling that sweet smile I know—everyone knows now—from the video. Then in my mental home video she's walking along the Charles holding hands with her robot, pointing out important buildings to him like he's a regular tourist and she's his guide. She seems carefree and happy, and I feel sick with the idea that I've destroyed that for her.

I feel even sicker picturing her lithe body splayed out in a gutter somewhere, perhaps the victim of some John Hinckley Jr.–style psycho who has become obsessed with Becky's story.

I start crying, hard. This isn't a game anymore—it's shockingly real. But I try to soothe myself by letting my inner voice say, You can't entertain those worst-case-scenario notions just yet. You don't have enough information to know whether or not this "disappearance" is something to freak out about.

Still, if Shapton's reporting hits the Internet without an update, or any hint as to where Becky West might have gone, I won't be able to leave my house, either—my front door will be surrounded by villagers with pitchforks and picket signs.

I need to think before I respond to this Shapton fellow. Since the *Post* does its own original reporting, my hope is that this is an exclusive and won't hit the rest of the world 'til tomorrow morning, in the next edition of the paper. But before I go ahead and assume that, I should check the latest Internet coverage of the case to be sure.

When my computer springs to life there are several IMs

from Moira clogging up my screen.

MoiraPoira (08:01:23): WHERE THE FUCK WERE YOU?

MoiraPoira (08:01:25): WHERE THE FUCK WERE YOU?

And so on, and so forth. For once I am not going to respond to her instantly, and I'm not going to fall back into the quicksand of my RSS feed, either. Somehow I'm going to try to figure out if Becky West is okay, and maybe even try to help find her.

I start by searching "Becky West disappearance." About three hundred pages come up, most of them porn-related, with headlines about Becky West's bra "disappearing." On the fourth page of results, I find a small squib on some MIT student's Facebook page from Wednesday night. The poster is a pretty Asian girl with black-rimmed glasses, one whose face is familiar from my Facebook stalkings of Becky. She's in a lot of Becky's photos, most notably one of the two of them rosy-faced at a college party, arms casually slung over each other.

Roberta Sasaki

Wednesday

Has anyone seen Becky recently? She was supposed to meet me for yoga today but she never showed up, and I couldn't find her at home. Did she disappear?

Like • Comment • Share

👍10 people like this.

This is probably what tipped off the *Post*. I try to tell myself that I've blown off yoga classes before just because I was tired, not because I was dead. But it doesn't help much.

I move on to Becky's Facebook page, which looks as pristine and innocent as it was on Tuesday when I first ransacked it. Her wall betrays no evidence of distress, besides a number of friends pledging their support to her:

Sara Klein

Tuesday

Becky, don't let any of this get you down. We know the real you and you are going to come out of this even stronger! Xoxoxoxoxooxoxox

Like • Comment • Share

👍 2 people like this.

Candace Woo-Rogers

Tuesday

We are here for you Beckster! Your gurls in Omaha have got yr back.

Like • Comment • Share

Danny Crandall

Tuesday

I'm so sorry. I love you.

Like • Comment • Share

👍 4 people like this.

I look back through her photographs. I stop at one in particular, from when she was a kid. She is with her three towheaded sisters, all wearing matching pink seersucker dresses and standing outside a corn maze. They're next to a sign that says THE MAIZE, spelled out in hand-painted cornstalks.

Something starts itching on my arms. I peer down and realize that I've broken out into hives. This physical manifestation of my guilt is too much to bear. How will I live with myself if something has happened to Becky? How will I face my own mother? She's had it hard enough the past two years without my making her feel like a failure of a parent.

I keep staring at those four very similar faces, trying to figure out which one is Becky. But I can't—all eight blue peepers look identical to me, and the longer I stare at them the more innocently judgmental those young faces look: pale and happy and excited about miles and miles of corn. I start scratching my arms deeply, like I deserve to feel the pain. Am I going to be held responsible by the public if something bad happened to Becky? Is there some kind of legal action that can be taken against me, like with those cyberbullying high school kids? Will I end up getting a teardrop tattoo with an unsanitized pen cap at Rikers? The now-familiar panic is churning in my stomach when my IM notification brings me out of my Nebraskan dream world.

Prettyinpink86 (8:20:01): Are you OK?

She is so full of shit I can't stand it. I've had enough. If I'm going to get fired anyway, and possibly be indicted in the disappearance of a blameless young girl, I might as well go full Monty and accuse Molly of being the hate blogger.

Alex182 (8:21:06): No, I'm not fucking OK, and you of all people should know that.

There's a long pause before Molly responds.

Prettyinpink86 (8:23:45): I'm not sure what you're talking about?

Alex182 (8:24:23): Oh come off it, Molly. Quit this nicey-nice bullshit. I know you're the one behind Breaking the Chick Habit.

Prettyinpink86 (8:25:14): This is a misunderstanding.

How does one scoff over IM?

Alex182 (8:26:01): Uh, right. I traced the IP address to Fort Greene, and I know you followed me to the Cactus Inn.

Prettyinpink86 (8:27:25): Lots of people live in Fort Greene, and it was just a weird coincidence that you ran into me at the Cactus.

Alex182 (8:28:22): OK, psycho. Whatever. I know you're lying, so just cut it out. You've made it pretty clear that you wanted my job from day one, sucking up to Moira like you have. This is just some pathetic ploy to bring me down and I won't fall for it.

I'm smiling for the first time in at least a day. After being on the defensive for so long, it feels good to be the one attacking for once.

Prettyinpink86 (8:29:59): If you'd just let me type for a second, you would know I was just trying to help you.

Alex182 (8:30:42): Yeah, right.

Prettyinpink86 (8:31:24): If you'd just LET ME TYPE, you would find out that the woman I was with at the Cactus Inn the other night is my old boss Shira Allen, from *People,* and that I regularly pump her for information that would help ALL of us at Chick Habit. She thinks of me as her little pet so she tells me a lot of stuff she's not supposed to.

I hesitate. Am I really going to buy that? It sounds too pat.

Alex182 (8:31:35): How can I believe you?

Prettyinpink86 (8:32:51): Because I'm telling the truth. If you'd shut up for a darn minute and stop accusing me of trying to bring you down, I could tell you that she gave me a really important tidbit about Becky West. That Robert Shapton guy from the *Post* has called all of us at Chick Habit, trying to reach you. If word gets out that Becky West is missing, Alex, you're going to have to hire a bodyguard. You'll have to go into hiding with Casey Anthony.

I don't want to admit that Molly's right, but what she's saying does sound reasonable.

Alex182 (8:33:31): OK, what's this "really important tidbit" that's so special?

Prettyinpink86 (8:34:24): The *People* that hits newsstands next week is going to have an exclusive interview with Becky West. They have her holed up in the Pierre Hotel so that no one else can talk to her—except for a very, very select group.

Alex182 (8:35:53): Who??

Prettyinpink86: (8:36:50): The group of MTV executives who are talking to her about the reality show they're planning about the West family.

Alex182 (8:37:24): Like a klassier version of the Kardashians?

Prettyinpink86 (8:37:52): Exactly.

Whoa. I just sit there for a few seconds, trying to collect myself. Here I've been driving myself crazy with guilt the past few days—and it turns out that crafty Ms. West is turning life's lemons into lemonade. Or I guess more accurately, turning life's coke binges into cold, hard cash.

Now I need to focus, because time is running out. Even though the *Post*'s website looks like it was made by a third grader in computer class, they might put the Becky West information up early if they think it's a big enough scoop. The *People* magazine issue won't be out until next week, and by then the *Post* narrative will be the one that sticks in the collective readers' minds: that Becky West was driven into hiding/was kidnapped/tried to off herself because of the humiliation of having that video published. And that it's all my fault.

First things first, I have to make things right with Molly. I've been mentally categorizing her as some devious, Tracy Flickian monster, when she's exactly what she appears to be: a hardworking Ohio-bred girl. She really just does want to help Chick Habit, and it seems like she's doing a sight more than I am.

Alex182 (8:39:21): Molly, I am so, so sorry.

Prettyinpink86 (8:40:34): It's OK.

Alex182 (8:41:52): I've been suspicious of you since you started working here, and it's not fair. You've only ever been helpful to me. This week has just made me completely crazy.

Prettyinpink86 (8:42:12): You have been pretty frosty, I guess. But it's OK. I accept your apology.

Alex182 (8:43:30): Thank you.

Prettyinpink86 (8:44:21): You know what you have to do now, right?

Alex182 (8:45:15): Continue to freak the fuck out?

Prettyinpink86 (8:46:45): No, silly! You need to go up to the Pierre Hotel and find some way into Becky West's room so that you can get her to spill about the reality show!

Alex182 (8:47:33): How would I do that?

Prettyinpink86 (8:48:11): You're going to have to figure that one out for yourself. Just make sure to have a digital recorder in your pocket!!!

Huh. Turns out under those emoticons and perkiness lies the quick-beating, ruthless heart of a fearless investigative reporter. I can't believe it didn't occur to me to go to the Pierre myself. I guess all these months of reporting exclusively from my couch have trained me to forget about exploring the wider world.

Alex182 (8:50:18): You're kind of amazing, do you know that?

Prettyinpink86 (8:51:37): Aw shucks. Are you going to really do it? Go up there and get the scoop?

Alex182 (8:52:22): I don't think I have any other choice.

I shuck off the muumuu, which hits the floor with a soft scratch. I find a bra, then rummage through my closet for a vertically striped cotton sundress with huge side pockets. I haven't worn it since last summer and when I throw it on over my head it's looser over my torso than I remember it being. It's the losing-your-goddamn-mind diet: Combine high anxiety, life implosion, and a potent cocktail of booze and sedatives and you will drop weight like a high school wrestler! No cauliflower ear required.

I believe my seldom-used digital recorder is in the old wooden desk in our living room, but all I see when I rummage around is used batteries and instruction guides for appliances we don't even own anymore. Finally I decide to just upend every drawer onto our grimy sisal rug. After dumping the third and final drawer, I see the dull silver of the recorder peeking out from under an iPhone charger and a take-out menu from a Chinese place that once gave me food poisoning. I grab it and press the record button. Miraculously, it turns on.

I shove the recorder in my pocket and head into the bedroom to look at myself in the full-length mirror. There is no obvious bulge in my pocket that screams "You're being bugged!" so I slide on my sandals and find my canvas bag. I check back at the computer one more time to get directions to the Pierre. Shit, I didn't realize how far uptown it is. But with midday traffic, it's probably just as convenient to take the subway.

I step out into the sunlight without bothering to put sunglasses on. Instead I let the warmth spread over my face as I walk a single block to the F train. The station is empty except for three Caribbean nannies gossiping next to tricked-out strollers holding their sleeping charges.

Thankfully, the subway arrives almost immediately, but I know it's going to be a long thirty-five-minute ride until I arrive at the Pierre. As we get on the subway, I let the nannies have the last two available seats while I hang on to a vertical pole and try to devise a game plan.

Molly sounded so confident over IM that I didn't really think through all the possible roadblocks. First there's the front desk. I'm sure they aren't just giving her room number out to any old person, so what do I tell them to get inside? What if Becky's under an assumed name? How do I figure out what it is?

An accordionist with a beret enters the car at Twenty-third Street. I turn my back on him as I continue to fret. If I succeed in getting up to Becky's room, what if she isn't there? Do I chloroform a housekeeper, steal her uniform and master key, and wait in the bathroom like they do in the movies? Probably not: There's a reason they never show the repercussions of thriller movies, or else nine-tenths of every Angelina Jolie action film would take place in a holding cell.

The accordionist is playing "Tears of a Clown" right behind me. I try to lean away from him, but he slithers around so now he's directly in front of me. He seems to have singled me out as his mark. Under the beret, he's got mime makeup on, with a garish smile painted on his chalk-white face. I try to shoot him a death glare, but he's not taking the hint. We're in the middle of a staring match when I hear the conductor announce my stop. Damn it! My longstanding mime hatred has confounded me again! I haven't adequately planned for my Becky confrontation because I was too busy trying to get that accordion-playing knob out of my face.

At Fifty-seventh Street I hop out of the subway. The station is muggy, and insta-sweat appears in the crooks of my knees and elbows. I run up the stairs to Sixth Avenue and head north by northeast, 'til I reach the grand façade of the Pierre, take a deep breath, and close my eyes.

I pluck each thought about Becky West out of my brain like a childhood game of "he loves me, he loves me not." I am sorry I've subjected Becky to this sort of intense national scrutiny; I am not sorry I tried to succeed at my job; I am sorry I let Moira pressure me into doing something I wasn't comfortable with; I am not sorry I tried to make my mom proud of me, even though it seems my efforts there were ultimately misguided; I am sorry I read Peter's report when I wasn't supposed to; I am not sure if I'm sorry we had that air-clearing fight. Maybe we needed that.

I look into the gleaming glass panes next to the revolving

door and lick my palms to smooth down any flyaways. I look, well, not great, but at least not insane. I stride into the Pierre with purpose, because I remember reading that the best way to fit in when you're too low-rent for your situation is to act like you belong; that's why they call rich people eccentric instead of crazy. So what if my hair hasn't been washed properly in a week and I'm wearing a dress that I bought from the Delia's catalogue even though I'm twelve years older than their average customer? If I own it, the front-desk ladies will buy it.

Two women are standing behind the concierge desk, their backs impossibly straight. They are wearing identical gray business suits and starched white blouses with small gold studs. One woman's name tag says "Christie," the other's "Astrid." Both are cool, Hitchcockian blondes. Christie seems more approachable—I can see that her tasteful beige manicure is ever-so-slightly chipped—so I go up to her.

"Can I help you?" she asks, smiling with robotic precision. She must smile like this at strangers at least a hundred times a day.

"Yes, I'm looking for a Rebecca West," I say confidently. I search her face for any signs that she recognizes the name, but there's not even a flicker in her eyes. She looks down at a computer screen and begins typing quickly.

"I'm not seeing anyone by that name staying here today."

"Hmm, that's strange," I say, stalling for time. "Perhaps she's registered under her mother's name? Darleen West?"

Christie's imperfect manicure clacks along the keyboard. "No, I'm sorry, that name isn't appearing, either."

"How about her sisters? Raina or Renata or Rachel West?"

Christie starts typing again, but her eyes keep darting back to me. I can tell she's starting to get suspicious. "Sorry, no."

I have a few more aliases in mind, but I'm afraid Christie is going to get spooked and call security. I decide to retreat. "I must have the wrong hotel. I'm a long way from Omaha!"

Christie nods silently. I hope that one bit of misinformation covers my tracks; if Christie happens to report me to the Wests, maybe they will just think I'm a relative or friend from back home trying to show some support.

I see a plush, golden-threaded couch in the corner of the hotel lobby just out of Christie's and Astrid's sight line and sink down into its welcoming cushions while I try to figure out what to do next. I can't very well knock on every one of the hundreds of doors in the building, or ride endlessly in the elevator in the hopes that Becky West decides to leave her room and hit the gym. Maybe this is the end of the road for me. The truth about Becky will come out eventually—it always does. In the meantime, I'll just have to take my lumps and the lesson learned. I learned it the hard way, with my ass literally hanging out there, but at least I know that Becky is safe.

I'm tearing up a little as I slump back across the black-and-white checkered Pierre lobby when out of the corner of my eye I see a familiar blow-out—light brown at the roots, getting progressively lighter toward the tips. I crouch behind a chair that's near the elevators and see the profile of one Shira Allen walking toward me.

Once Shira's passed by I duck out from behind the chair and

follow her over to the elevators. She presses the up button, and I try to stand far enough away from her that she doesn't realize that I'm there. Her nose is in her iPhone the entire time, though, so I could probably be playing "Louie Louie" on a bagpipe without attracting her attention.

I get on the elevator after she does and watch her press the button for the seventh floor. I push the button for the eighth floor, just to cover my tracks. I hear her say something quietly, and I catch my breath. But then she jabs at her phone again and I realize she was cursing because she just lost another game of Angry Birds.

As the doors are about to close, I watch Shira take a left. I can't just follow behind her—my tread is too heavy to tiptoe successfully. So I take the elevator to the eighth floor and make a left, just like Shira did. I find the stairwell nearest to the elevator and sprint down it, skidding to a stop just as I reach the seventh floor. I open the door to the hallway a tiny, quiet crack, just in time to see Shira lift her head up in front of a door to my immediate right. I close the door just as quietly, but I can still hear Shira's knock on the door and a feeble voice replying, "Who is it?"

"It's Shira. I'm just here to take a few more notes before this issue goes to press."

"Okay," says the little voice, and the door opens slightly, and Shira slips in.

Maybe I am like a really dirty, out-of-shape Jolie character, because I spot an unattended housekeeping cart in the hallway and grab the skeleton key that's hanging off the side, attached to a Smurf key chain. I don't want to have to break into Becky's room—that does seem like crossing a line that I have managed thus far to avoid—but it's a pretty good backup plan.

I stand in the doorway to the stairwell and wait to hear Shira's flats on the thick hotel carpet. After what seems like an hour—though it's probably five minutes, tops—I hear the door open again.

"Thanks for coming," says the little voice, not without enthusiasm.

"Besos," Shira says, and I hear the puckery sound of air kisses waft toward me.

The door closes and I watch as Shira's back gets smaller and smaller down the long hallway. I wait until she's out of sight before I walk up to Becky's room and knock confidently on the door.

Chapter Thirteen

I don't hear anything from the other side of the door for a full minute. Just as I'm about to walk away from room 714, I hear that little voice say, "Shira?"

"No, it's not Shira." My heart starts beating more quickly. What am I going to tell her instead?

"Who's there?" the voice asks, a slight tremor creeping in.

"It's Alex," I blurt out. Damn it. I should have given her a fake name.

"Oh! Come in!" the voice says, to my total shock. The door opens and Rebecca West is standing there, three feet away from me. Unlike Savannah Guthrie, who looked so much smaller and tidier than I had expected, in person Becky West is much more robust. She looks like a beautiful farmer's daughter, her long blond hair in a loose braid and her face devoid of makeup. She's wearing black yoga pants, a fitted tank top, and flip-flops. I look down at her feet and admire her clear pedicure. I'm trying to avoid making eye contact because I'm scared.

When I do finally look up, she's smiling at me. How can she be smiling at me? Didn't I just cause her to have the week from hell?

"I didn't know you'd be coming so soon. I would have tidied up for you," Becky says. I look around the room. It's nearly spotless. The only sign that a person has been living here is a pair of worn Converse upended under a chair. Darleen West really has drilled her girls with good manners, I'll give her that much.

"The room looks great, don't worry," I say tentatively.

She grins back at me. "I'm so glad you guys are interested in me and my story. I was having a pretty rough day when I got that call from your boss. Guess MTV really does make everything better."

Aha. Molly's intel about the Kardashian-style program was 100 percent correct. Becky thinks I am an MTV lackey coming to work out some detail of her TV show. I don't want to affirm her assumption and outright lie to her but I don't want to announce myself as the blogger who posted her video, either.

I'm trying to figure out my next move when I realize that neither of us has spoken for longer than is comfortable. Becky's looking at me with a politely questioning expression, so I blurt out, "Do you mind if we sit? I'd like to ask you a few questions for background for my boss." I even take out my digital recorder and wave it in her face. No surreptitious taping necessary, and nothing I've said aloud so far is a lie. This isn't illegal, is it?

"Of course," Becky says, giving me a practiced smile like a QVC hostess.

Whoever is paying for Becky's digs spared no expense. She's in a master suite, and we sit down on a brocade sofa that probably costs more than my rent. A verging-on-gaudy chandelier dangles above us, the glass casting shards of light onto Becky's clear face. She crosses her ankles demurely as she sits. She's so perfectly poised I wonder if she's received media training in the past few days, or if she's just naturally this way, or if this is the result of Darleen's meticulous mothering.

When my conversation partner is awkward, I always get awkward; I'm generally a pretty good talker, but big empty silences make me blurt out randomness to fill the void (Do you like dogs? What's your sign?). The opposite seems to be true with Becky West. Her noblesse oblige raises my level of confidence and discourse, and I'm able to just launch into it. I press record on my little device and nudge it toward Becky on the ornate glass table in front of us.

"Describe for me the days leading up to the release of the video," I say, crossing my own legs at the knee.

"I was working at an MIT robotics lab for the summer, creating a robot that is capable of cleaning your entire house. Sort of like a Roomba on steroids. My boyfriend, Danny, was living with me at the MIT dorms. We were having a really great time," Becky says. She's lightly smiling as she tells me this, and it's clear that she's told this story before several times. There are no extra words or natural pauses.

"And then?"

"And then I was at the lab on Wednesday until around six. My phone doesn't work in the lab because it's in the basement. When I walked out of the building and turned on my phone, I had forty-seven missed calls. My first thought was that something had happened to one of my sisters."

Oof. I push down the guilt. I can't tell if Becky notices my discomfort because she just continues on with her story.

"But the first voice mail I got was from Mother's lawyer, Gil. He explained precisely what had happened."

"Your mom didn't call you first?"

"My mother is an extremely busy woman," Becky says curtly, her back straightening.

"Didn't it bum you out that you didn't hear from her directly?"

"Of course not," Becky says. "Listen, I know a lot of people say a lot of things about my mom, but she really does just want the best for us. That's why she wrote that book. She really believes in her philosophy and just wants to share it with the world."

I deride this internally at first. Becky has obviously been trained like a show dog by her domineering mom. There's no way she really feels that way about Darleen.

But then I think about it for a minute. Becky does seem incredibly centered, especially for someone who has just had her life upended. Maybe Darleen's methods have something to them.

Besides, Darleen is still her mother. No matter how complicated that relationship is—and I truly have no idea what that must be like—of course Becky's going to defend her mom to some stranger. I think about how livid Darleen's comments about working moms made me—I took them personally, as if she were talking about my specific mother, when she wasn't. I can't imagine what it must be like to have at least half the media calling your mother a monster. I start to feel a smidge of retroactive shame for slamming Darleen so hard on Chick Habit.

Once again, I realize I haven't spoken for a weirdly long time. Becky is still waiting patiently for my next question, her expression open.

"So . . . then what did you do?" I ask quickly.

"I went back to my apartment so that I could look at Chick Habit myself. I've read the site before. I used to even like it."

It never occurred to me that Becky was a reader. I never think anyone I write about reads the site—I wouldn't be able to be so hard on them if I did. My organs cringe but I push on.

"Do you have any idea how the video got online?"

"I know exactly what happened."

I look at her expectantly. Becky twists a lock of baby-fine hair in her right finger and, for the first time in this half-fake interview, stares off into space. This is a chink in her heretofore unflappable demeanor. She doesn't look hurt, exactly, but I wonder if that's the subtext.

The silence is killing me, so I say, slightly too loudly, "What happened?!"

Becky takes a deep breath, and then the story comes tumbling out, as if she's been storing it up for just this moment. "My boyfriend's nutbag sister, Cassandra, had been visiting us over the weekend. She basically hated me on sight, and I have no idea why. Danny's always so nice to her even though he knows she's a crazy person.

"We were supposed to go to Fenway Park with her on Saturday—I went out of my way to get really good tickets—but she said that she wanted to stay in and rest. She claimed she wasn't feeling well." Becky winces. "I should have known she just wanted to snoop around."

"So she found the video?" I ask, already knowing the answer.

"Well, it was just sitting there on Danny's desktop. She didn't exactly need to be Sherlock to find it."

"And you're positive she sent it?"

"Positive. Danny loves me. He would never betray me this way. I don't know what his sister's problem is. I think she's just jealous because she has no life. She uses their family money to run some magazine about revolutionaries that twelve people read. She's always talking about 'exploding' people's expectations." Becky puts air quotes around "exploding" and rolls her eyes. "She really believes her stuff is going to change the way people think. As if anyone cares about whether the word 'seminal' is sexist.

"But I still can't understand why she sent it to that Chick Habit website. She's always talking about how much she hates it." A tremor creeps into Becky's voice and she abruptly stops talking, plastering on that shopping-network smile instead.

As I look across the sofa at her, those huge baby blues betraying the emotion she's trying to hide, I realize what's been missing from my job, what I've been shoving away all week, maybe all year: empathy. I came here expecting to expose Becky as just another fame whore, but now that I'm just a few feet away from her, I can't help but like her. Besides, she might not even be signing on as a reality TV star if I hadn't posted the video in the first place. I can't condemn her for something I helped create.

Part of me wants to admit to my deceit right now, to tell

Becky that I'm the one who published the video. But I'm too scared. I feel like I'm in too deep, and it's easier for me to just play along.

"After it went up, what happened next?"

"Danny and I had a big fight, and I dumped him. Which is the worst part of this entire thing. It wasn't really his fault." She sniffs and adjusts herself in her seat, dropping the grin. She's composed now but not happy.

"*That's* the worst part? What about the world seeing your boobs? What about the drugs?" Damn it. So much for sounding professional.

Becky shrugs. "Having the world see the video was embarrassing, I guess," she says with a sanguine expression. "And my mom was super super pissed. After I talked to the lawyer, she eventually called me and read me the riot act. But as I explained to her, everyone my age has embarrassing videos and photos lying around, and if they ever become famous they're just going to come out. Look at what's happening to all those politicians, and they're in their forties. I really think this is a net positive."

"A net positive?" I repeat. She sounds like she's reading from a PR guru's playbook.

"Of course," Becky says, her plastic smile returning. "Would you be here arranging for my family's MTV show if that video never got out?"

"I guess not," I tell her.

She must be reading my dismay at her lack of genuine upset, because she turns her whole body toward me and puts her cool fingertips lightly on my arm. An expression of deep concern washes over her face. "Do you think it would play better if I were more upset about it? Because I can be sadder," she says gently, and just as the word "sadder" comes out of her mouth, her eyes start to well with tears.

I spend another ten minutes asking Becky more questions, but they drop out of my mouth without much oomph or consideration. When I stand up to leave, Becky gives me a big warm hug. She's almost a head taller than me and her lanky arms drape lightly across my shoulders. She smells like Ivory soap and, somehow, water. "Thanks for coming by!" she says.

"Don't thank me," I tell her, wanting to be honest at least once in our conversation.

"Um . . . okay!" For a half second Becky looks confused, before she tames that emotion with her ever-present smile.

I take two steps away from her but then abruptly turn back around. "Are you really going to be all right?" I ask her.

"Of course," Becky says. "We West women are resilient." She smiles once more, politely, then closes the door.

While riding down in the elevator I consider everything I've just seen and heard. I'm still trying to parse the experience of being face-to-face with someone I've thought so much about as a moving image on my computer screen, comprised of pixels and sound. Certainly Becky is more calculating than I ever imagined, but she's also just another twenty-year-old with a complicated relationship with her mother. How much of this charade is Becky and how much of it is just her responding to Darleen's expectations? Even though my mother and Darleen West are like night and day, I've definitely pushed myself harder and farther because of what I thought my mother wanted for me.

As I walk back across the grand checkered lobby of the Pierre and out into the sunlight, I realize that I don't think Becky's canniness absolves me. Though it's going to work out for her in the end, I still regret publishing the video. If I had gotten the full story first, if I had done the investigating and spoken to Becky and Darleen and Danny and even this shadowy Cassandra figure—would that have made it okay? Maybe, maybe not. But I could at least tell myself that I had tried to be fair.

I cross Fifty-ninth Street and head toward a bench right outside the bounds of Central Park. I find a place far enough away from the carriage horses and their barnyard stench where I can sit and collect myself. I play back a little bit of the interview to be sure that it recorded, and Becky's girlish lilt is clear and fresh. I don't know what to do with it. Should I just take the Internet drubbing I clearly deserve, allow the blackmailing BTCH to publicly humiliate me, and protect Becky's (probably quite lucrative) deal with *People*? Or should I spill Becky's whereabouts and let the Internet draw its own conclusions about her behavior?

I can't decide just yet so my mind drifts back to Becky's boyfriend, Danny. How must this be affecting him? I imagine him up in Boston, walking gloomily next to the Charles under an overcast New England sky. Even though she's a master manipulator, I bought that Becky really had feelings for him, and I know that losing your first love is a special kind of devastation. This makes me wonder what Peter's doing right now. Is he at work, plugging away and pushing out all thoughts of me? Is he distraught, sniffling over his financial models? While I'm picturing Peter's office and his sleek desktop, I suddenly shift to a mental screen shot of Becky West's Facebook wall. Danny Crandall—the one who said simply that he was sorry and that he loved her. That's her boyfriend.

Wait a minute. Cassandra Crandall. Cassandra Crandall. Why does that name sound familiar? I'm thinking about that alliterative name as I rummage through my canvas sack for my iPhone and go straight to Facebook to look her up.

Her full profile emerges immediately. It turns out we're Facebook friends. I have a strict policy of not friending anyone I don't know personally, so she must be someone I've met before and don't remember now. She's from Palm Beach, Florida, and she went to Andover—that means she's not a Manning kid. Then I notice she's in the Wesleyan network, so we must have gone to college together.

The photograph she uses for her main image is one I vaguely recognize. It's not of Cassandra—it's a grainy photo of a wan woman with strawberry blond hair tucked into a bandanna. It looks like it's from the late sixties. Is she one of Charles Manson's girls? Yep, that's definitely Squeaky Fromme.

I scroll down to the rest of Cassandra's photos and try to find some that are of the girl herself. Most of her photos are of other sixties radicals who liked to blow shit up: Weather Underground beauties Kathy Boudin and Bernardine Dohrn in short skirts, Angela Davis and her huge afro. She also has a photo of the patron saint of all literary girls of a certain age and education: Joan Didion, wearing her trademark giant sunglasses and severe expression.

Finally, I see a photo of Cassandra herself. She's a shrimpy little thing, wearing Lucite frames and a too-long dress that looks like it was salvaged from the trash. She's giving the black power salute with her tiny fist. I can't tell if it's ironic or not; judging from her other photos, it isn't.

The sun beats down on my shoulders as I try to place Cassandra's face. It suddenly occurs to me: She was at Cheyenne's show! She's the one I worked with at the newspaper whose name I never remember! Oh Jesus, that tiny midget fist: She's Deloser! The one who hated me so much from our French hypertextualism class!

I go back to her main page and switch to the "Info" tab to see where Cassandra lives. I almost drop the phone when I see her address listed in clear black characters on my screen: The Phthalo, 79 Carlton Avenue, Brooklyn, NY 11205.

Cassandra is the hate blogger. *And* Cassandra fed me the Rebecca West video. But why does she despise me so much? Because I never remember her name? That doesn't seem like enough of a reason for her to have devoted hours and hours to mocking and harassing me, for her to have created an elaborate website. And why did she feed me the video and then tell me to take it down? That just seems schizophrenic.

The time on my phone reads ten thirty. Now that I know that Becky West isn't dead or seriously injured, my immediate priority is making sure that Cassandra doesn't post whatever mysterious incriminating materials she has on me. I have thirty minutes to get to Fort Greene and convince Cassandra to halt whatever she's doing.

I ask the bellman outside the Pierre to hail me a cab. He puts his arm up and immediately, just like in the movies, a taxi pulls up and screeches to a halt. I climb into the back of the car; tell the driver to take the Manhattan Bridge into Brooklyn, and fast; and we're racing downtown within moments.

Chapter Fourteen

As we're rumbling over the bridge, I listen to the Q train whoosh past us, and I wonder what I'm getting myself into. Cassandra seems pretty obsessed with ruining me—there's no telling how she might respond to whatever I have to say. Should I tell Jane where I'm going? Make the cabbie stop at a bodega so I can pick up some pepper spray? The only thing I have time to do is text Jane:

> Alex Lyons (10:48 AM): I'm going to the Phthalo. If you don't hear from me in an hour, call the cops.

Hopefully the police won't be necessary. I do have three years of kickboxing classes at my local gym—surely those evenings with Misty will help me out if I need to get physical!

We pull up to the glitzy, modern façade of the Phthalo at 10:53. I throw a twenty and a ten at the driver and rush into the lobby.

Even though this is a pretty fancy building, there's no doorman anywhere to be seen. A gardener is tending to the enormous Japanese rock garden that takes up most of the entryway, but he completely ignores me as he draws intricate patterns in the sand. There is a directory to the right of him, and I find a Crandall, C, who resides in unit 3R.

I am too impatient to wait for the elevator, so I take the stairs up to the third floor and turn right, where I find a heavy gray door with a batik of Patty Hearst, replete with beret and machine gun, plastered across it.

I ring the doorbell once. There is no answer. I ring it again. Still nothing. I don't even hear anything stirring behind that thick door. It didn't occur to me that she might not be home and my panic notches up another level. I'm sure I would survive my sex tape taking over the Internet, but I really would prefer for my most private grunting to remain, well, private.

I start banging on the door and screaming. "Cassandra Crandall! I know you're in there! Open this door right now!" I keep banging and banging—it's 10:56, then 10:57, then 10:58. "I will bang on this door until you open it, so help me God!"

At 10:59, the door swings open, and the small, wild-eyed figure of Cassandra Crandall stands before me. She's wearing those Lucite glasses, and her bony body is clad in ratty madras shorts and a hole-filled black sweatshirt. Her face has the wan color of someone who hasn't been outside during daylight hours in weeks, which is to say we have similar complexions. She squints at me—the light of the hallway must be too bright for her mole eyes.

"Who are you and what's your problem?"

I'm momentarily speechless. Does she really not know who I am? After everything she's done to me? But before she can close the door in my face, I barge into her enormous pad—and turn my digital recorder on, just in case.

"I'm Alex Lyons," I say once I'm firmly in the apartment. Keep your cool, girl, I tell myself. Don't let her see you sweat.

"Oh," she says, rubbing her eyes. "You woke me up."

"Oh? That's all you have to say to me right now?" I'm so angry that I'm immediately shouting at her. Good job at maintaining that calm, dummy.

"Give me a minute to collect myself," Cassandra says as she takes off her glasses and cleans them with the tatters of her shirt.

This gives me time to take in my surroundings. There's no doubt that this is a nice place—there's exposed brick everywhere and huge bay windows that are covered with dark curtains. The tin ceilings have been meticulously created to echo the architecture of the older buildings in the neighborhood. But though the bones of the apartment are lovely, the place itself is a mess. Because the curtains keep out all natural light, the apartment has a thorough mustiness. There are yellowing newspapers everywhere and cheap prints thumbtacked to the mostly bare walls.

I glance back at Cassandra, whose lips are now quivering with . . . fear? Anticipation? She's clearly waiting for me to say something.

Only one word comes out of me, almost by its own volition. "Why?"

"Why what?" she says, goading me with a superior smirk.

"A million whys!" I can't help myself; I'm shouting now. "Why did you create that hate blog? Why did you send me that video of Becky West? Why did you try to get me to take it down almost immediately? Why do you keep threatening me? Why are you such a *fucking loon*!?"

Every "why" seems to hit Cassandra directly in the gut, and she flinches with each question. She looks so small and ineffectual that I believe she's just going to break down and apologize to me on the spot. But instead her face stiffens and her mouth becomes a hardened circle. Her eyes narrow and she looks like she might spit on me.

"If you're going to be rude, I'm not going to answer your invasive questions," Cassandra snaps.

I catch my breath. If this is how she's going to play, I will calm myself down. "Fine. Will you please explain the motivations behind your actions of the past week?"

She smooths her holey sweatshirt as if it were the finest silk and calmly explains. "I started that hate blog because you—all you Chickies, but especially *you*, Alex—have this amazing platform that you could use for *real* social change. But instead you clog it up with celebrity tweets and your own self-absorbed bullshit about boys. I thought if I created Breaking the Chick Habit, you would see the error of your ways and start posting about things that really matter."

I don't entirely disagree with her, but I don't want to give her the satisfaction of knowing. "So? Start your own website if you want to change the world."

"I *have* started my own *nonprofit* website and my own quarterly magazine. It's called *Logos*. But it doesn't get the kind of traffic that your trash gets. I bet twenty-five people read the ten-thousand-word feature one of my writers did about her experience living among the Langi women of Uganda, but tens of thousands of people read your two-hundred-word post about vagina crystals or whatever."

"Vajazzling?"

"Whatever. Yes," Cassandra says, getting visibly angry now. Dots of white spittle are starting to collect in the corners of her mouth. "It's infuriating."

I can't believe this. *She's* infuriated? I'm the one getting threatened! "If you had sent me that article about the Langi women or 'whatever,' I would have been happy to link to it," I tell Cassandra, trying to make my voice drip with as much smugness as possible.

"Fuck *you*!" Cassandra screams, whatever composure she had quickly going out the window. "I *did* send it to you! Just this week! And you ignored it." She's right, I realize, dredging up a vague memory from Monday—God, that seems so long ago now! I open my mouth to defend myself, but Cassandra's rage is unstoppable. "You've always been like this! Even when we were in college, you got all the breaks! You don't give a shit about the Langi, and you probably didn't give a shit about those women at that domestic violence shelter in Bridgeport, either. I was the one who spent a full year covering the journey of one undocumented immigrant in New Haven! My piece about Jose deserved the Silent Spring Prize for advocacy journalism! Not your piece!"

"What are you even talking about?" The fury radiating from Cassandra is starting to unnerve me. I'm wishing I had stopped for that pepper spray. "That was three years ago! And college prizes don't even mean anything in the real world."

It occurs to me as I say this that Cassandra doesn't really live in the real world. From the looks of this apartment, she doesn't go outside, and she clearly doesn't have to pay her own bills if her work time is spent running a nonprofit website that twelve people read and she's not even awake at eleven A.M. I decide to dial back the tone of this conversation to see if I can get her to calm down.

Putting on an even, distant, diplomatic voice, I tell her, "At Chick Habit we do try to include a wide variety of subjects. Yes, our readers may enjoy a post about the latest trends in pubic hair, but they also like to read about serious issues women across the world are facing. It doesn't have to be all one or the other." It occurs to me as I'm speaking that I actually believe what I just said. It's just the recent quota pressure that's made my posts exclusively frivolous.

I look closely at Cassandra to see if she's relaxed at all, and at first I can't tell. But just then her eyes narrow again and she screams, "*Bullshit!* Alex, that is such bullshit. The world will only change through revolutionary action. Not through satisfying advertisers with stories about makeup."

That sounds scarily familiar. Where have I heard that before? Then it hits me. Cassandra is the commenter Weathergrrrl. It all makes sense now: The Kathy Boudin photos in her profile, her grandiose notion that she can shame Chick Habit into being the kind of site that she wants to read.

"Does sending me a video of your brother's girlfriend topless really qualify as a 'revolutionary action,' Weathergrrrl?" I ask her.

"Oh, that," Cassandra says, unclenching for a minute and even cracking a smile. She doesn't seem at all surprised that I've identified her by her commenting handle. "I knew you wouldn't be able to resist publishing that one. I figured that sending it to you would kill two birds with one stone."

"What do you mean, 'kill two birds with one stone'?" I am completely befuddled by this—and the fact that Cassandra's using the word "kill" in any context isn't exactly soothing. In fact, I feel a chill run through me.

"Well, I'd read everything you'd written about Darleen West, and I agree. She's an agent of evil who does not respect the dignity of the proletarian woman." I want to ask what Cassandra really knows about the proletarian woman, but I stifle it and let her continue. "I knew you wouldn't be able to resist showing Darleen for the hypocrite that she really is. So I'd be destroying Darleen's political career and toying with you at the same time."

"But what about your brother? Didn't you care that he loves Becky West? Don't you want him to be happy?"

"Not especially," Cassandra says, pushing her glasses back up the bridge of her largish nose. "My brother is a simpleton who has never understood the need for revolution. He is content to spend his spare time playing fantasy football and drinking watery mass-produced beer. He and those troglodytes we call parents have made no attempt to understand the struggle."

Translation: The Crandall parents have always preferred Danny and Cassandra isn't over it. I am starting to feel slightly sorry for this misfit waif.

"But what about Becky? What did she ever do to you?"

"That she is the spawn of that hateful woman makes her part of the problem," Cassandra says. "We will burn and loot and destroy. We are the incubation of your mother's nightmare."

That must be a quote from someone else, but I can't place it. Still, I'm losing my interest in playing ball with her. "Okay, crazy," I say. "So you got what you wanted. You got me to publish the video. Darleen's reputation is tarnished, and I'm getting death threats. So why did you then ask me to take the video down? And why are you threatening me with these alleged 'incriminating videos' that you have on me?"

Cassandra snarfs an ugly laugh. "That was just to mess with you. It didn't really matter whether you took the video down or not. Even if it's no longer on Chick Habit the damage has been done to Darleen West. That video's everywhere."

I let that sink in for a second. I've been going crazy for the past few days with fear and guilt, while Cassandra was just sitting here, cackling her evil little cackle and picturing me twisting in the wind. All because I wouldn't link to her article about the Langi women and because I won a journalism prize in college.

"Fine," I say. "So you were just messing with me. Game, set, match: Cassandra. I've spent the last few days terrified about this entire ordeal, and I've been reconsidering my job at Chick Habit. Do you really have to humiliate me further?"

"Why not? What have you ever done for me?" Cassandra asks.

Nothing. I've never done a thing for her. She's right. I try offering the one thing she wanted in the first place: my platform.

"How about this. I'll link to the piece about the Ugandan women, and I'll post to every subsequent issue of your journal, too. I'll even let you guest-post once in a while." I sincerely doubt Moira would ever let this happen—but I'm desperate.

"It's too late for that now. Like I even want some capitalist pawns sending my journal traffic anyway." Cassandra can obviously smell the desperation and has no desire to settle.

I try one final salvo. "Can I at least see whatever these materials are before you release them to the World Wide Web?"

I realize something else as I'm speaking—I've been focused on the idea that the incriminating material is my sex tape, but I still don't know how Adam could have gotten Internet access to send it—he never responded to my e-mail so I assume he's still off the grid. And self-centered as Caleb is, and bad as that breakup was, I'm starting to believe he wouldn't have made some creepy inappropriate "piece" about me—his computer seemed clean, and weirdly, I trust him.

But Cassandra went to college with me. She could have anything: a photo of me from Wesleyan's notorious naked party, snapped surreptitiously; an audio clip of me saying something racist-sounding that I meant in jest; a video from some freshman-year party when I was too drunk to remember what happened.

Cassandra looks at me for a minute and I guess decides to give me a break. "I'll get the video. It's in my laptop in the bedroom," she says.

I'm shocked by her acquiescence but relieved. I guess she's already gotten everything she wanted—her entire scheme went just as she planned—so why push it further? "Okay," I say gratefully.

I watch her as she scuffles off to the back of the apartment, hunched like a miniature Quasimodo. To busy myself while I wait I wander over to those beautiful bay windows, move aside the curtains, and check out Cassandra's view. Her apartment looks out on a perfectly kept courtyard with a mosaic fountain in the center. A slender woman in her early thirties is sitting on a bench near the fountain. Her blond hair whips gently in the wind and she's wearing a chic black maxi dress. A cherubic baby with a floppy pink sun hat is perched on her lap. The woman stares into the infant's face with a look of unyielding pleasure while she bounces the baby up and down on her knee.

I am absorbed in the innocence of this scene, its purity and clarity of purpose. There are no ulterior motives here, no complications or upsets. Just a clean, human interaction between a mother and a daughter. I'm feeling a pang of jealousy for something so uncomplicated. I must have been standing there for at least five minutes when I hear a loud crash against those gorgeous hardwood floors. The sound is coming from Cassandra's bedroom, and so I rush there to see what the ruckus is.

The bedroom is pitch-black when I get there, except for a bright shard of light against the floor. I look up to see where the sun is coming from and see Cassandra's skinny leg sticking out of the window, her foot almost on the fire escape. She's trying to flee the scene? But why? She's won the elaborate game she constructed. Why would she run away just at the moment of ultimate triumph?

I don't understand it, but I need to prevent her from getting away. I sprint over and yank her back into the room with one swift motion.

"Where the fuck are you going?" I scream at her.

"Um, I just wanted some air?" She seems scared of me now, and she's breathing quick little rabbit breaths. Probably because I just forced her back into the room with one comparatively brawny arm.

"That's not why. Tell me the truth." I say this so strongly that Cassandra starts to cry.

"I don't have anything on you," she blurts out.

"What?"

"I don't have anything on you. No sex tape, no dirty photographs, nothing. And believe me, I tried to find something."

"So you really were just fucking with me for the past four days?" I have to stifle the hysterical laughter that's welling up in me. After all this fear and self-loathing, there was nothing at the center of it.

Cassandra sighs and sits down on the bed, the tears still coming. "I guess so. Yes. I remembered the smiley-face tattoo from college, and I assumed that everyone has some naughty business lurking somewhere in their past. I assumed right in your case, obviously."

I stare down at her. How does she still sound smug, even through tears? I look around at her bedroom while I'm trying to figure out my next move. The vaulted ceilings and crown moldings really are lovely. This place must have cost at least $1.5 million. Then it occurs to me—if I'm going to get Cassandra to do what I want, I need to hit her where it's going to hurt the most.

"Here's what's going to happen," I tell her, pulling the recorder out of my pocket and waving it in front of her face. "I've been recording this entire conversation. I'm sure Mr. and Mrs.

Crandall back in Palm Beach would be really eager to hear about how their daughter is spending her trust fund. If you agree to remove Breaking the Chick Habit from the Internet, I won't send your mom and pops this file."

Cassandra looks truly horrified at the prospect of having her financial security cut off, and so she says quietly, "Okay, okay, I'll delete it."

"Good. I'm going to stand over your shoulder while you do it so there won't be any funny business." I gesture toward her computer.

"Okay." Cassandra stands and trudges slowly toward her glass-topped desk.

"Let's speed it up a little, shall we?" I keep my hand firmly on her left shoulder as she moves her fingers deftly across the keyboard. I watch as she deletes the blog and then I make her transfer the Breaking the Chick Habit domain name to my Go Daddy account. Just to be extra careful, I make note of the password she types into her WordPress blog: weathergrrrl, of course.

Once I'm satisfied that BTCH won't be updating ever again I remove my hand from her shoulder and allow Cassandra to swivel toward me in her chair. She scowls at me and crosses her arms, but we both know I've got her. "I'm going to ask you one more question," I say.

"What?"

"Was it worth it? Causing all this chaos?"

A creepy, shit-eating grin spreads across her withered-apple face. *"Viva la revolución!"* she cries.

"You've gotta be fucking kidding me," I tell her. I turn promptly on my heel and head for the door. Just before I'm about to close it behind me, I hear her shout one more thing.

"Bet you'll remember my name now!"

I stand, dazed, outside the Phthalo for what could be five minutes or could be twenty, running back over all the events of this week. In a sick way, I respect Cassandra. She may be a nutcase, but she also really believes in her twisted causes. Besides empathy, that's the other thing that's been missing from my work: being able to stand by it.

What privacy means now is an ever-shifting line—the old universal standards have yet to be replaced by a new code of conduct, and we're all just muddling through. So all I have to go on are my own moral standards. If I had listened to my instincts about Becky West, I never would have run that video. I would have deleted the e-mail and moved on with my day. If I had listened to my instincts about Peter, I never would have read that stupid report. All this moral equivocating has been exhausting.

As I'm realizing these things, I come to the revelation that I've been circling all day. It's not the job that's the problem. It's *me* in the job that's the problem.

I text Molly:

Alex Lyons (12:43 PM): You should post on Rebecca West's reality show later today, if you want to. You deserve the page views for this one. It's your scoop, after all.

Molly Hawkins (12:44 PM): OMG YAY! That is awesome. I can't wait!

I hope this gives Molly a leg up with Tyson Collins and that if the sale goes through, she keeps her job. She deserves it more than I do. She does the real work, instead of just hiding behind a clever sentence or two. Moira may still fire me, since I've been AWOL for about twenty-four hours, but I no longer care.

All of a sudden I miss Peter something awful, like a shot through the chest. I want to tell him about my crazy day—he's the only one I ever want to share my highs and lows with. I think about calling him but remember how angry he was last night and decide that I should probably give him a little more space. He has a lot to focus on at work right now. He can deal with me later.

I decide to walk all the way home, even though it will take me nearly two hours and I will have missed another half day of work. After the week I've just had, I deserve some fresh air.

MONDAY MORNING, NINE MONTHS LATER

Chapter Fifteen

My alarm clock goes off at seven thirty. I'm alone in bed, and I reach over and turn it off. I'm wearing a proper nightgown, a white, floaty affair that makes me feel like an extra in *Valley of the Dolls*, in a good way. The sun is already streaming through the gauzy curtains I installed. I hop out of bed, stretch my arms, and walk into the kitchen.

Peter's already made coffee, and he's sitting at our long white table, reading a hard copy of the *Wall Street Journal*. A copy of the *Times* lays across the place mat opposite him. When he sees me enter the room, he gets up to pour me a cup. "Good morning!"

"Hello, honey." I smile and give him a hug and a kiss, and we sit down at the table to drink our coffee and read the paper together.

That's right—Peter and I are still together. He didn't speak to me for two weeks after the Becky West debacle, and even though it was torturous, I gave him his space. I spent a lot of nights at Jane and Ali's place, watching bad reality television and crying over many different kinds of smoked meats. Jane was the most wonderful best friend a girl could ever ask for—full of real talk, as ever. She told me that she was glad Peter had left, because it forced me to take a hard look at myself. In the moment, of course, I wanted to smother her with a pillow. But I knew she was right.

Those fourteen days made me realize just how deeply I had taken Peter for granted, how I had betrayed his trust by reading that report, and how my job had brought out the worst parts of my personality.

On that fourteenth day, Peter came home after work. We cooked dinner together and opened a bottle of wine. By the time the oven timer went off on the roast chicken, we had demolished the wine and were back in bed together. As we ate the chicken afterward, both of us clad in Peter's soft old T-shirts, I apologized for my behavior. Peter did, too, for not telling me earlier about how he felt my job at Chick Habit was affecting me, and affecting us. That's what he had been trying to talk to me about for the whole crazy week. "I was trying to be supportive, but sometimes that means being brutally honest," Peter said.

About that job: I went home after my blowout double confrontation with Rebecca West and Cassandra Crandall and did a full day of work. Moira could have fired me after those few days of insubordination, but she didn't; the Rebecca West post brought the site so much attention it would have been bad press. Not that Moira was pleased: She screamed at me for so long that afternoon that I ended up putting my iPhone on speakerphone and playing solitaire while she ranted without interruption.

Furthermore, after all that drama about the Omnitown

deal, it fell apart at the last minute. Peter never told me any of this—it's still against the law—and I never brought it up with him, but I read a short article about it in the business section of the *Times*.

Molly did publish a meaty post that day about Becky West's new reality show. She even got Shira Allen to cough up the proposed title: *West Knows Best*. That scoop got her two hundred thousand page views, a promotion to associate editor, and a side gig commentating about celebrities on VH1 shows.

As for me, I tried to create some boundaries for myself at Chick Habit. No more histrionics; no more Googling myself and being upset about the results; no more squabbles with Rel or Tina or Molly. I did the best I could, and whenever I was on the verge of taking myself too seriously, I would remind myself that Chick Habit was just a job.

It was still a job I cared about, though; despite everything, from Becky West to my mother's non-expectations, I realized that blogging was where I really did want to be—and I tried to do work that I was proud of. That doesn't mean I started exclusively following Cassandra's agenda, writing straight-faced posts about sad foreign ladies and their worthy plights. I did some of that. But I also continued to do slide shows highlighting Ke$ha's fugly fashion sense and wrote searing indictments of women-hating politicians. What I wrote could sometimes be construed as mean—but I always tried to be fair. "Nice" is different from "good," as Stephen Sondheim says. My new rule turned out to be: Don't write anything you wouldn't say to a person's face. Sober.

I made some other changes, too: I asked Moira if Molly

could take the first post of the day, so that I could be slightly less crazed—and to my surprise, she agreed. I also started showering before noon every day and even putting on a bra at least three days a week. I retired the ol' muumuu: It now hangs in the back of my closet. Whenever I see it, I remember that work isn't my entire world and that there are lots of different outfits that would like to see the light of day. I even started leaving the house for lunch occasionally, eating many different sorts of non-salad-based things while seated at tables with other live humans for company.

Sometimes those humans are even Rel and Tina. In the weeks after our respective tiffs, I invited them out to drinks and explained the whole Becky West/BTCH saga. They both impressed me with their easygoing forgiveness. I had been especially scared that acid-tongued Rel would hate me forever, but she understood why I had tweaked out so hard. She and Tina work on the Internet, too, after all—they both saw how I could lose perspective, and fast.

I never told anyone about my altercation with Cassandra. Rel and Tina noticed that the hate blog had disappeared, but they never asked me about it. They just assumed whoever was writing it got bored and moved on to hating bigger and better things.

For several months after that July day, I was anxious that Cassandra would find some new and inventive way to harass me. For a while, every time I'd open my inbox I'd dread a threatening e-mail from her. But I haven't had a whiff of her since. She defriended me on Facebook and deleted her profile. The website for that magazine she founded, *Logos,* has disappeared as well. I heard through the Wesleyan grapevine that she sold her apartment and moved to Kinshasa, where she now goes by the name Ayana. Who knows if it's true. Perhaps her revolutionary fervor goes over better in the Congo, but somehow I doubt it.

And what of Becky West? Molly's post about her reality show didn't sour the deal with MTV or with *People*. Just the opposite: It made the American appetite for all things Becky even more insatiable. The *People* issue with Becky's sad-looking face on the cover was one of the most popular newsstand buys of the summer (just behind the cover with the woman whose face got eaten by a chimp). Becky became America's favorite tabloid daughter and took an indefinite leave from MIT and her beloved robots. Her three sisters took leaves from their respective august institutions of learning and the whole lot of them moved home with Darleen so that MTV could film *West Knows Best*, a *Father Knows Best* update for the "End of Men" era. The show premieres next month; I've seen ads for it plastered all over the subway, the West sisters' angelic faces beaming down at me on the F train.

Becky and I didn't speak after that morning in the Pierre. I'd like to think that if we did see each other again she wouldn't hold a grudge. It worked out well for her in the end. But who knows how she really feels. I don't think even she knows, deep down.

Though I never heard directly from Becky, I heard from Darleen's lawyers. Again. And again. And again. For the first time in Chick Habit history, Moira and our lawyer agreed to take my post down four months after it had been published, just to make Darleen go away. By then, it was only a token takedown—any curious Internet surfer would be able to find the video on a torrent somewhere, and the post had received ten million page views and put Chick Habit on the map in a way that it hadn't been before.

As much as I had mixed feelings about publishing that video, it turned out to be a boon for my career. Suddenly the editors of those $2-a-word glossies knew my name and started assigning me short celebrity profiles and reported cultural essays. They wanted some of that trademark Alex Lyons sass, but the pieces of mine that ended up in the magazines were edited down to be both bland and utterly unrecognizable as the work I had handed in. No matter: I really enjoyed getting more than an hour to work on an article (sometimes I'd even get weeks!) and the checks didn't bounce.

And then, a month ago, I was offered a job managing the website of one of those glossies, at nearly twice my salary plus health insurance. I would go into a real office every day, and ride the subway and interact with people and speak aloud regularly. More important, I would get to pick and choose what web originals to run. Though it is celebrity oriented, the magazine is also known for its profiles of politicians, musings on Wall Street, and dispatches from the Middle East. I could offer the same mix of stories I was trying to achieve at Chick Habit, but with a much bigger budget. It was an opportunity that was too good to pass up.

When I got the job offer, I couldn't wait to tell my mom the exciting news. Things between us had been strained since that crazy week: She felt responsible for pushing me into a career that was making me miserable, and I felt guilty for making her feel responsible. Despite the fact that we both work with words for a living, neither of us could muster the right ones to say to each other.

I decided to go up to Connecticut to tell her the good news in person. I wanted her to see how genuinely thrilled I was about the job offer. I wanted to give her real credit for all the creative encouragement she gave me.

She picked me up at the Metro North station and took me home. The conversation between us in the car was stilted. When I asked her how the new crop of freshmen was she said briefly, "Oh fine. Same as they always are," and kept her eyes on the road.

When we got home she put up a kettle to make us chamomile tea, which is the first thing she always does whenever I come home. We sat across from each other with steaming mugs and I told her about the offer. She took a sip from her mug—a wonky, handmade piece from my seventh-grade pottery class—and nodded. "Well, that sounds nice," she said.

"Mom, aren't you happy about my new job?" I ask her, a little wounded that she's not kvelling.

"I'm happy if you're happy, puffin," she said, her expression unchanging.

"I am really, really happy about it. I swear," I said, reaching out for her hand. It was warm and dry, just like I remembered it from when I was a kid.

She squeezed my hand in return. "Are you sure that you're not continuing on this path just so that I can live vicariously through you?"

"I promise. This is for me."

She sighed and her expression finally relaxed. "That makes me happy, then, yes."

We sat in comfortable silence for a few minutes, blowing on our tea, and that's when I mustered the courage to ask her what had been on my mind for years.

"What about your work? I know you have that thesis sitting up there in your desk. You could still finish it. It's not too late."

Mom put down her mug, smiled, and sighed wistfully. "I think that particular ship has sailed. But maybe when I retire in a few years, I'll start writing again." She paused and then added, "Your father and I had a great marriage, and I miss him every single day. I don't blame him for giving me that ultimatum about my thesis—I chose to give it up. But when he was alive, I was too embarrassed to try to write again. Now I'm ready to go back to it."

"That's really great, Mom," I told her, starting to tear up. "I'm so proud of you."

"Maybe I'll even start my own blog," she said, smiling.

I laughed out loud. "Maybe you should."

Even after everything that had happened, it was surprisingly difficult to leave my job at Chick Habit. I was grateful to Moira for the opportunity, and also for everything she taught me along the way. The job had been sort of like a mental and emotional boot camp, and I felt prepared for anything that could come my way.

When I gave my two weeks' notice, I told Moira that I thought publishing that Rebecca West video was ultimately a mistake for the site. "I don't think we have to be Pollyannas," I said, "but I think we should be careful about how we construe the term 'famous.' Unknown children of famous people should be off-limits."

To her credit, Moira sat and listened to my moralizing without interrupting. "Are you done now, love?" Moira asked after I had been speaking for a good ten minutes. When I nodded, she said, "Good. I'm glad you got that out of your system. You know I never forced you to post anything you didn't want to post. It was your choice to put up that video, and even though you feel uncomfortable about it, it was the right decision."

I opened my mouth to protest, but Moira continued. "You have to realize that this is what being a journalist is about. I always remember that Janet Malcolm quote when I encounter people like you, Al: 'Every journalist who is not too stupid or too full of himself to notice what is going on knows that what he does is morally indefensible.' We writers are snakes, and don't you forget it. If you wanted to do something that was always 'right,' you should have become a dentist."

"Al?" Peter says to me, waving his hands in front of my face. "Isn't it time to get a move on? You don't want to be late for your first day on the new job!"

"Damn, you're right!" I say, heading quickly toward the bathroom. I poop without the aid of a laptop, take a shower, blow-dry my hair, and put on a tasteful amount of makeup.

I laid out my outfit the night before: A DVF wrap dress that says "sexy competence," my nicest matching underwear, and a trench coat. Peter's fastening my dad's beaker cuff links while I put my shoes on. I gave them to him right after we got back together—with my mom's sincerest blessing.

Peter and I leave the house together and hold hands on the way to the F train. It's a breezy spring morning, the sun is high and bright in the sky, and I'm so thrilled to be getting up and out of the house for work that I could almost float all the way to Forty-second Street.

When I arrive at my new office building, I get my pass at the front desk and the magazine's executive editor, Joe Aaronson, comes and meets me at the elevator bank on the twentieth floor, kissing me on both cheeks in welcome. Joe is in his fifties and has been around the industry since the days of the three-martini, three-hour lunch. He exudes a sort of natty largesse that I find unfamiliar but appealing. "Let me show you to your office," he says. "I'll have my assistant bring us some lattes."

Assistant! Lattes! I feel like I'm eons away from my dumpy brown couch and my sugar-sweet bodega coffees. I follow Joe down the hall to a small, windowless cubbyhole several minutes from the front door.

"It's not much but it's all we have open right now," Joe tells me.

"It looks great," I say, and I mean it. I could not be more excited to have a little place of my own.

An officious-looking twenty-two-year-old in a nubbly pencil skirt and sensible heels comes in a minute later with two china cups full of foam.

"Thanks, Annika," Joe says, closing the door behind her. "Sit!" he says to me, directing me to the chair behind a brand-new Mac.

"Thanks," I say, taking a seat.

Joe sits down across from me. "We're all so happy you decided to come on board with us," he says. "We really want you to hit the ground running."

"Great! I am raring to go myself!" I say enthusiastically.

"There are a few meetings I want you to sit in on this morning," Joe says. "But that's all just bullshit. Here's what I really want to know."

"Yes?" I say, leaning toward him.

Joe smiles broadly, even eagerly. "Do you have any more Becky West–type exclusives up your sleeve?"

Acknowledgments

Sad Desk Salad is a work of fiction, but it would not have been possible without the wonderful experiences I had working at both Jezebel and Slate's section for women, DoubleX. All the women I worked with were beyond generous, smart, and compassionate coworkers—and nothing like Alex's peers. Thank you to Hanna Rosin, Meghan O'Rourke, Emily Bazelon, Kate Julian, Nina Shen Rastogi, Anna Holmes, Tracie Egan Morrissey, Moe Tkacik, Dodai Stewart, Jessica Coen, Jennifer Gerson, and Megan Carpentier for making my workdays a delight.

Many other colleagues were incredibly supportive while I was writing this, in particular David Plotz, Daniel Engber, Michael Agger, June Thomas, Julia Felsenthal, Heather Murphy, Seth Stevenson, and Noreen Malone.

I am deeply grateful to early readers Nathan Heller, Marisa Meltzer, and Lucinda Rosenfeld, all of whom helped shape the book into something much deeper and smarter than it would have been otherwise.

Acknowledgments

My agent, Elisabeth Weed, is an indispensable giver of advice, edits, and all-around care. She worked tirelessly to get this book out there in the best shape possible, and is a font of wisdom on just about everything, from emotional sanity to acupuncture treatments. Her tireless assistant, Stephanie Sun, was always helpful and provided a smiling face and a can-do attitude.

Kate Nintzel, in addition to being a delightful drinking buddy, is the best editor around. She knew exactly where to fill the holes in this manuscript, and her suggestions were always spot-on and brilliant. The rest of the staff at William Morrow, including Meredith Burks and Mary Sasso, have been a complete joy to work with and I'm so grateful for their hard work on this.

Thank you to my family and friends—Richard and Judith Grose, David and Charlotte Winton, Jacob Grose, Anna Magracheva, Judson Winton, Meghan Best, Wendell Winton, Leah Chernikoff, Willa Paskin, Mary Lydecker, Kate Lydecker, and Liz Stevenson—for encouraging the crazy idea that I could write a novel in five months while holding down a full-time job without having a nervous breakdown. And they were mostly right.

But most of all I want to thank my husband, Michael Winton, for being my biggest fan and greatest solace. And, of course, for putting up with me.